SWEEP LOTUS

SWEEP LOTUS

An Elias McCann Mystery

Mark Zuehlke

A Castle Street Mystery

THE DUNDURN GROUP
TORONTO

Editor: Barry Jowett
Copy-editor: Jennifer Bergeron
Design: Andrew Roberts
Printer: Webcom

Library and Archives Canada Cataloguing in Publication

Zuehlke, Mark
    Sweep lotus : an Elias McCann mystery / Mark Zuehlke.

ISBN 1-55002-532-5

I. Title.

PS8599.U33S84 2004   C813'.6   C2004-903711-0

1   2   3   4   5   08   07   06   05   04

We acknowledge the support of the **Canada Council for the Arts** and the **Ontario Arts Council** for our publishing program. We also acknowledge the financial support of the **Government of Canada** through the **Book Publishing Industry Development Program** and **The Association for the Export of Canadian Books,** and the **Government of Ontario** through the **Ontario Book Publishers Tax Credit** program.

Care has been taken to trace the ownership of copyright material used in this book. The author and the publisher welcome any information enabling them to rectify any references or credit in subsequent editions.

J. Kirk Howard, President

Printed and bound in Canada.♲
Printed on recycled paper.
www.dundurn.com

Dundurn Press
8 Market Street
Suite 200
Toronto, Ontario, Canada
M5E 1M6

Gazelle Book Services Limited
White Cross Mills
Hightown, Lancaster, England
LA1 4XS

Dundurn Press
2250 Military Road
Tonawanda NY
U.S.A. 14150

Readers familiar with Tofino, Ucluelet, and Pacific Rim National Park may find some discrepancies between their world and that of Elias McCann. This is as it should be, for Elias's world is as fictional as the people who populate it.

chapter one

During the dark hours of morning, dense fog laced with heavy threads of icy, wet drizzle crept in off the Pacific Ocean. Six hours later, closing on noon, the heavy weather showed not the slightest sign of lifting. I trudged across sludgy sand, water sluicing off my old canvas hat and coat and pearling in my beard. The strong smell of salt off the chuck was overwhelmed in places by the sulphurous odour of rot emanating from great tangled balls of bull kelp and other seaweed cast ashore during the most recent storm. Slate grey surf, frothed with angry foam, sloshed against the beach. There was no horizon, just the press of fog against the tree- and shrub-dressed headlands, upon which the shadowy presence of glass slab and cedar-walled beach-front houses could be detected but not defined.

I walked cocooned in a grey world seemingly devoid of life. The only sound was the long, eternal drumbeat roll of the inward washing waves followed by the slow sucking hiss as each receded in turn. Gravel and sand sighed outward in a mournful, timeless, operatic lament. No gulls shrilled, no shorebirds flushed from the surf line in chittering flocks. Even the ravens normally perched amid the twisted branches of storm-battered firs and hemlocks held silent. I walked down the middle of a track marked on the sand by two sets of tires — one the wide, rough tread of a sport-utility vehicle or truck, the other a car's narrower, smoother print. It was a trail that ran straight and true to the far end of the beach, where death waited.

The dead are always patient, so although my pace was purposeful, I did not hasten toward this meeting. Service as Tofino's coroner has as yet failed to harden my spirit and stomach to the realities that accompany sudden mortality. Each time, I must steel myself anew before entering the presence of the dead. It was this reluctance to approach the death scene that had prompted me to leave the old 1967 Land Rover in the beach access parking lot rather than use the excuse of official duties to disobey the "No Motorized Vehicles Beyond This Point" sign. I walked and let the mist cleanse me.

As I drew closer to the southern end of the beach, the red and blue flash of a rack of emergency lights materialized out of the fog. The nose of Sergeant Gary Danchuk's RCMP Blazer canted inland, its bumper facing seaward. Lined up alongside the Blazer was a police cruiser, lights also flashing. Next to the vehicles a small crowd had gathered, everyone protected from the elements by varying forms of rain gear that ranged from old rubber slickers to state-of-the-art Gore-Tex coats with matching pants. A couple of dogs squatted on their haunches next to two of the people. Constable Anne Monaghan, wearing a yellow police slicker, faced the group. Passing through the cluster, I nodded a greeting to Bess Witherspoon while brushing a finger across the tip of her Labrador's muzzle. Bess met my eyes bleakly, and so too did Charlie, the dog.

I wondered why Bess was here. Although she lived in a house just inland from the ridge overlooking the beach, it seemed out of character for her to join a congregation of onlookers at a death scene. None of the others were familiar to me. But most of the houses fronting this beach had been bought or built by people who made their money far removed from Tofino, so this did not surprise me as it might have a few years back. The turbulent beauty of the landscape surrounding Tofino and its deceptive small-town ambience has drawn an ever-increasing number of people to build seasonal recreational homes or even to move here permanently. Most waterfront areas suitable for housing development are chock-a-block full of oversized homes lived in by people with more money than three or four normal Tofinoites might see in a lifetime. But I can hardly cast aspersions on these outlanders, for in many ways I am one of them.

"It's a bad business, Elias," Monaghan announced wearily. Stray strands of blonde hair straggled lankly out from beneath her ball cap, and water dribbled down her cheeks. She looked cold and pale. I suspected, however, that the paleness had little to do with the discomfort caused by the foul weather. "Never seen anything like it." I thought she shuddered, and a responsive chill ran up my spine. "It was Bess who found her. Out walking Charlie. Just about tripped over her in the fog."

"Where?"

"Other side of the cars. You'll find Danchuk and the others there. Better go and take a look. See if you can get the okay to cover her up with something, will you?"

Leaving Monaghan to maintain the scene's security, I approached the three figures that formed a rough semi-circle around a still indistinct object. Scattered out behind the object were what appeared to be a series of strange structures resembling some crude and mis-shapen Stonehenge. Drawing closer I realized the structures were nothing more than jumbles of drift logs and bits of lumber roughly piled together to construct a semblance of protection against the worst of the rain and wind, but they would never keep anybody completely dry. Not even the addition of various torn orange and blue plastic tarps tied this way and that to create roofs and seaward-facing walls added much weatherproofing.

Like probably everybody else in Tofino, I knew this place as the One Earth Family's crude campsite. They called themselves the Family for short and had come from down island late in the spring. Surprisingly they had stayed on even as fall hardened its grip with ever more frequent rains and storms that lashed hard upon the backs of those lacking dry, heated shelter. I joined the three officers, who like Monaghan all sported the garish orange, yellow, and black slickers favoured by Royal Canadian Mounted Police officers fearful of being struck down by motorists while conducting road-side checks. Sergeant Danchuk offered a scowl and jerky nod by way of greeting before turning his gaze toward the body lying on the sand. Constable Josinder Singh touched the brim of his cap in a two-fingered salute, while Constable Norman Tom merely offered a sad smile that showed no flash of white teeth from within his round, brown face.

Stepping in between Singh and Tom, I glanced down and reflexively sucked in a hard breath at the horror to be found there. I looked upon the body of a young woman lying face up. She was naked. Eyes wide open, staring sightlessly up into the foggy sky, unmindful of the drops of water forming on her face and running across the brown pupils to trail like tears down her cheeks onto the sand. Her long blonde hair, plaited into cornrows into which multi-coloured wooden and glass beads had been woven, fanned out around her head and was thickly matted with sand. There was no horror in how she looked in death, for she had been an attractive woman, despite the gauntness brought on by hunger that had stretched her skin as tight across her ribcage as a drum hide. No, the horror lay in the bands of barbed wire wrapped tightly around her from ankles to shoulders and in the brutally deep gash that encircled the precise centre of her neck.

"Jesus," I hissed.

From where he stood on the opposite side of the young woman's corpse Danchuk growled, "You up to this or not, McCann?"

I took another long breath and raised my face to the drizzle for a moment, letting its icy bite help stave off the lurking nausea. Then I forced myself to look again at the woman. "Is this how you found her?"

"We ain't about to move her," Danchuk retorted. "Call's already in. Forensic team is on the way from Nanaimo. Damned fog meant they couldn't fly in. So they're coming by car." He made a show of pushing back a jacket sleeve to consult his watch and twisted his mouth in thoughtful consideration. "Should be here in ninety minutes or less."

I considered the scene before me, trying to think clearly, to notice everything that mattered and then to remember it. There was the way she lay on her back, legs locked hard together by the encircling wire. Her arms were bound tight to her sides, forcing her into a stance akin to that of a soldier standing at attention.

Then there was the terrible throat wound. Her mouth was open, as if frozen in a scream. Between her body and the three police officers the damp sand was surprisingly devoid of footprints or other tracks. A line of large paw prints that were undoubtedly Charlie's approached the body on the right and then milled about uncertainly until being joined by footprints that looked to match Bess's gumbooted tread. Both these prints retreated in a direct line that ran off and disappeared under the two police cars. The stride leaving was far longer than that of the approach. I pictured Bess and her dog sprinting down the beach toward the nearest stairway or trail leading up to a house, and using a phone there to report her discovery. Bess was a retired elementary school teacher. A calm, serious sort, little given to panic.

There was one other set of footprints that approached almost to the body from where Danchuk stood, executed an about-face, and then retreated back by virtually the same route. Next to the body was an imprint likely left when the person crouched down on a knee for a closer look. "Your footprints, Gary?" I asked in as civil a voice as I could muster. There was a job to do and a duty to perform, so I was determined to try to set aside mutual animosities.

"Yeah, went in close to confirm she was dead. Not that there was much chance she wouldn't be, having her throat slit like that. Bastards."

Although I wondered what bastards he referred to, this didn't seem the time to pursue the matter. I looked again at the woman's body and realized a familiarity. "I've seen her before. She's one of the street kids who panhandled outside the liquor store or the co-op. One of the drummers."

"We made her, too," Singh said. "Not that we have a name. She never gave us that whenever we moved them along. I think she went by Sparrow or something. Move them from one place and they just set up in another."

"Wanted to put them on a bus out of here, but everyone kept sweating about not violating their civil rights and constitutional freedoms. Malarkey," Danchuk grumbled.

"Okay if I take a closer look?" I asked him.

He shrugged uninterestedly. "Step where I did and don't disturb the body. Should be okay then. Don't see what you're going to learn. Ain't like you've got any training."

Choosing to ignore the jibe, I walked around to where Danchuk was and then tried to place my larger foot into his almost dainty little footprints to avoid further disturbing the scene. He was right, of course. For I am a coroner with no medical or forensic expertise at all. Rather peculiarly such knowledge is unnecessary in British Columbia for a community coroner. The Coroner's Act merely cites that a community member in good standing must fill such a position. There is also the inherent requirement that said person have sufficient time on hand to attend death scenes at any time and on any day and be willing to engage in such grim work for relatively meagre remuneration. Still, lack of training aside, my job is to ascertain the cause of sudden deaths in the Tofino area, and I am not one to shirk a duty assumed. And since becoming Tofino's community coroner almost three years ago, I have learned far more than I ever desired about the nature of such deaths.

So I knelt beside the woman who may have assumed the street name Sparrow and considered her corpse. While I did so, Singh and Tom got busy erecting strands of yellow RCMP crime scene tape in a wide square around Sparrow's body, using bits of driftwood stabbed into the sand for posts to elevate the tape to waist height. Danchuk let his minions apply themselves to this task unsupervised, preferring instead to take up a position about five feet away from the body, from where he could closely watch my every move. Always suspicious of me, he apparently feared I would somehow tamper with his crime scene.

Digging into the game pouch on the inside of my Filson jacket I extracted the palm-sized microcassette tape recorder that Vhanna had decided this past Christmas was an absolute necessity for one entrusted with a job such as mine. I had seen no use for it in the various straightforward death investigations lately attended, but this was anything but routine. I had a murder and no shortage of significant and complex details. Remembering them all unaided would be impossible. And the heavy drizzle would quickly reduce any ink scrawled into a notebook to an indecipherable smear on so much soggy pulp. Palming the recorder to screen it from the worst of the moisture, I clumsily keyed the record button and then engaged the pause button until I had something worth saying.

Looking past the glistening galvanized barbed wire entangling the woman, I considered her closely despite feeling a creeping unease at her nakedness. Although malnourishment had eaten the flesh off Sparrow's body, she had fairly heavy bone structure. Given a normal North American diet she would have been prone to plumpness. I noted small purple stretch marks around her stomach and waist and on her breasts that indicated she had once carried significantly more weight than had recently been the case.

Like many young people, she had used her body as a personalized canvas upon which she had spattered tattoos, and various tender points of flesh were pierced with bits of jewelry and steel. Thin metal rings adorned the outside corners of both eyebrows, a diamond-coloured stud pierced her left nostril, a silver bud was centred in the flesh below her lower lip, and a red drop-earring dangled from her navel. Crescents of studs and rings marched up the length of each ear from lower lobe to the rounding of the helix cartilage at the very top. Perched high on her left breast, the tracing of a thin black needle stabbed right through a dusky red heart and tiny red drops of blood sprayed off the needlepoint down toward her nipple. Just above the upper line of her pubic hair, a dove with a strand of thorns gripped in its beak flew in the direction of her navel. In grim irony, tattooed strands of black barbed wire encircled both biceps. But the barbs there had only two prongs, one on each side of the thick weave of the tattoo wire. They lay gently on the skin, wicked in appearance but mundanely benign when compared to the brutal reality of the gashes the four-pronged barbs of real wire had carved into Sparrow's tender flesh.

Once a soldier, I had worked often enough with military wire, both the standard barbed variety, similar to what cowpunchers string on fencelines to pen in cattle, and the razor-edged concertina wire commonly used to confine inmates inside government penitentiaries. The former had been used to create perimeters around positions where the threat from the outside world was deemed minimal and the wire intended only to deter thieves or errant children. The latter had served as a front-line defensive obstacle at roadblocks and for bunkered gun positions. Both types of wire were vicious in their own ways, difficult to work with, and required the use of heavy gloves to avoid painful lacerations.

The wire encircling Sparrow's body was of a standard type I had seen during those days: two galvanized strands of thick iron wound together and interspersed with half-inch-long barbs in a twisted four-prong pattern spaced at intervals of about three inches. The wire was supplied in rolls that increased in length by increments of fifty feet. Even a fifty-foot roll was almost too heavy for a single man to lift. Barbed wire is hard to stretch out or wrap around a post for it inclines to go its own way, constantly seeking to twist into coils of its own design. How anyone could wrap another person so methodically and completely without ending up almost as ravaged as the victim puzzled me. Yet there was no sign on the surrounding ground that the killer had been dripping blood or having flesh flayed from his body as he carried out the crime.

Tripping off the pause button, I murmured a brief description of the barbed wire and the manner in which it was wrapped about Sparrow's body into the recorder's built-in mike. I kept the player close to my lips and my voice at little more than a whisper in order to prevent Danchuk from overhearing. Finished describing the physical characteristics of the wire, I added that each barb appeared to have been dragged back and forth approximately an inch or so diagonally across her flesh with the result that her body bore multiple superficial gashes. Each gash had drawn some degree of blood, so her body was smeared erratically with red splotches from ankles to shoulders. I noted how the blood had dribbled in thick strands down her sides, and yet the sand upon which she lay was barely stained.

When I had first bent over Sparrow's body the stench of rotting meat that quickly starts emanating off a corpse had been almost overwhelming, and I had considered asking Danchuk to fetch a surgical mask to help filter out the worst of it. But such a request would surely have been met by some scathing sarcasm and a delay in my being able to inspect the corpse. Besides, I no longer even noticed the odour, for after about three minutes of exposure to the stench of death my olfactory nerves had simply gone numb. As long as I remained in close proximity to Sparrow's body this would remain the case. If I walked away and cleared my head, then returned, another three-minute endurance test would ensue until the nerves again shut down.

I wondered how long ago Sparrow had been murdered, but there were no conclusive surface clues to go by. Her face and jaw were stiffened by rigor mortis, but it did not appear to be present elsewhere. As this process extends from head to toe in a basically sequential process, this could indicate that she had been killed only a few hours ago. Normally rigor sets in somewhere between two to six hours after death. But there are a host of variables that render it a very poor time indicator. The person's weight, physical condition, and the climatic conditions in which the death occurs are among factors that influence when rigor begins and for how long it persists.

One thing that seemed decidedly odd was the manner in which postmortem lividity had set in. Sparrow lay on her back, arms trussed at her sides. The moment she died, her heart would have stopped beating and arterial and veinal blood flow ceased. Slowly the blood should have begun settling and pooling along her back from head to shoulders and down the length of the back of her legs and arms, turning the skin in these areas an increasingly deep purplish red. Because she was lying on her back, this lividity would not be visible except where the lower parts of her body just edged free of the sand. Yet Sparrow's feet and ankles were coloured entirely purplish, as were her hands and wrists. There was also a sharp purpling of the skin around her pelvis, buttocks, and thighs.

I recalled Doc Tully's autopsy report on Margaret James, one of my first investigations. The poor old soul had passed on sitting in her easy chair watching a television cranked up to almost full volume. And so she had remained undisturbed until a frustrated neighbour knocked on her door nearly a week later to register a complaint. Tully had noted that postmortem lividity was present in her buttocks, pelvis, thighs, feet, and ankles. This was entirely consistent with someone who died sitting in a chair. Sparrow's body showed very much the same symptoms, but she lay on her back.

Having finished recording these observations, I turned my attention unwillingly to Sparrow's throat, forcing back the bile that threatened to rise in my own. Despite having seen many types of violent death as a coroner and having in my soldiering past witnessed more horrific combat-inflicted casualties than should have been the lot of a supposed peacekeeper, Sparrow's death wound was the worst I had ever encountered. Not because of the nature of the gash, for this was remarkably thin and precise, almost surgical in how it formed a narrow line circling her throat. Whatever weapon the killer had used to inflict the wound had sliced deeply into her neck to create a distinct groove. Surprisingly little blood had drained out of the gash, more a gentle weep than a steady flow. Looking more closely, I noted that a very slight trickle of blood was still escaping from the wound.

It was only when I bent closer to the body that I saw a peculiar irregularity in the preciseness of the gash. This came in the form of regular points slicing either upward or downward from the edges of the wound and matching it in depth of penetration. Leaning in more closely I looked this time not at the throat wound but at Sparrow's face. Perhaps it had been the fog or, more likely, the presence of so many red splotches of blood on her body that had prevented my seeing how her face and the part of her neck above the wound were as florid as that of a binge drinker.

Slipping the tape recorder back into a pocket, I extracted a pair of surgical gloves and tugged them on. "What you think you're doing, McCann?" Danchuk barked suddenly. "Don't go disturbing the body, hear."

Shaking my head, I replied, "Don't worry, I'm not about to." Then without waiting for a response I gently reached out and tugged down slightly on the lower lids of Sparrow's eyes. Just as I had expected, the lower whites of each eye were webbed with lines of blood where the capillaries had ruptured.

Pulse quickening, I turned my body so it masked my actions from Danchuk's increasingly dithering bulk. Then I formed my hand into a loose fist and carefully slipped it under the back of Sparrow's neck. Slowly I extended my index finger out of the fist and was not surprised to feel it contact something thin and metallic. Wiggling the finger to one side I touched a barb and released my breath as I extracted my hand from under her neck and rocked back onto my heels.

Standing up, I turned to Danchuk. "Nobody slit this girl's throat. Whoever did this strangled her with a strip of barbed wire." Looking past the sergeant, I gazed at the surf slowly rolling in great grey swells up onto the beach, and the grey fog that hung above them. There was no malice there, just nature's implacability. "Gary," I said, "whoever did this stripped her, coiled her in the wire, and then, while she fought to get free, garrotted her."

Danchuk looked at me hard and then lowered his eyes to the nude woman's body. I saw his jaw grind. Having completed the stringing of crime scene tape, the two constables were drifting back toward us. "It gets worse," I continued. "They moved her here. She was murdered somewhere else."

chapter two

When I finished explaining the absence of blood on the sand and the postmortem lividity anomaly, Danchuk sullenly conceded the likelihood that the body had been moved. "I think we can track back to the actual murder scene," I added.

"Forget it, McCann. We wait for the forensic team. We go tromping about and some material evidence might be damaged."

It is an immutable truth that Danchuk immediately rejects any idea I advance. This necessitates much needless debate, and I have long since learned to curb my temper and try to appear calmly reasonable. "Take a look around, Gary," I said.

Always curiously responsive to direction, Danchuk's square head swivelled obediently this way and that on a stocky neck. His forehead furrowed as he peered at our surroundings with grim concentration. Then his little blue eyes fixed their gaze upon me with a mean glint.

"Nothing to —," he started to say.

I cut him off. "This drizzle is turning to rain. Half an hour from now we could have sheets of rain that will wash the trail away. That'll mean launching a major search to sweep the entire area meticulously, and how many officers is that going to require? How are you going to explain away the fact that you could have moved on this earlier and spared everyone such an effort?"

Danchuk blinked, and a little flash of pink tongue flicked across his bottom lip as if to recover some spittle. His mouth started to open to utter what was probably a scathing rebuke, but then snapped shut with an audible click. I could almost hear his brain grinding from one cog to another as he tried to weigh the consequences of action versus inaction. Obviously if he sat tight and maintained the integrity of the crime scene it was unlikely any higher authority could fault his decision. But if he did allow a trail back to the actual murder site to be washed away his inaction might be considered a failure to demonstrate initiative. He could emerge looking like a dutiful, if unimaginative, constable rather than a resourceful sergeant who capably commands an isolated detachment where the burden of decision making often rests heavily on the shoulders of the officer in charge. Danchuk longs for a promotion, one that will deliver him from the evils of Tofino and take him somewhere that is larger, less wild, and a true haven for Christian evangelists such as him and Donna, his long-suffering wife. Somewhere like Chilliwack, with its valley of dairy farms, sprawling suburbs, shopping malls, and endless churches vying for the title of being more extremely righteous than the others.

For cops there is opportunity to be found in any investigation of a violent, mysterious murder. An aggressive, successful investigation by which the Mountie gets his man can lead directly to promotion, or at least a transfer away from backwater detachments. But should the investigation be fumbled, said Mountie may find himself consigned to an obscure post until retirement. Chilliwack or Tofino. I could see Danchuk weighing the odds. Being a good minion would hardly do. More likely that following such a course would result in his being left to gather moss in Tofino.

His hesitance was irritating. I could feel opportunity literally trickling away as each spatter of intensifying rain struck the sand and threatened the track I sensed would lead us to where Sparrow had died. "Gary, I'm going," I said softly.

Although he scowled at me, Danchuk said, "Okay, let's do it." The words made him sound somewhat like a soldier in a bad war movie heading forth to attack a particularly vicious-looking enemy bunker. He barked over a shoulder at Singh and Tom to stay put and then marshalled close behind me as I walked slowly into the maze of driftwood and tarp structures that the Family had called home.

I scanned the sand carefully, noting the sign running back through the camp from the spot where Sparrow's corpse had been dumped. During my final days in the army I had been a paratrooper in the 1st Canadian Airborne Regiment. We had been trained for small unit operations behind enemy lines where avoiding detection while setting up ambushes was a skill imperative to survival. Footprints are always a problem in such operations because the opposition will assuredly be wary and watchful. So we had learned many techniques for obscuring or eliminating signs of our passing or presence. One relatively crude method was for the last man in a column to sweep away all the footprints made in soft soil with a branch. This is slow, tedious work that also leaves a clear impression that will be visible to any fully alert and well-trained pursuer.

A soldier who is both good at hiding track and blessed with the necessary time will take steps to obscure the pattern left by the sweeping away of footprints. Sticks and pebbles will be scattered about, leaves returned to their former positions, grass clumps bent or flattened will be carefully straightened and separated by a gentle caress. The column of soldiers will also zigzag to avoid leaving a straight trail that is harder to clean. A dozen soldiers can simply disappear without trace of their passing through an area. Fortunately whoever had moved Sparrow's body lacked such skill. The sweeping was perfunctory and thorough, but blatantly obvious. Danchuk grunted dismissively when I showed him the distinctive signs and then cast me a thoughtful sideways glance. I realized suddenly that the sergeant was imagining such skills might be useful to an adulterer and wife murderer. Even all these years after my wife's tragic suicide, Danchuk continues assiduously to seek proof that I murdered Merriam. His belief in my guilt is unshakeable. And it chafes him raw to have to work alongside me.

As I moved past each of the crude shelters I glanced into the little cavelike openings that served as doorways. Some had fire rings inside, and in one a few charred chunks of half-burned driftwood still smouldered. Food wrappers, unwashed tins, and dirty bits of clothing lay strewn carelessly throughout the campsite. There was nothing else. No fresh food, no sleeping bags, no packs, none of the ubiquitous bongo drums they had played with noisy enthusiasm and scant skill while sitting for hours on the beach facing the sea or panhandling in small clusters out front of the businesses downtown. In a few places next to the makeshift shelters the sand had been hard packed in oblong or square shapes by bodies sleeping inside tents and the ground there was less sodden, as if the Family had only recently pulled up stakes and decamped en masse. But had the others left before or after Sparrow's murder? Given the still smouldering fire, it seemed probable that their departure had taken place within mere hours either way.

"One or more of them killed her and then they all ran for it," Danchuk growled when I asked aloud why they would all leave in such obvious haste. "Should be out hunting them down instead of traipsing around here. Ass-backward approach." Yet he made no move to initiate a pursuit.

We left the camp and ventured to the borderline, where tall beach grass and dense clumps of salal competed for space to set roots into the sand. The sweeping marks ran straight up a sandy track, passing between near impassable stands of low-growing, vivid green salal. The brush was heavily beaded with water that brushed off onto our pant legs and jackets as we moved single file up the track and entered a stand of storm-twisted and cracked Sitka spruces and hemlocks that ran up toward the headland.

Moments later we came upon a four-foot-high barbed wire fence that consisted of five strings of wire set about ten inches apart and fastened to thin steel fencing stakes that could easily be hammered into the ground with a sledge hammer. The stakes were set eight feet apart, and the fence marched off in a straight line to block access from the beach to the woods. A small sign tied to each fence section read: "Trespassers will be prosecuted by order of Dagleish Property Development Corporation." Where the trail we followed bumped up against the fence, the wires had been cut to leave the full eight-foot gap between two stakes wide open.

"Maybe should get a warrant first," Danchuk muttered.

With the darkening shadows cast by the trees and the fallen needles lying thick on the ground, it was getting harder to follow the track. But I could still make out signs of a branch having been swished back and forth to wipe out a footprint here and there and occasionally detected the slight impression that a foot might have made in the soil. I stepped through the gap, and after a moment I heard Danchuk shuffling along behind.

Until she passed away last winter this had been Tempest Ashton's land. Shortly after Tempest's death, her children in Vancouver had quickly entered into a development deal with Darren Dagleish to subdivide half the property into several exclusive acreage properties, while the remaining half was to be transformed into a deluxe resort hotel. Vhanna tells me that Dagleish is rumoured to have guaranteed the children not only a higher than normal value for the property but a percentage on the selling price of the estate properties and a stake in the hotel's profits in order to seal the deal.

Tempest had been in her eighties, but was strong and wiry as an old Garry oak until she simply dropped dead while chopping firewood out behind the old house. Fortunately, her son, Jack, had arrived for a visit that very night, so her body was not much disturbed by wildlife when Danchuk and I arrived at the scene. There was a bloody dent in Tempest's forehead, apparently incurred when she fell face first against the chopping block. After a routine autopsy, Doc Tully determined that the injury had likely come within seconds of her heart having simply lurched to an abrupt stop.

It was her husband, John Ashton, who had given Tempest her nickname. He said it was because she was quick to anger and became a force to be reckoned with if ever crossed. Her real name had been Valerie, but once John took to calling her Tempest a year or two after their wedding in the 1950s everybody else followed suit.

John Ashton had been a fisherman who augmented the meagre life that occupation afforded by selectively logging timber on the twenty-acre property and running it up as lumber in a small mill set next to their house. Two years before I moved to Tofino, Ashton and his eldest son, twenty-year-old Richard, had gone out to sea in his thirty-foot trawler in the dead of winter when a weather report predicted a two-day hole between the passing of one storm and the blowing in of the next. Sufficient time, John was certain, to scoop up some herring and safely return. A gamble for sure, but one Ashton had always won in the past. The weather and sea off Tofino is notoriously unforgiving and unpredictable. The Ashtons were half a day out of harbour, and well offshore, when the second storm came broiling in on a quickening wind. Shortly after dawn of the next morning the boat was discovered capsized and washed up as a splintered wreck on a beach in Pacific Rim National Park. There was nobody aboard. The bodies of John and Richard were never found.

Jack, the Ashtons' other son, graduated from high school a year later and quickly departed to study computer sciences. On the day he discovered his mother's body, Jack Ashton told me that he now owned a computer software company that was developing a state-of-the-art record-keeping system for use by financial service firms managing high-end corporate and business bankruptcy asset liquidations. He was very enthusiastic about his product, and it was difficult to affect polite attentiveness to his incomprehensible descriptions of its prowess and robustness, which were terms he used repeatedly to reinforce highlights of its operational capability. My concern at the time had been to determine which other family members needed to be advised of Tempest's passing rather than discussing computers, something of which I remain blissfully ignorant by determined choice. Both Danchuk and I were relieved to hear that he would try to conact Janet, his younger sister, who he assured us was the only other living relative of any closeness.

Although I had moved to Tofino before Janet left, I didn't remember her. But having no children of my own, I have until recently paid scant attention to teenagers, thinking them generally sullen, self-absorbed, and far too impatient to become old before their time. Tully, however, as a long-established family doctor here and also the town's perennial mayor, recalled that Janet and her mother had not got along. The girl preferred boys and partying to attending school, while Tempest believed in hard work and frugal living. After running off several times in her early teenage years, Janet had finally gone for good when she was sixteen and her father ten years dead. Tully believed she had never returned and commented that it was fortuitous that Jack had happened to come home when he had, for he was seldom seen around either. Tempest had never remarried, had lived alone after Janet ran off, and had eked out a living by single-handedly continuing to log and mill mature timber harvested from the property. As the years wound past and her body grew frailer, she steadfastly continued to accept no help. At some point, the logging must have become too much for her. On the day I attended her death the mill lay dormant, slowly rusting away.

The increasingly obscured trail suddenly broke out of the woods into the grounds surrounding Ashton's house. In the months since her death, buildings and equipment had greatly declined. The roof of the big cedar shed housing the sawmill was sagging and buckled open in the centre. Many of the two-storey house's windowpanes were cracked or broken, and the yellow exterior paint was blistered and peeling. A 1970s-era Ford pickup truck listed down on rusting wheels only partially wrapped inside deflated tires. The woodshed door dangled outward from a single hinge. Weeds and brambles now thrived where there had once been lawn, while the gravel of the driveway and parking stand had sunk away into sticky mud.

Given the state of disrepair, the presence of a modern travel trailer parked near the entrance gate came as a surprise. It was an aluminum Airstream — the kind of rig rich Californians drag laboriously up the narrow, snaking highway from Port Alberni that terminates on the edge of the continent at Tofino. Vinyl wheel covers meticulously protected each of its tires from the rotting effect of sunlight on rubber, and its exterior glistened as if from a recent shining. Next to the trailer stood a grey four-wheel-drive pickup that squatted on dual rear wheels like some enormous hard-shelled bug. The truck's hood was open. A gangly man in a blue uniform with badges on the shoulder stood on a small stepstool in order to gain sufficient height to be able to peer in at the engine. A big air filter was balanced carefully on one side of the engine cowling, and a couple of large hoses rested on the other.

Danchuk and I shrugged at each other. Neither of us knew the man or had any idea what he was doing on the Ashton property. The trail was again easily detected, running across the muddy driveway in a straight line to the woodshed. Next to the shed a short length of thickly needled cedar branch had been carelessly tossed aside. Undoubtedly a cursory examination of the branch would reveal that its needled fronds were coated in sand and grit. I pointed the line of the trail out to Danchuk silently. Although he nodded understanding I could tell by the furtive darting of his eyes that Danchuk could not detect the trail even now.

So far the man hovering over the truck engine was unaware of our presence. My interest was to see what lay inside the woodshed, but when I started that way Danchuk gripped my elbow in a firm hand as if placing me under arrest. I scowled down at him, but Danchuk just met my eyes levelly with his own. Then he turned me towards the truck and released my arm. Deciding this was not the time to ignore the sergeant's obvious command, we walked side by side over to the truck.

At the sound of our approach, the man looked over his shoulder. He had a long, thin face that went well with his slender-fingered hands, from one of which dangled a hose clamp while the other held a big screwdriver. The shoulder patch on his blue rain jacket consisted of a white shield, within which the word "Security" was written in gold letters bordered with black. A thin yellow lightning bolt cut between the "u" and the "r." The man sized up Danchuk's police slicker and cap at a glance, flitted his eyes over me in a nanosecond, and then returned his attention to the inside of the engine compartment. "What can I do for you, Sergeant?" he said through gritted teeth while trying to pry the clamp onto a hose with the screwdriver.

Danchuk's eyes narrowed into thin slits, a sure sign that he didn't care for the man's manner. Generally a Mountie expects to have the full attention of whomever he approaches, and no Mountie likely expected this more than Sergeant Gary Danchuk. Normally, seeing Danchuk having his sense of official importance go unrecognized would have caused me some satisfaction, but there was a dead girl and a trail that led to a wood-shed standing not forty feet from where this man calm-ly changed the air hoses and filter on his truck.

"You can start by telling me who you are and what you're doing here," Danchuk said. The hard edge in his voice must not have been lost on the man, for he paused in his efforts, set the screwdriver down, picked up a rag and wiped his hands clean, and then stepped down from the stepstool to face us. Holding out a still grimy hand, the man introduced himself. "Jeb Simms. I'm the securi-ty guard here for Mr. Dagleish. Live in the trailer there." He had watery blue eyes shot through with red veins and an Adam's apple that bobbed when he spoke. There was a nasty line of purple scabs on the back of his prof-fered hand where something sharp had opened a thin gash from the knuckle of his ring finger clear back to his wrist. "What brings you here?" He dropped the hand that neither Danchuk nor I accepted and then glanced towards the beach and the woods with a puzzled expression. "You come up from the beach?"

"Mr. Simms," Danchuk said, "there's been a mur-der down there." I could see Danchuk was eyeing the cut on Simms hand, thinking hard on it. "You mind if we take a look around the buildings here?"

Simms shrugged and then looked thoughtful. "Well, I'm not sure, Sergeant. Maybe I should talk to my boss first. See how she wants this handled."

"She?" Danchuk asked.

Simms nodded. "Yeah, Ms. Walker. She's in charge of Mr. Dagleish's security in this operational sector." He was starting to puff up with officiousness, his lanky frame noticeably straightening. "Let me see if I can raise her on the radio." He started off toward the cab of the truck and then turned suddenly. "Who do I say is want-ing to look around here?"

Danchuk's face reddened as he fought to check his temper. "Sergeant Gary Danchuk. Tofino Detachment Commander of the Royal Canadian Mounted Police, Mr. Simms." He gestured toward me curtly. "And this is Tofino coroner Elias McCann. You raise Ms. Walker and I'll speak to her."

Perhaps sensing Danchuk's impatience, Simms nodded sharply, opened the truck door, and snagged a radio handset from a bracket mounted under the dashboard. "This is Pegasus 3 to Mother Ship," he said, while shooting us a sheepish glance. "Come in." After a moment or two of static crackle, Simms repeated the message. More static, and then a woman's voice responded. "Mother Ship here, Pegasus 3."

Simms ran a tongue over his lips. He seemed suddenly nervous. "Ah, Ms. Walker, there's a police officer here wants to check out some of the buildings. Thought I should call." Danchuk tapped Simms on the shoulder sharply and reached out for the handset. The security officer hesitated a moment, then shrugged and passed the handset over.

Danchuk identified himself with full formality and then gave a brief rundown on the fact that he was investigating the discovery of a body on the beach in front of the Ashton property. Walker expressed her regret about the death, but questioned how it could be connected to the Dagleish Development Company's property. "The property is secured by fencing, Sergeant."

"Fencing that's been cut open, Ms. Walker," Danchuk snapped. "And we've got signs that the body may have been moved from this property to the beach area. So we'd appreciate your cooperation here, Ms. Walker, without having to go through the formality of acquiring warrants."

There was a long silence. "Tell Simms that I'm about ten minutes out from there right now. You can proceed, Sergeant. Dagleish Development Company policy is to always cooperate with any authorities."

Danchuk thanked her and as he passed the handset back to Simms asked, "How'd you come by the cut on your hand?"

Simms glanced at the wound and grimaced. "Snagged it on some wire. Those damned people living down on the beach keep breaching the perimeter and just trooping through here from the beach up to the road whenever they feel like it. Have to fix holes two or three times a week. They're living above the high tide line on our property, too. Been trying to get Ms. Walker or Mr. Dagleish to let me just wire up the beach area and get a court injunction to clear them out of there if we have to. But they keep telling me to be patient and that the bad weather will move them on soon enough." Simms looked like he didn't put faith in that strategy. He brushed a tentative finger over the dried blood on his hand. "Don't know why we have to use barbed wire anyway. Doesn't seem to keep anybody out more than page wire would. Just damned hard to work with, always getting cut."

There was an old house near the hospital that Dagleish had also recently bought. I recalled a barbed wire fence strung around its perimeter and generously covered in "No Trespassing" signs so that the place rather resembled a concentration camp. Apparently Dagleish took keeping people off his property seriously. But at the same time it seemed contradictory that he would allow the One Earth Family to camp unmolested on his beachfront.

"You catch any of those people trespassing on your land?" I asked. "Cutting the wire?"

Simms nodded. "Yeah, the old guy, the one who acts like their leader, and that mouthy blonde girl are the worst. Just walk through here like it's their God-given right. She's the worst one. Always saying we've got no right doing anything with this land. Plain crazy, if you ask me."

"You confront them?" I ignored Danchuk's scowl. He would consider my questioning Simms to be meddling in police business. But there was a death and it was my duty to investigate it. The Coroner's Act gave me the right to pursue that investigation pretty much any way I liked. Right now I liked to see what was to be learned from a security guard with a barbed-wire-induced gash on his hand.

Simms was nodding his head forlornly. "Told them I'd have them arrested. But the girl would just laugh and strut right by as pretty as you please. What was I going to do, wrestle her to the ground and cuff her?" He shook his head and snorted. "I reported to Ms. Walker and she said that, so long as they didn't really hurt anything, it was better to just leave them be. Piss-poor idea if you ask me, but nobody ever does."

When I asked him what the girl looked like, he pretty much described Sparrow. I wasn't surprised. When she was among the panhandlers outside the liquor store, Sparrow had occasionally rebuked passersby for lacking the generosity to drop coins in her proffered knit hat set out in front of where she would sit cross-legged and slap loudly but ineffectually on her drum. I had also noticed how the other young people in the group tended to follow her lead as they moved from one panhandling site to another.

"You see who cut the fence this last time?" Simms denied having done so and said it had been a section over on the south edge of the property where an old deer trail ran through the woods down to the beach. One of their favourite ways across the property, but one that he had recently seldom bothered patrolling because of his instructions not to cause a fuss.

Danchuk looked from me to Simms darkly, as if trying to decide who was more suspect. "We'll have some more questions for you later, Mr. Simms." The security guard assured Danchuk that he would be available at the sergeant's convenience.

While Danchuk concluded his warning to Simms, I headed for the woodshed. Checking the cedar branch laying next to the shed, I saw the fronds were matted with damp sand and bits of vegetation. For sure somebody had used it as a crude broom. Although I doubted that it would be possible to lift fingerprints from the branch, I was careful not to touch it. Danchuk grunted in acknowledgement when I pointed out the telltale signs on the branch. Then he stepped past me to look in the woodshed. "Jesus," he said.

Joining him, I saw three rolls of barbed wire stacked one upon the other in the back corner of the small, rough, plank-walled building. Attached to the wall next to the wire were various tools: an axe, a shovel, a steel rake, a winch and cable, pruning sheers, and a wheelbarrow. Tipped over on its back in the very centre of the shed was a small, simple, straight-backed wooden chair. The woodshed had no floor, and around the chair the dirt was stained dark. I saw what looked like thick smears of blood on the white paint-chipped surface of the chair. There was also the coppery scent of blood in the air mixed with the stench of feces. In one corner was a ragged pile of clothing, an old orange external-frame backpack bulging with hidden contents, and an hour-glass-shaped drum that looked very much like the one I remembered seeing Sparrow playing outside the liquor store.

Danchuk unzipped his slicker and pulled the handset of his mobile radio free of its clip on his shoulder. A moment later he was learning from Monaghan that the forensic team had just arrived. Danchuk told her he would send me down to lead the team up. "I'll stay here," he said. "Keep an eye on Simms and on this." Danchuk was glaring hard over to where Simms had just finished installing the new hoses and air filter. As he banged the hood shut on the truck, a black Toyota Forerunner rolled into the yard and parked next to Simms. The door opened and a tall woman with straight, shoulder-length red hair stepped out. She wore a black Gore-Tex rain jacket, knee-high yellow gumboots into which the legs of her black rain pants were stuffed, and somewhat bizarrely carried a short black quirt tucked under her arm in the same manner in which a British general might sashay about with his riding crop while inspecting an honour guard.

As the woman walked toward us, Danchuk moved to intercept her halfway. He obviously didn't want her to see inside the woodshed, but I knew this wasn't to protect her womanly sensibilities. The less anyone besides the investigators knew about the contents of that shed the better for containing information that might prove critical to the investigation. "Sergeant Danchuk," the woman said, "I'm Roberta Walker, Pacific Rim Sector Security Chief for Dagleish Development Corporation." Almost my height, she towered over Danchuk so that he was forced to look up from under the brim of his cap like a ten-year-old as he shook her black-leather-gloved hand. "I've talked to Mr. Dagleish," she said, "and he has instructed that we are to give you whatever assistance we can." With a flourish, she pressed a gold embossed business card into Danchuk's palm.

When she looked over at me curiously, I introduced myself and declared my job title so she would understand my right to be present. She had green eyes and high Slavic-looking cheekbones. Her gloves stayed on when she offered a firm and brief handshake. She appeared unmindful that the drizzle was getting her hair wet. There was about Walker a slickness in the way she comported herself that seemed better suited to the corporate boardroom than managing property security in a backwater like Tofino.

My friend Stan Jabronski owns the community's only private security firm and also pinch hits as Tofino's volunteer fire chief. He's a big, hard-muscled man with grey hair razored down in a close crewcut. Fiercely loyal to and protective of his customers, Jabronski is also a rough, no-nonsense professional. He has a black belt in karate and is known to have a deft hand with a riot stick. When he's out on the security prowl, Jabronski drives a vehicle studded with radio aerials and mounted with spotlights. The sleeves and chest of his jackets are rife with zippered pockets into which various flashlights, binoculars, communication systems, specialized tools, and other gizmos are squared away. He carries a web belt of gear that, but for the lack of a Smith & Wesson pistol, could be mistaken for Danchuk's.

Except for her quirt and elegant business cards, Roberta Walker, by contrast, appeared entirely unarmed. Yet there was no mistaking that she was the lady in charge. Glancing over at Simms, I noticed that he had fetched a web belt of his own from somewhere and strapped it on so that he was now armed with a long-handled flashlight and walkie-talkie. He was standing at parade rest next to her SUV like a soldier manning his assigned station, with his eyes fixed on our little group gathered in the middle of the muddy drive.

A group that I knew must quickly be reduced to merely two, for Danchuk was looking impatient and there was a team of forensic investigators at the beach that needed guiding up to the woodshed. So off I went, following the ill-swept trail back to the beach, where on the damp sand a dead girl still lay bound in barbed wire.

chapter three

The RCMP forensic team commander introduced himself as Nickerson and offered neither a rank nor a first name. He stood six-foot-six and, despite being completely bald, wore no hat. Every few minutes he ran a big paw across his scalp to swipe away the drizzle forming into thick drops there. Like the rest of his team, Nickerson had on a pair of white coveralls and was speaking through a surgical face mask. When he offered one my way, I accepted. The rotting meat stench had grown much worse in the time I had been away from the beach. Sparrow's body still lay uncovered on the sand. Two of the team members were gathered around her like scavenging gulls, one meticulously photographing the scene while the other took measurements and what looked to be soil samples from next to the body.

Beyond the forensic team, Monaghan and the other Tofino Mounties continued to man the perimeter. Backed in alongside the detachment vehicles stood the forensic team's unmarked black station wagon. Its rear gate was down, and numerous steel equipment cases were open on the inside deck. The thickening precipitation had driven away the onlookers. There was just a long expanse of grey beach shrouded in heavy fog thick with strings of drizzle. I shivered and yearned for home, to be sitting next to the fireplace, sipping a glass of single malt Scotch, with Fergus sprawled contentedly at my feet. Why on earth had I ever let Tully talk me into this grim duty?

"They've got everything in hand here, for the moment," Nickerson said cheerily. "Damned good people. Not the sort to have to be led by the hand. Hardly need me around at all. So we might as well go up and check out this other site where you think the murder might have happened." He clucked rather disapprovingly, as if the murderer had cheated. "Certainly didn't happen here. You're right about that, Mr. McCann."

I told him to call me Elias, and he nodded congenially. Jerking the face mask down so it hung around his neck, he then set off up the path with great distance-gobbling strides that left me scampering to keep apace. "Do you like the bush, Elias? I love it. Just can't get enough. Nothing better than stomping along some trail through a damned big dripping rainforest. Love getting over to this side of the island. Never get enough chances. Too much bloody work. Christ, but this is a pretty little grove, don't you think? Look at that Sitka. Bet it was young when the Spanish galleons were in these waters. What do you think?"

Panting along in his wake, I had only opened my mouth to form a reply when Nickerson veered off into a cursory discussion of salal and the delicious flavour of the jelly that could be made from its berries. Which he loved, though not as much as the Saskatoon berries his wife had made jelly out of when they were stationed in northern Alberta back when he was a young constable. That was a few years after he immigrated to Canada from England. Devonshire. Fine country for rambling and where he had developed his love of tramping in woods. "Nothing like here, mind you. Christ no. Nothing in the Old World like this."

When we barged out of the woods into the Ashton compound Nickerson suddenly quieted and appraised the scene with deliberate concentration. Danchuk had taken shelter on the porch of the house. The engine of Roberta Walker's SUV was running, and the windows were steamed over. I assumed that she and Simms were inside. There was still some trace of the sweeping marks that had not yet been washed away, so I pointed these out to Nickerson and described how we had followed them up here.

"Where did you learn that?" he asked.

It was a different Nickerson now. Still direct and cheerful, but now he listened, and I felt nothing said would be forgotten or any salient point missed. I told him about a misspent army youth, and he clucked in what could have been either approval or not. "Let's see the shed, shall we?"

The increasingly thick fog had robbed the day of much of its light, so Nickerson pulled a flashlight out of a pocket as he approached the woodshed. He flashed the beam around the inside, bending his long frame over awkwardly in the cramped entry to closely examine the stains in the dirt and the tipped chair. "Looks like you're on the money, Elias." To Danchuk, who had just walked up, he said, "Sergeant, get two of your people up here to string some tape around this building. It's just become a crime scene."

Danchuk started snapping orders into his handset at Monaghan in a tone that implied she had somehow messed things up. Nickerson was on his knees, carefully scanning the dirt of the shed under the flashlight's beam. "Swept the inside too. Thorough buggers, weren't they?"

I knelt down beside him, looking for any sign of footprints. There was nothing. "Buggers?"

Nickerson nodded vigorously. "I expect so. She may not have weighed bloody much, but I don't see one man carrying a corpse wrapped in wire like that for that far unaided. Get cut to pieces in the doing of it, I'd think. Wouldn't you?"

"Now I would," I said, believing him right. "Would it be possible to examine the pack?" I explained that we still didn't know the woman's identity and suggested that she would probably have some identification inside it. Nickerson considered the request by examining the ground hard up beside the shed's wall. "Once my people have photographed the whole thing and sampled the contents, I'll have it fetched out of there. That should be soon enough." I nodded agreement.

There was nothing more for me to do, so I left Nickerson and Danchuk by the woodshed and wandered over to escape the rain by standing on the covered verandah that stretched the length of the side of the house facing seaward. When I tried the front entrance door, the knob turned. Out of curiosity more than any belief that the house might hold any clues about the murder I stepped inside.

Although Tempest Ashton had been dead only a few months, her home had the forlorn emptiness of a place abandoned for generations. Not a stick of furniture decorated the place. No pictures hung on the wall, nor were there even any picture hooks or nails still puncturing the plaster. The once-beige carpet underfoot was now blackened with mildew, as the moisture rolled in through the shattered windows, and the interior paint was peeling off in strips from the walls and ceilings. All the fixtures had been removed from the bathroom and kitchen. Where a wood stove had once stood there remained only a rusting metal floor plate and a hole in the wall leading to the chimney flue.

"The family sold everything that wasn't fixed down," Roberta Walker said from behind my shoulder. "There wasn't much of an estate besides the property itself."

Prodding the floor plate with the toe of my boot I noted how the spikes pinning it down gave slightly as if the floorboards were beginning to rot. I thought about the land that John and Tempest Ashton had worked and so obviously loved, this house built by their own hands and maintained by Tempest after her husband's death. Value there for sure, both financial and spiritual. But nothing of either John or Tempest was left. It was as if it had always stood empty. I wondered what thoughts had passed through her son's mind as he had overseen the stripping of possessions from the building. For I presumed that would have been the case. When we had talked on the day he found Tempest dead by the wood chopping block, he had indicated that his sister was nowhere to be found and that there was no other immediate family.

Deciding what to do with the property of a deceased parent, I knew, posed a daunting task. To sell everything off was perhaps no worse than my decision to keep many of father's Edwardian furnishings and leather-bound books. There had been the little farm in the Comox Valley, a remittance man's idyll with its lush green pastures, white barn trimmed in red, and the Britanny Spaniel breeding pens. Angus had known nothing of farming, so it never prospered. Angus had known only of guns, of hunting, of sporting dogs, and of the heartbreak that came when an older man settled down with a younger wife who left him days after his only son was born. There were, of course, the quarterly cheques that arrived from the family business back in Britain, and so his lack of ability in agriculture mattered not. Like his furniture and books, I had been unable to bring myself to sell the place after his death, even though for many years I had professed to despise it, and my relationship with Angus had been restive and difficult at best. When Angus died I chose to rent the farm to someone imbued with far more ability than either Angus or I ever possessed for nurturing life from soil — a young couple who grew chemical-free hay they then fed to some Jersey cows, who in turn chugged out organic milk, which they then transformed into organic cheeses and other all-natural dairy products. They paid a reasonable rent and endowed me with welcome gifts of cheddar and Stilton whenever I ventured to that side of the valley.

"How did the windows get smashed?" I asked. Shards of glass crackled under my boot soles as I walked over to one that looked out toward the mill and woodshed. Nickerson's people were gathering around the shed.

"Vandals. Happened before the family entered into the development agreement with Mr. Dagleish. After Simms was stationed here, it stopped. I imagine it was kids looking for somewhere warm to party. There were a lot of bottles and other stuff that had to be cleaned out." The way she said other stuff gave the impression of things seamy and best not described. Tofino has its share of the young, restless, and wild. Entirely possible they would have tried to use an abandoned house for parties. Someplace dry would be welcome.

Finding nothing of interest on the main floor, I climbed the stairs to the bedrooms there. They numbered four, and at the end of the hall stood a bathroom. Like its mate downstairs, this too had been stripped of plumbing fixtures. Years before, when the children were just youngsters, Tempest and John had apparently wallpapered the upstairs bedrooms to reflect the age and sex of whoever slept within. The biggest room had a soft green flowered motif that would have once been bright and cozy, but was now yellowed and fading. Tempest and John had presumably slept there. Richard's room sported bold alternating navy and aqua stripes that ran from ceiling to floor and would suit perhaps a teenager headed toward young manhood. Conversely, Jack's combined a mosaic of antique steam trains and lithe 1950s diesel trains all dashing toward some distant destination along tracks that buckled perilously upward beneath the steel wheels and extended only a smidgen of distance aft and stern of each well-spaced engine. The trains were grey and set against a pinkish background that I assumed had once been a sharp purple. Then there was Janet's room, where Pooh, Piglet, Owl, Eeyore, and all the other happy campers of Hundred Acre Wood were at home to provide a warm and safe haven for a young girl. Throughout the rooms, the wallpaper was badly faded now, blistering away from the wallboard underneath, and yellow and brown with moisture and mould.

Not a scrap of furniture, clothing, books, or anything else remained in the bedrooms. The upstairs windows were also cracked or shattered, and in Janet's room several rocks lay scattered across the pale pink carpet, evidence of the force with which the vandals had worked their damage upon the place. I wondered idly what a growing young girl might have thought over the years living in this house alone with Tempest after her father and oldest brother had perished at sea.

"When Tempest died, Jack didn't know where to find Janet. Did he ever find her?" I asked.

Walker was leaning against the doorjamb, hands shoved into her coat's slash pockets, quirt dangling from where it looped around her right wrist. I noticed a red and grey flowered silk scarf coiled loosely around her throat. "Our dealings are all with Mr. Ashton," she replied. "He's never mentioned the sister." She looked around the room kind of sadly, as if she too felt the grim spirit of loss permeating the place. "Are you done here?"

I followed her downstairs and out onto the verandah. Monaghan was standing over by Danchuk with a big roll of yellow police tape in one hand. The two faced each other like a couple of gunfighters intent on a close-range shootout. Danchuk's head was thrust out and his mouth was moving while he pointed this way and that to indicate the perimeter he wanted created. Monaghan held herself very straight and tight, her expression absolutely neutral. After only a year with the detachment, the young constable was so tired of Danchuk's hectoring ways that I knew she had taken to applying for every possible posting that would take her elsewhere.

Several months ago on Vhanna's sweeping deck Monaghan and I had faced down a crazed, knife-wielding maniac intent on opening our guts in the way he had done to several other victims. Monaghan had drawn her service pistol and emptied the entire clip into the man at point-blank range, an act that left her emotionally stunned for weeks after. In the aftermath Monaghan and I had become friends and comrades-in-arms in conflict with Danchuk — a classic "your enemy is my enemy" scenario. Danchuk, of course, could dump a lot more trouble on Monaghan's day-to-day life than he could on mine, and the pressure was taking its toll. "Nunavut," she had told me over coffee at the Crab Pot Café earlier this week. "Churchill Falls. I'd go there in a flash. Polar bears and ice floes be damned, anything to escape Fearless Leader."

Methodically, Nickerson and his forensic team were busily working over the woodshed's interior. This was the first time in my short career as a community coroner that I had been involved in a formal murder investigation, and the manner in which the forensic team conducted itself was impressive. I doubted much would escape their scrutiny. They seemed to be endlessly taking samples that were carefully deposited into various plastic bags or vials. I had no idea what the purpose of it all was, but knew there would be a report soon enough that might resolve my investigation. For while the forensic team sought to find clues that would ultimately help with the apprehension of a murderer, my duty was only to determine the cause and circumstance of Sparrow's death. Then I must decide what recommendations might arise from this to prevent such a death being repeated. Given the bizarre nature of this killing, I doubted there would be much to recommend. And I already had a pretty good idea of the cause and circumstance.

Sparrow had died in the woodshed. That was certain. How was less clear. But it looked as if she had been stripped of her clothes and forcibly restrained and bound in some manner to the wooden chair in the centre of the shed. Sparrow's murderer had then tortured her by coiling a long, vicious length of barbed wire tightly around her body from throat to toes. And at some later point, he had taken a shorter length of the barbed wire and cruelly strangled her. Then, as Nickerson believed, the murderer and an accomplice had for some reason carried her corpse to the beach and dumped her in front of the ramshackle shelters in which the One Earth Family had been living.

Had the Family been gone already? Was it members of that group who had murdered her? Or was it Simms with somebody helping him? Both were possible. But I sternly reminded myself that it was not my job to find the killer. Twice now I have ended up in pursuit of a murderer and, although in both cases successful, the result has been a worsening of my already poor working relationship with Danchuk. It was important this time that I not head off on a tangent that would put me at odds with the sergeant. Better to stick to my business and to that alone.

Which, I decided, led to having a look inside Sparrow's backpack. As promised, Nickerson's people had retrieved this from the woodshed and leaned it against one of the verandah's support posts. Spread out next to the pack was a wide blue plastic tarp. Before I had a chance to walk over and ask Nickerson for permission to delve into the pack, the forensic officer strode across the yard and up onto the verandah with one of his assistants double-timing along in his trail to keep up. Nickerson offered a great-toothed grin and handed over a pair of plastic surgical gloves for me to pull on. "Wondered where you had got to. Sergeant and I were just going to take a look inside here." He gestured at the short woman with black hair and olive skin who had been following in his wake. "Simone's been through it already and collected fibre samples and such, but let's be careful to disturb everything as little as possible, alright?"

Danchuk and I gathered around him, and we all stared down at the pack as he rolled the flap-style lid back to expose the contents. "Dark as Hades, isn't it?" he said cheerfully. Whipping a small penlight from a pocket, Nickerson stuck it between his teeth and lit up the inside of the pack. "Travelled light." He suddenly pushed the pack toward me and handed over the light. From another pocket, Nickerson produced a tape recorder much like the one that Vhanna had given me. "Okay, carefully remove each item, one at a time, so that

I can describe it and keep a record of how everything was positioned. Put the items down on the tarp, so they don't get any dirt on them. Top items first, of course, and then work downward, if you please. Sergeant, if you could hold the pack upright so it doesn't tip."

Although his nostrils flared at being relegated to the pack holder duty rather than to the apparently more important task of emptying the pack, Danchuk obediently grasped the upper edges of the metal frame. Danchuk was never one to confront a superior. He marched where he was told to march and made damned sure everyone beneath him in the chain of command did likewise in tune to his orders. "Straighten it up just a little more, Gary," I said, although it was already flagpole straight. It moved fractionally. "That's good."

Looking in, I saw that Sparrow's pack was a disorganized jumble, everything heaved in just willy-nilly. "Was this how things were when the samples were taken?"

"Yes. Simone made a point of keeping everything just the way it was. She just did some preliminary sampling where it was possible to reach items without disturbing them. We'll get more thorough samples back at the lab." He bent so his big shoulder bumped against my own and peered into the pack. "See what you mean."

"See what?" Danchuk growled. "Looks like a filthy bunch of rubbish to me. They were all a dirty bunch. Lived like pigs."

Nickerson caught my eye and winked. "Sergeant, it looks very like the pack was given a toss."

"A toss?"

"Sorry, bit of British slang. I mean that someone searched the pack and just threw the contents back in afterward. Careless."

"But were they looking for something or not?" I asked.

"And, if so, did they find it?" Nickerson said, finishing my thought. Then he shrugged. "Well, we probably can't know that. So let's just see what we've got here and hope there's something useful. Be good to know who she was."

Now that I was to start the task, I found myself hesitant to do so. There seemed something unseemly about going through Sparrow's small assortment of personal effects. Yet another invasion of someone already badly violated. Reluctantly, I picked up the first item and lifted it from the pack. "Pair of wool hiking socks. Grey with red stripe around top. Size six or thereabouts," Nickerson said into his tape recorder. More clothing followed. A yellow T-shirt, U.S. Army jungle-patterned camouflage fatigues, a green wool sweater sporting multiple small holes, two pairs of manly looking women's Jockey underwear. One soiled, the other dingy but clean. Then a tattered paperback copy of Samuel R. Delaney's *Dhalgren*, a post-apocalyptic novel that I remembered struggling through while standing down from watches on the Nicosia Green Line for no better reason than there was nothing else to read. A thin brown wool blanket and blue sleeping bag with a musty-smelling flannel interior lining. Small pair of scissors, a jack knife, a toothbrush in a plastic holder with tube of toothpaste attached to it by an elastic band, a bar of soap in a plastic container, and a little leather pouch that contained some odd bits of jewelry and a half-smoked roach. Danchuk snorted knowingly when I produced this.

There was a multicoloured striped toque of the kind favoured by Rastafarians. Underneath this, I unearthed a silver metal plate, mug, bowl, and set of utensils. A plastic shopping bag from Tofino's Co-op Grocery was half filled with a few bags of herbal tea, some mushrooms, an onion, two red apples, a morsel remaining from a cheap chocolate bar, and a couple of rice cakes. Finally, in the very bottom of the pack, I found a plain spiral-bound notepad with a cheap pen stuck into the coil to keep pad and pen together. When I flipped the notepad open the first page was devoid of any ink. All the other pages were likewise blank. But the pad was only half there. Of the first half of the pad only a few shreds of paper attached to the coils remained. Someone had carried off whatever Sparrow had written. "Damn," I muttered.

"Too right, old chap," Nickerson agreed. "Whatever secrets the girl might have scribbled in there are gone now."

I thanked him for his work and Danchuk just scowled — his meaning unreadable.

Nickerson and I carefully repacked Sparrow's meagre belongings. "Anything in her clothes?" I asked.

He shook his head. "No, just another doobie in her jeans pocket, a stick of chewing gum, and a couple dollars in change. She either carried no identification or …" He didn't need to complete the thought.

When Nickerson's team concluded their work in and around the woodshed we gathered up the samples and equipment to return to the beach. Walker's vehicle still stood in the yard, engine running, wipers periodically sweeping back and forth to clear the rain beading on the windshield. The woman's shadowy form sat behind the wheel, Simms in the passenger seat.

Our little group proceeded in single file back along the trail that had been taken by the murderer or murderers. Wet, cold, and bedraggled we proceeded in silence. Even the seemingly irrepressible Nickerson appeared uninterested in conversation. As we passed through the abandoned camp I thought of the threads of smoke that had been drifting out of the fire ring in the one shelter. Ducking through the narrow entrance, I crouched over the small pile of still hot ash and poked it gently with a stick.

"Nickerson," I called. "Can you take a look at this?"

Seconds later his big head popped through the entrance and he wriggled in alongside me. The roof was so low that we were both on our knees in the damp sand. Taking the stick from my hand he delicately lifted one charred flake of material and grunted. "Paper, I think. Sally," he shouted, "bring some containers. We've got a pile of ash to gather up here. Still hot."

A moment later a small Asian woman slipped in beside us, and I backed out of the shelter to give her and Nickerson more room to do their work in the cramped space. When they emerged the forensic team leader patted me on the shoulder lightly. "Good work there." He wiped the rain off his head and face tiredly. "Hot fire, though. I doubt we'll be able to read anything of it. Swept his way in and out of there just like he did everywhere else. A right thorough bastard."

chapter four

Fully seven hours after its discovery, Sparrow's body was gently zipped into a body bag, placed on a stretcher, and loaded into an ambulance for transport to the hospital. A forensic pathologist had accompanied Nickerson's team and now waited there to perform the autopsy assisted by my good friend Dr. Reginald Tully. My presence was mercifully unnecessary, for either the pathologist or Tully would report their findings to me later that evening or, depending on how long the procedure took, the following morning. So I shook Nickerson's hand, nodded curtly to Danchuk, and tapped a finger to the brim of my Filson in silent salute to Monaghan before trudging off down the beach toward the Land Rover and home.

A steady rain was falling, and a biting wind whipped off the ocean to blow the water in under my hat brim and spatter my face. Gratefully I crawled into the Land Rover, turned the ignition key, shoved a thumb down on the starter button, and mashed the gas pedal to the floor while gentling the choke lever out to find the necessary trim to bring the old girl to life. The starter whirred, and the engine shuddered and spat and then settled into a rough idle that rattled the small cab. Built in the 1960s, when British vehicle manufacturers were still British-owned and turned out quality products built by skilled craftsmen, my Land Rover is a far cry from the modern SUV-style urban runabouts with all their comforts and state-of-the-art operational systems. She harks back to an era when Britain's influence spanned the globe and there was need for a vehicle that could traverse Saharan dunes, grind over Himalayan passes, wade through flood waters in the swamps of Borneo, or drag a Yorkshire farmer's plow across a muddy field. I could easily afford to replace her with some modern piece of computerized machinery made of plastic and thin steel, but she has been with me a long time. And though her engine and transmission are in decline, the solid aluminum body is as stout as the day she clattered off the assembly line. So I scrounge parts to effect repairs and stoically tolerate her mechanical eccentricities.

What the Land Rover will not do is hurry. She turtles. Slowly scuttles along the road at a steady, noisy gait. With darkness falling, a cold rain pattering loudly on the roof, and heavy humidity fogging the windscreen inside and out, I pleaded silently with the defroster to finally yield up some heat while I wiped a rag repeatedly over the window to clear a vision hole. The two individually controlled windshield wipers beat back and forth in their typically out-of-synch manner, managing only to smear the rain rather than sweep it aside. This forced me to bend over the steering wheel with chin almost on the dash to see anything.

I wound along a narrow access road, greasy with running water, until it eventually intersected the highway, which offered only marginally better driving conditions. The wind pummelled the side of the Land Rover, and the rain blew down in great, thick sheets to ricochet up off the pavement. Every dip in the road was running with a freshet, but the Land Rover waded through with such a slight waver that I saw no need to get out and engage the four-wheel-drive lugs.

Finally we rolled along Tofino's main street, dimly lit by a straggle of ill-placed streetlights. At every passing street corner and in front of the scatter of businesses lining the road a motley assortment of election placards had been speared into the ground or nailed to utility poles. A few bore the name of our current mayor, Reginald Tully, and these simply read: "Re-Elect Mayor Reginald Tully." The lettering was bold and red. But these signs were grossly outnumbered by the others, which exhorted Tofino's electorate to "Vote Monica Klassen Mayor, Your Voice For Prosperity!" in bold blue lettering. It seemed my good friend and doctor faced a stiff re-election fight. One he was welcome to. As I turned onto the gravel side road that ran past one of the government docks, I wondered why on earth anyone would want to be mayor of a town filled with the lot of idiosyncratic characters that call Tofino home.

When I drove up a short rise to where my cabin overlooked the wide waters of Duffin Passage, with Meares Island on the opposite side, it was impossible to see any sign of the ocean below. There was just blackness so thick that I could barely see the glow of the light over the cabin door as I climbed out of the Land Rover and ran for shelter. The moment the door opened Fergus pressed out against my leg, and I bent to give him a quick scratch behind the ears. A shake of his head jangled the dog tags at his throat, and he let out a small chuff of complaint at the sight of the rain hammering the yard. Then, with surprising speed for an aging dog, Fergus lumbered across the open yard and rustled off into a dense clump of salal and ferns growing under the cedars that run down toward the water. A few minutes later, business attended to, he re-emerged and, brown and white coat dripping, hustled back to the protection of the small outside porch. I waited for him to give his body a hard shake to throw off the worst of the water and mud before letting him back inside.

Fergus was part of the last brood produced by my father's Brittany Spaniel breeding stock and was just a puppy when Angus died. He was the scrawny weakling of the brood, with a little crooked jaw that gave his mouth a somewhat querulous expression and meant he would have no particular purebred value despite his lofty heritage. Because he was so small his eyes had seemed enormous, and when I had held the pup up in my arms he had nibbled hungrily on the collar of my jacket and delicately licked my cheek. Merriam and I had agreed there and then to take him home. Fergus had rebounded quickly, becoming strong and healthy on an indulgent diet and much loving attention.

Something he obviously felt had been missing this day, for Fergus walked directly across the kitchen to his empty food dish and equally depleted water bowl to give both a good rattle with a smack from a big, catlike paw. I quickly filled the bowl with water and poured a couple cups of dry gourmet chicken-flavoured dog food into his dish. After lapping up some of the water, Fergus turned to noisily crunching food while looking over his shoulder at me and then directing his gaze instructively toward the Franklin stove standing in one corner of the kitchen.

Having shaken off my Filson coat and hat and hung them on a peg, I could feel the damp cold of the house and had to agree with Fergus that the next order of business was getting some warmth back in the place. Pulling the cast iron doors open, I crumpled a wad of newspaper and lay it on the hearth, then sequentially piled on cedar shavings, slivered cedar kindling strips, some larger pieces of cedar, a couple of good-sized chunks of split hemlock, and atop it all a small alder log. Striking a wooden match, I lit the paper at the base, and soon the sound of crackling and popping cedar filled the room. Once everything was heartily ablaze, I closed the Franklin's doors and savoured the warmth already radiating outward from the stove.

Meal over, Fergus was sidling around my legs, taking an unseemly interest in the various scents that lingered on my jeans and shirt. Although aging, his sense of smell remains keen and he is unduly attracted to the odours imparted by corpses — whether they be animal or human. To his disgruntlement, I put the clothes into the wash and headed for the shower. Eliminating the stench of death from my sinuses, body, and clothing has become a familiar routine. The clothes can be renewed by a regular wash, my canvas Filson coat and hat purged by a liberal dosing of a commercial odour eliminator, and myself by a thorough scrubbing with lemon-scented shampoo and bath soap. When I emerged in fresh jeans and corduroy shirt, Fergus lifted his nose, tested the air, and sniffed with haughty disappointment before stretching out on a mat next to the stove and staring pensively over toward his dishes.

Having no intention of feeding anybody but myself at this point, I chose to ignore the unwarranted hint that he was being underfed and turned instead to fixing a steaming, spicy curry. This was the last step, a surefire method for neutralizing my sinuses. Dinner done, I washed up the dishes, poured an after-dinner snifter of cognac, lit a fire in the living room fireplace, and settled in my father's large old leather chair that stands alongside the hearth. All my slights apparently forgiven, Fergus sidled across from the kitchen to curl up on a rug set before the fireplace specifically for his comfort.

It would be nice, I thought, if everyone were as easy to get along with as Fergus. But, of course, that was not at all the case.

The knife-wielding Chinese Snake Head whom Anne Monaghan had killed last summer had mortally wounded Vhanna's cousin, Kim, mere moments before her shots felled him. By the time Monaghan and I reached Kim's side, nothing could save the young man. We tried to stem the blood gushing from the deep slash in his guts, but there was so much internal bleeding that our efforts had been in vain. Kim had died quietly, murmuring not a word and emitting not a single moan of pain during the few short minutes it took for his life to drain away. He was gone by the time Vhanna finished mounting the stairs that led from the beach up the almost sheer cliff to her deck above.

Sprawled like a broken doll on the sandy beach below was the body of the knife-wielder's accomplice — back and neck broken by his striking the beach after plunging from the deck. He had come up the loser in a short melee with Vhanna. A Tai Chi combat adept, Vhanna had knocked him over the railing only to be dragged along in his wake when the Chinese Snake Head grabbed her elbow and pulled her over the rail with him. Ever nimble, and strong out of all proportion to her small, lithe body, Vhanna snagged an outgrowing tree branch to still her fall. The man didn't. So a killer died and a survivor lived. The woman I love is not easy to kill. Something her assailant was not the first to learn, although as far as I know he was the first to die in the learning.

Vhanna had bounced up onto the deck with a look of wild elation flaring in her brown eyes and teeth flashing in a warrior's grin of triumph. Every muscle was tight and pulsing from the adrenaline burning through her veins. A long, silent moment had ensued as she absorbed the sight and import of Monaghan and I crouched next to Kim. Slowly she had smoothed her long, straight black hair with the fingers of one hand and then hesitantly crossed the deck to where her cousin lay. I reached for her, but Vhanna rested a palm on the back of my hand and pushed it gently, firmly aside. Then she knelt in front of Kim and lightly closed his eyes. "Leave us," she said in a voice that was no more than a whisper.

Monaghan and I had quietly withdrawn into the house, leaving Vhanna with the cousin she had so recently found and now had lost so brutally. The constable had gone out the front door to call in a report on the police cruiser radio, while I stood before the living room's vast plate glass window and watched a line of whitecaps roll in beneath a brilliant blue sky to strike the white sand. Sky, water, sand — a view full of peace and gentleness that lay at odds with the reality of death that had visited this home and remained on the deck in one corner just out of my line of vision.

After Kim's death, Vhanna decided his cremated remains must be returned to their homeland for scattering in order that his soul might have some hope of attaining peace. She would not hear of my accompanying her. It was a duty that was hers alone. So with the leaves just beginning to yellow after a few crisp nights as early warning of fall's approach, I had driven Vhanna and the little Chinese urn bearing Kim's ashes to Vancouver and watched her disappear through the security gates to board a plane for Phnom Penh. This was Vhanna's second trip in as many years to that tormented homeland from which she had escaped. The first time she had gone in search of surviving family, a journey that had ultimately turned up Kim. Now she went to bury her last relative. The rest were undoubtedly lost to the Khmer Rouge genocide that had left millions of corpses strewn across Cambodia. A tragedy of global proportions, a nation left to waste, and a family of Cambodian Chinese swept away like ashes on a breeze.

Except for a ten-year-old girl who escaped to make her solitary way through putrid jungle swamps and over the mountains of Chuor Phnum Dangrek to eventually reach the refugee camps in Thailand. She had witnessed her father's murder on April 17, 1975 — the day the Khmer Rouge came to Phnom Penh to begin the slaughter and enforced evacuation of the city's entire population to the countryside as part of a crazed scheme to transform Cambodia into a Communist agrarian utopia. Her Chino-French mother had succumbed to starvation. Her family was scattered and lost. Most probably ended up brutally executed and dumped in the mass graves scattered across the countryside or left to rot in the ditches alongside the road that the columns marched down as part of a nightmarish trek to nowhere.

Vhanna never speaks of her experiences under the Khmer Rouge. I know these few scant details only because she once — and once only — confided them to her foster father, Lars Janson. Lars and his wife, Frieda, had been working in the refugee camp to which Vhanna was brought after her escape across the border into Thailand. Eventually they brought her to Canada and settled in Tofino, a happy outcome for a young refugee.

The indelible marks these childhood horrors have left on Vhanna's soul are beyond my comprehension. And I fear that each return to Cambodia, with all the suffering that persists there still, serves only as a scalpel to reopen the wounds and inflict a deeper cut on her psyche. It had been less than a month since her return, and in her eyes I sensed a brooding sadness that might be impossible to ease away.

When Lars and Frieda found Vhanna in the refugee camp she was living alone in a storeroom closet rather than sleeping in the common room set aside for orphans. There was little life left in her, for she had taken to foraging on her own rather than joining the queues for the paltry meals of rice and soup that were the normal daily fare. Vhanna never explained to Lars why she had withdrawn as she had, and it was only through his and Frieda's patient nurturing care that she recovered from malnutrition and slowly came to give them her trust.

I believe Vhanna sought refuge in that storeroom closet because it was an environment that she, and nobody else, controlled. Same with the decision to forage for her own food, no matter how poorly she succeeded. During her long trek through the wilderness, Vhanna had lived on grubs, wild fruits, and the roots of plants. She developed a necessary self-reliance that only strengthened over the ensuing years, so that she is now always quick to remind people that she is entirely capable of taking care of herself without interference from others — particularly me.

Although self-sufficiency is a truly admirable trait, it can at times lead to unnecessary personal costs. Vhanna's unwillingness to share any emotional pain with others leads her periodically to shut people out of her life at a time when she could most use their support. Upon Vhanna's return from the pilgrimage to Cambodia with Kim's ashes, she had withdrawn into her Tofino refuge, the great house on the beach. Her phone directed callers to leave voice mail messages that were not returned, and no invitations to drop around were issued. In the past I would have attempted to force the issue by appearing unannounced at her door with predictably disastrous results. When Vhanna seeks seclusion it is folly to force myself upon her, even with the noble intent of offering comfort. So this time I had been staying away, allowing her to decide when to reach out to me.

But always in these times I remain hopeful, possessed of an eternal optimism — a trait Vhanna believes is one of my character flaws, setting me up for only greater disappointment. Fergus shares this trait, so both our heads cocked hopefully when the phone rang.

Approaching midnight, it seemed a bit late for unexpected callers other than Vhanna. A night owl, she has on occasion phoned with an invitation or to suggest her coming by for a visit. Either offer is always fine by me. So it was more than a little disappointing to hear Reginald Tully's voice requesting that I make myself immediately present at the hospital. "There's some things that I can show you better than explain," he said. "Sorry," Tully added, for he knows how much I hate these forays into pathology hell.

Tully awaited me in an examination room with pale green walls and a mud brown linoleum floor. Sparrow lay on the stainless-steel autopsy table, covered by a rubber sheet. "God's tooth, what a night, eh?" Tully said, as I shook my coat and hat off in the hallway and tossed them onto a chair by the door before entering the room. He wiped his bottle-thick glasses with a napkin, held them up to the light to inspect his handiwork, and slipped them back on. I was trying very hard not to be affected by the foul rotting stench filling the air and studiously ignored the sad form stretched out under the sheet.

"You'll get a more thorough written report from the forensic pathologist probably in a day or two, but I thought I should go through this by way of filling you in on general information." Tully tugged his glasses off and rubbed his eyes as he does often when perturbed or troubled by something. "And there's things you can surmise in this work but don't want to put in a formal document. It's a grim bloody business, Elias, I'll tell you that."

Without further ado, Tully carefully slipped the sheet off Sparrow's corpse. I gritted my teeth. There was the normal wide "Y" incision extending across the chest from shoulder to shoulder and then slashing down the front of her abdomen to the pubis, so that all internal organs could be removed top to bottom and then examined. "We haven't done the craniotomy yet for reasons I'll show you." That explained why Sparrow's face and skull were untouched. Usually her skull would have been sawed open across the crown and then peeled forward to expose the brain for removal, leaving the frontal scalp lying like a flap over her face. The indirect combined effect of the "Y" incision and the craniotomy is to strip the autopsy subject of virtually all identity, reducing the corpse to an anonymous human carcass. So far, Sparrow had been spared some of that loss.

Tully started with the wounds caused by the barbed wire that had been wrapped around her corpse — cut away at the beginning of the autopsy after being carefully photographed and examined in meticulous detail. Tully confirmed that the nature of these wounds indicated that Sparrow had been alive when her attacker wound her up inside the barbed wire and that she had been seated, presumably on the white chair found in the woodshed.

He pointed to her wrists and handed me a large magnifying glass. "Look closely." I peered at her wrists and after a moment noticed they were circled by a narrow red line and that in places along that line the skin had been broken. "There are similar laceration and bruising marks on her ankles," Tully said, "that are consistent with the kind of wound that would be left if her hands and feet had been tied together by thin lengths of rope." With Tully directing my eye, I was able to quickly detect the markings on her ankles.

"Now, look at this." Moving gently and carefully to ensure the corpse stayed on the narrow autopsy table Tully turned Sparrow face down. He pushed her thick cornrows of blonde hair up from the base of her neck to expose a large purple bruise on the back of her skull. "Looks like she was struck by a blunt object." Tully let the hair drop back in place. "We suspect an unseen assailant armed with some kind of club struck her from behind in order to knock her unconscious. She was then dragged to the woodshed, bound by her ankles and hands to the chair there, and then ultimately murdered."

He went on to confirm that she had been garrotted with the strand of barbed wire and that this was the ultimate cause of death. "From the deep wire lacerations on her lower arms and lower legs, it's evident that she had regained consciousness at some point and was struggling right up to the end," Tully said grimly. "She didn't die easily."

It took a pretty cold-blooded killer to strangle so viciously someone who was fighting for her life. During my airborne days we had trained in such killing techniques for the purpose of covertly silencing enemy sentries. But we were always made to understand clearly that it took a desperate situation for the average soldier to find the hardness of heart to take another soldier's life in this manner.

There was a tendency to relent, to loosen the pressure the moment the victim ceased struggling, hoping he had been rendered unconscious and that that in itself would suffice. Such an act of mercy could prove a grave mistake that provided the enemy soldier the opportunity to emit a warning cry or even to break free and fight back. Better to use a knife for up-close work or even shoot the sentry at close range with a gun and just be done with the job.

I mentioned some of this to Tully and he grunted agreement in the way of one not wanting to be distracted from the task at hand. "There's another thing. You probably wouldn't have noticed it out there because it's fairly subtle. We measured the depth of the lacerations made by the barbed wire that was wound around her and found it varied, being deepest across her breasts, stomach, upper parts of her arm, and across her back, particularly along the flanks. It didn't seem sensible that her murderer could have just randomly tightened these strands more than those on her lower body with his hands alone."

Tully went over to a tray set on a stand and carefully withdrew a length of barbed wire that had an identifying tag taped around it. "We couldn't remove the wire all in one length, so it's cut up into sections and numbered so that each can be linked to the next part to reform the total strand." He set the piece of wire down on the stand. It looked entirely unremarkable, except for the fact that each barb was darkly stained with dry blood. "You would see it if you were looking at all the strands still wound around her body." Carefully he withdrew three more strands and lay them out one above the other.

"They each have a kink in them," I said softly. Set out flat in the manner that Tully had placed them each strand of wire was like a short stretch of river, and in the precise middle each looped to form an oxbow.

Tully nodded enthusiastically, and I realized that despite the gruesome nature of the work he was proud of this discovery. He strode back to the table and gestured toward me with the magnifying glass. "Take a look at her back, focusing on the spine."

I did as ordered and soon noted that the lacerations cut into her back by the barbed wire seemed deeper and more widely spread than elsewhere. Even more so than was the case for where the wire had circled tightly around her flanks and hips. "Absolutely correct, Elias," Tully said. "The forensic pathologist and I believe that not only was the girl wound in the barbed wire, but that the upper strands were wrapped around some kind of object that was fitted up against her spine. Her killer was then able to alternate the tension of the wire circling her body by turning that object like a crank. Twist it one way and the barbs cut more deeply, twist the other and they marginally retracted."

"What kind of object?"

"We're not sure. Could have been a wooden pole or a length of pipe. Something like that."

"He wanted something from her," I said.

Tully nodded. "Either information or just to hear her plead for mercy. Who can know?"

I thought about that. "Reginald, was there any evidence of a sexual attack?"

He shook his head. "No trace of semen or any form of forced vaginal entry." Tully paused, as if considering something. "There was, however, a degree of vaginal scarring such as would result from forced entry some years back, probably when she was in her early teens or just past puberty." Tully shrugged. "Additionally, there are a number of scars on her body, particularly stomach and breasts, that indicate her having been cut with a very thin knife or razor blade at about the same age.

These cuts aren't deep, barely flesh wounds. The sort of injuries a terrorized teenager could probably successful ly hide from parents, teachers, and friends by treating them herself with Band-Aids and keeping them hidden until the cuts healed. It's a common enough story. Probably half the young girls living on the streets were sexually assaulted at home by some relative or another and forced to keep it secret by persuasion, threats, or physical punishment. A good motivation for running away and taking to the street life."

Tully was undoubtedly right about this, but what had happened in this girl's past likely had little or no direct bearing on how she came to be killed. I was interested in her murderer and what the means he used to take Sparrow's life told us of him. "If he had been torturing her purely for sport, you would think he would have at least attempted a rape."

The doctor considered this, which led to a careful cleaning of his glasses and wiping of tired eyes. "Hypothetical, Elias," he finally allowed. "First, we don't know for certain that the killer was even male, although I imagine that to be the case. So, assuming the killer was a man, don't forget the sexual innuendo suggested by her having been stripped of her clothes before he started working her over. This could be a sex crime even without there having been a rape." Tully turned the body back over onto its back and replaced the rubber sheet covering. "That's all I've got for you. We've taken a lot of samples that might yield DNA evidence later. But that's beyond what you need. I just wanted you to be clear on how she was murdered." His tone hardened. "Whoever did this is cruel, calculating, and probably sadistic."

Tully peeled off his surgical gloves and disposed of them, then shrugged out of the surgical gown and dropped it into a laundry bag. As he began washing up,

Tully noticeably stifled a yawn. "Bloody late night and I have to look all chipper and confident in the morning for a Chamber of Commerce breakfast. They call them Power Starters, if you can believe it. Probably won't even be able to get a decent plate of bacon and eggs. Quiche or something."

"How's it look?"

"Early days." He looked worried, though. "It's not that I'm particularly attached to the mayor's chair after all these years of sitting in it. But I don't want to see someone in charge of our town that would turn it into Disneyland, either. Trouble is she's got the ear of the business community and is offering up a bag full of promises. Lower taxes and less controls that hamper progress. As likely as not what she's offering is just a bed of fool's gold more than pay dirt, but it's the sort of stuff guaranteed to spark the dreams of your entrepreneurs, and that's the vote that usually counts in these elections. Stability is what we need, and that means not running toward change for change's sake."

He was starting to get wound up, so I comforted him by saying he had my vote and should save his energy for the morning. Tully laughed and poked me in the shoulder with a knuckle. "Your vote. Will you even come out and mark a ballot? Are you even registered?"

I had no idea. Tully was right. I had never voted in the past. Scarcely could be bothered turning out for provincial or federal elections, let alone municipal ones. Tully had been the mayor for a decade, longer than I had lived in Tofino. His mayoralty had seemed immutable. "It'll work out, Reg." Tully snorted at my empty assurance.

We walked out of the hospital into the slanting rain, shook hands briefly, and then jogged toward our respective vehicles.

chapter five

I spent a restless, largely sleepless night punctuated by occasional descents into disturbingly vivid and confused nightmares. Wrenching awake from the last just before dawn, I abandoned bed for shower. But the haunting images torn from the subconscious were too intense to easily escape. There was the familiar Nicosia plaza torn by a blast of fire and steel, and a little Cyprian girl whose blood gushed over my hands even as I tried to stem its escape with one quickly saturated bandage after another. Over the years this girl, whose name I never learned, has faded into death before my eyes during hundreds of dreams. She remains suspended in a time warp within my psyche. Had she lived, the girl would be approaching the middle of her years. Did her parents still live, grieve, and light candles of remembrance in her memory at the cathedral? Was she remembered and idealized by her brothers, sisters, aunts, uncles, and cousins? Had her death served to stoke the flame of ethnic hatred in their hearts or led one family to extend the hand of forgiveness across the barriers that split Greek from Turk on that idyllic but tormented island?

I had worn the blue beret there, and we had come to enforce a peace bloodily shattered by an outpouring of violence that raged throughout the summer of 1974. All these years later I still recall with absolute clarity the chaotic firefights that ripped across Nicosia's Green Line — the armed barrier that divided a city into two ethnic ghettos. It is the curse of soldiers, I believe, to live so intensely during combat that those memories are indelibly etched upon their souls to be carried to the grave.

The dream itself always leaves me shaken, but this time seemed worse than usual. For even as I stared down into the girl's dark, questioning eyes and urged her to stay with the living, her hair had lightened and twisted into cornrows until I was looking into Sparrow's lighter brown eyes. Then the eyes had slowly morphed, assumed Vhanna's elliptical almond shape, only to thin even more, and I no longer strove to prevent blood escaping from the Cyprian girl's chest but pressed hard on Hui's frail chest to expel water and bring her back from drowning. A race I had won, but not this night. Helplessly I had watched the light fade from Hui's eyes, and even as I cried out I lurched awake, wiped the sweat from my chest, and threw back the duvet.

Paws braced on the edge of the bed, Fergus stared across at me with concerned eyes. When my breath steadied and heartbeat slowed, I patted him and offered reassurance that I was okay. Dubiously he shook his head so that his ears flopped about and the dog tags rattled, before wearily trudging across the room to climb back into his big wicker basket bed.

I reminded myself that the dream was that and only that. Unlike the Cyprian girl, Hui was alive and well.

When I had found her floating in a tide pool near the wreckage of the freighter she had been on the verge of death. But I had managed to bring her back from that edge. Vhanna and I had successfully won her refugee status and hoped soon to have Hui confirmed as a landed immigrant. Until that status was secured there remained the lingering worry that some tragic circumstance might see Hui deported back to a homeland where her future would be dubious at best. Mercifully, Lars and Frieda Janson had agreed to once again take a traumatized child from distant Asia into their home and serve as her adoptive parents. Neither Vhanna nor I had for a moment entertained the thought that our tenuous relationship could offer a child a stable environment. Nor did either of us believe ourselves good parenting material. So we serve as pseudo-godparents, a role that we can each act out in our separate ways.

Since the day that I scooped her from the grip of the tide pool's icy waters, Hui has undergone a major transformation from frightened refugee and shipwreck survivor into an almost typical precocious Canadian child. How she came to be on that ship remains a mystery. Did her relatives in the Fujian region of China sell her to the Snake Heads? Was she kidnapped?

Most of the illegal migrants who washed up from Fujian Province on a series of dilapidated freighters during that long summer were summarily rounded up and deported back to China — men, women, and children. Hui was spared this fate because the Chinese government was unable to find anyone who would claim to be related to the girl or to have any knowledge of her parentage. Return to China would only have resulted in her placement in some squalid orphanage, so the immigration authorities had relented and granted Hui refugee status.

As the first glow of dawn dusted the house in a soft light, I woke Fergus, and together we strolled down a muddy track that passed beneath the dripping branches of tall firs, hemlocks, cedars, and the occasional massive Sitka. The rain had blown itself out sometime during the night, but the sopping cedar boughs released a divine herb-like scent that mingled with the smell of wet earth and rotting leaves and needles. Occasionally the trees bordering the shoreline thinned, permitting brief glimpses of fog lying low on the water beyond. The upper reaches of Meares Island, heavily cloaked in its old-growth forest, rose seemingly out of the very heart of the fog. And beyond the island Clayoquot Sound's mountains towered, each cloaked in great expanses of precious timber. Overhead, thick, scudding black clouds were being shredded into long strings by high atmosphere winds. By noon the sky might be clear or, just as likely, a new storm front could have blown in.

At first Fergus remained by my side to demonstrate his comradely concern, but eventually the lure of possible sport proved too great. He ran ahead in quest of grouse or squirrel. The occasional noisy rustle of brush or cracking of branches underfoot betrayed his whereabouts and served to warn off any game long before Fergus might actually overrun it. Now elderly, Fergus has lost much agility and more than a little speed. His dashes are now short-lived and more a lope than a sprint. And in recent years my shotguns remain more often than not back in the gun locker rather than tucked in the crook of my right arm as we wander these familiar woods. Today, given the cold, my hands were shoved into the deep pockets of the Filson and I gave no thought to the prospect of downing either duck or grouse in the name of sport or nourishing meal.

I attempted instead to affect a carefree presence of mind, but, whether due to the events of the past day, the lingering effect of the nightmare, or both, my mind churned with troubled thought and conjecture. There was Sparrow's murder and my duty to investigate its cause. Did that duty not imply making efforts to determine how the murder had come about? I knew the strict answer of officialdom. It was the coroner's duty to determine cause of death and then either by investigation or formal inquiry to present appropriate recommendations to avoid such a death's recurrence. I could presumably recommend that barbed wire be outlawed or that all homeless women be assigned a guardian angel to protect them from deviant evil. But beyond the pointless or ridiculous I had little idea what manner of useful recommendation might result from this tragedy. Sparrow was dead. Nothing could have prevented that beyond her being rescued before the murderer finished his grisly task. Officialdom aside, I wanted to know the why of Sparrow's death rather than just the how of it.

By now Fergus was so far ahead, somewhere near the tide line, that his crashing about sounded like only a soft rustling. I whistled for him to return and eventually, in his own good time, Fergus slithered out of the brush. He had the sloppily happy grin that only a bush dog who has been pawing in mud and scrabbling over logs and through thorns to scatter myriad wildlife before him can muster. His coat was dripping a black brew of water and slimy mud, ears a matted tangle snarled with various types of burrs, paws gummed with great saucers of congealed mud and sand. It would take a good thirty minutes with comb, brush, and scrubber to get him fit to be let back into the house. I scolded him halfheartedly and he took the effort for what it was, refusing to look even slightly contrite. But he stuck close as we walked briskly homeward.

After rendering Fergus somewhat presentable and ensuring that he wouldn't scatter much grime through the cabin I let him inside. He sashayed over to his mat by the fireplace and stretched out with a contented sigh, obviously hoping that I would whip up a warming blaze there to dry his coat. A dog's vision of the perfect climax to what had so far been an ideal morning. Instead I stoked the fire in the Franklin stove and then picked up the phone.

Nicki, the Tofino RCMP dispatcher-cum-receptionist-cum-typist, answered on the second ring. "Sugar, where have you been?" she asked. "I've been calling and calling. Actually," she said with a chuckle, "I just called a few minutes ago and got only a long string of rings. Thought you were going to leave your answering machine on. You really should get a cellphone. After all, you're an important person."

Glaring at the answering machine, I noted nothing wrong. The red power light was aglow. Yet there was no flashing signal indicating a message having been taken and the number indicator registered zero. I flipped up the lid and groaned. "Sorry, spooled out to the end. It doesn't rewind automatically anymore." I pressed the rewind button and the cassette whirred busily back to its start position. Barely a year old and already acting up. I had much preferred life without such technological marvels, but Nicki and Vhanna had conspired to convince me that a coroner required such gizmos for easy contact to be assured. They had won the answering machine campaign, but I had so far successfully staved off their cellphone offensive.

"What's up?" I asked.

Her voice dropped a few octaves. "Well, first his nibs is all hot and bothered and wanting your presence pronto at the office here. Although right now he's over at the coffee shop scarfing down a doughnut." Hence Nicki's careless banter. When Danchuk is out of sight, Nicki, who stands just under six feet tall and has a penchant for three-inch stilettos, always delights in mocking her boss.

I was, however, genuinely puzzled. Danchuk usually tried to keep me well away from police investigations. "He wants to know what your plans are regarding that poor girl," Nicki said by way of explanation to my unasked question.

"Where are things at there?"

Nicki's voice lowered to a whisper. "Shouldn't be telling you this, but all the troops from away have departed with no plans of returning."

"The investigation is to be handled locally?"

"You got it, sugar. Which means by his lordship."

I asked Nicki to tell Danchuk I would be in later that morning. Then I climbed the stairs to the open loft that serves as my bedroom and small office. Sitting at the small oak desk that is wedged against the railing so I can do paperwork while enjoying a view out the front windows to the water and also look down upon the living room and kitchen, I pulled open a file stuffed with blank forms. It took just a few minutes to complete the paperwork declaring my intention to investigate the death of one Jane Doe who had died by violent means the previous day. To avoid having to stop at a photocopying shop, I neatly and laboriously penned out original, identical documents for my file, another copy for Danchuk, and a final one for Dr. Carl Harris, the regional coroner in Nanaimo. That one went into an envelope to be sent off by courier later, while the other I would serve on Danchuk personally.

As I drove into town my stomach started rumbling, so I started eyeing the various restaurant options. For a place with a permanent population of barely more than a thousand, Tofino is rather well served in this regard. One payoff of being a world-class tourist destination is a proliferation of services and amenities far surpassing that of the other small towns and villages clinging to the rugged shoreline of Vancouver Island's isolated west coast.

Today one of the old waterfront hotels had a parking lot clogged with vehicles, among them a fire red Jeep Cherokee and a slightly rusty blue Cadillac. The latter was Tully's car, which reminded me that the Chamber of Commerce was holding its meet-the-mayoralty-candidate breakfast this morning. Not pausing to weigh the merits of my actions, I squeezed the Land Rover in alongside the Cherokee. By offering Tully the support afforded by my presence I would also get the opportunity to see Vhanna.

Adding my old-fashioned dull brown coat and hat to a rack of multicoloured Gore-Tex items, I mixed into the throngs of people making their way from the lobby into the banquet room. We shuffled forward in a long, crawling line, as each person had to be granted entrance by the chamber's long-suffering clerk, Wilma Effertson. She jealously guarded the door from behind a card table on which lay a stack of plastic name tag holders, squares of paper that could be inserted into said holders, and a large black felt pen for writing names on the paper. A small cash box was set precisely in the centre of the table, and once she had been given a five-dollar bill to deposit into the box, she would issue a ticket and name tag. Her lips pursed dubiously when I stepped up to the table. "It's a member-only function, Mr. McCann," she said stiffly. Wilma Effertson never forgets or forgives a scandal. Merriam's suicide and the rumours of my affair with Vhanna were the perfect grist for her scandal-mongering soul and fodder for her dislike of the prime villain in the piece.

Although I normally go out of my way to keep what is a far truer dirty little secret from becoming public knowledge, it appeared that if I wanted to gain entry to the banquet room there was no choice but to expose it. Leaning close to her ear, I whispered, "Wilma, I've been a chamber member for years. I just don't attend meetings."

Her eyes narrowed and she looked ready to argue, but just then Crab Pot Café owner James Scarborough patted me on the shoulder with a friendly hand. "This rascal giving you a problem, Wilma?" He then vouched for my duly paid-up member status, insisted on paying for the breakfast, filled out my name tag and attached it to my shirt, and then ushered me past her table into the banquet hall. "This is a moment to celebrate," he said with a laugh. "You're coming out of the closet."

I had no doubt that the moment the meeting was concluded Wilma would scurry back to her office and scour through the membership ledgers. To her chagrin she would discover that I was indeed a paid-up member. As I am a silent partner in Scarborough's café and a number of other Tofino business ventures, including Jabronski's security firm and her own Artemis Adventures, Vhanna has insisted that I support the local business community by joining the ranks of the organization that represents their common interests. I know better than to question Vhanna's business acumen. She is my financial adviser, and, despite my best efforts, her careful guardianship of my ever-accumulating wealth only makes it grow all the more exponentially.

While Scarborough guided me to a table groaning under a long row of shiny coffee urns, I quartered the room and finally sighted my quarry. Even from the back she looked wonderful, and my pulse quickened at the sight of her. Vhanna's long hair had been combed out to run straight down the length of her spine, and she wore a black sports jacket, black jeans, and thick-soled Doc Martens. Despite her being relatively tall, Vhanna's slender frame gives a first impression of fragility. A totally illusory impression, of course, as a vigorous lifestyle endows her body with a supple and powerful strength.

With tepid coffee poured into a grey porcelain mug, I joined a small knot of local restaurateurs who had gathered around Scarborough to debate the merits of serving patrons wild salmon versus farmed salmon. Their attempts to balance the entrepreneurial advantage provided by serving up penned fish evenly alongside concerns for protecting the ocean environment and its Pacific salmon stocks from potential devastation by diseases or encroachment by escaped Atlantic salmon seemed akin to trying to count the numbers of angels that might dance on a pin.

Quickly excusing myself, I prowled toward my selected prey. Closing in, I was surprised to see that Vhanna was in discussion with none other than Roberta Walker. Standing next to Walker and facing mayoralty candidate Monica Klassen was a man I didn't recognize. But hulking next to the politician was Jack Ashton. Walker, Klassen, Ashton, and the unknown man were all dressed like outlanders lifted straight off the hard concrete of Vancouver's Georgia Street or Toronto's Bay Street. Tofinoites are a relaxed bunch, and even the most avid homespun entrepreneur was unlikely to conform to the dress codes of big city business. Throughout the room, denim and practical footwear abounded. Many a man sported a ponytail, while various women featured closely shaved heads. All very west coast British Columbia. So the Vancouver-looking coterie were the non-conformers. Walker wore delicate spike-heeled black sandals, a fashionable black dress with a string of pearls around her throat, and an expensive-looking linen jacket draped over her shoulders. Her lustrous red hair was piled up on top of her head in an artful coil, and makeup stunningly delineated her cheekbones and catlike green eyes.

The man's charcoal jacket and pants and white shirt were of a fine, crisp linen that only a minimum of $1,500 will buy. His thick grey hair swept back from a high, light-catching forehead in a studiedly casual manner that only regular attention from an expensive stylist could maintain. He had the chiselled good looks and cleft chin of a big studio leading man, the lean but solid frame of a dedicated swimmer or runner. After Walker made introductions, the carefully applied firmness of his hand on mine spoke of controlled power without any obvious macho posturing. "Dagleish," he said, "Darren Dagleish. Roberta told me about the sad business out at the Ashton property." The developer shook his head in commiseration, as if Sparrow's murder constituted a personal loss for me. "Tragic. And a hard blow for Jack," he said, while placing a fatherly hand on the younger man's shoulder.

Ashton wore a pair of grey dress pants and a black turtleneck sweater stretched tautly across his broad chest. His blonde hair was cut short, gelled into a measured imitation of tousled disarray, and blocked to square precision across the back of a coarse head set squarely on a short, powerfully muscled neck. A large nose protruded bluntly from between narrow eyes, the pupils of which were almost obsidian. His lips were thick and fleshy.

The first time ever I saw Ashton he was standing at the foot of his mother's corpse. He had stared down at her twisted form with an expression of puzzlement, as if unable to comprehend how she had come to be lying there unresponsive and dead. In one hand he held the splitting maul with which she had been chopping wood. It was a heavy thing with a blunt cudgel opposite the cutting blade. I had been struck during the ensuing examination of Tempest's corpse with the thought that the man must have inherited his features from his father rather than from that fine-boned and attractive woman. He looked like a man who should wrest out a living by working a chainsaw or pulling nets from the sea rather than from the intricacies of keyboard movements.

"How's the software project coming along?" I asked him now as my hand was crushed flat inside his great paw.

He grimaced, and his eyes were as flat as dimes. "Bad time for the technology industry right now, I'm afraid," he grunted. "Nortel's crash has taken the wind out of all of us. Fuckers."

"Fortunately," Dagleish said cheerfully, "Jack's on board with us for the development of the family land. You can never lose on land. That's because it's real, solid. Put land and imagination together and you can only prosper."

The man seemed to measure each word carefully before releasing it into space with clear and perfect enunciation. There was a slight accent, a hint of some elite British public school perhaps, that defied placing. He smiled, revealing a precise line of perfectly white enamel. Although I marked him as being in his late fifties or even early sixties, his face was tanned and touched only around his bright blue eyes by the slightest webbing of wear lines.

Dagleish and Walker were an elegant and exotic couple, and there was an intimacy in how he lightly rested a hand on her lower arm and the way their shoulders brushed together that suggested a relationship closer than that of employer and employee. "I was just discussing with Ms. Chan and Ms. Klassen my vision for the hotel on Jack's property and how I hope to be able to draw on Ms. Chan's expertise to assemble the ideal outdoor experience packages for the guests that will form our client base. There are a lot of exciting opportunities."

At that moment Scarborough's sharp whistle brought all conversation to an abrupt halt. "Food's ready," he announced loudly, "so form up and dish up. Once everyone's settled we'll hear from our mayoralty candidates." There was a general push toward the buffet table that our little cluster did not join.

"Would you care to sit with us, Ms. Chan?" Dagleish asked.

Vhanna glanced quickly my way as if uncertain what to do before turning to Dagleish wearing a polite smile. "I would be happy to."

"Mr. McCann?"

What I wanted was to talk to Vhanna, but there would be no chance for that in this company. And I had no desire to hear more of Dagleish's plans for the Ashton property or any of the other properties he had been acquiring around Tofino. "Sorry, I can't. James is holding a spot for me at his table." To Vhanna, I said, "Maybe we can talk after."

She nodded in a way that seemed more indicative of dismissal than agreement. I had the disquieting feeling that Vhanna had feared I might accept Dagleish's offer. Perhaps she worried that I would do something embarrassing that might threaten her opportunity to cut a business deal with the man. Turning my back on them, I went over to the buffet and squeezed into the line beside Scarborough. "Mind if I join you?"

He glanced over to where Vhanna and Dagleish's party ambled slowly toward the buffet line with the air of people who cared little about the provisions on offer.

Dagleish and Vhanna had heads close together and seemed engaged in earnest discussion. Roberta Walker was hanging back with her eyes fixed on Vhanna's back as if she peered down a gun sight at a target. Monica Klassen trailed behind the others in the meek manner of a house servant.

Hefting up a plain white plate, I focused my attention on fishing out a few tangled rashers of bacon from one silver heating dish, some factory-diced hash browns from another, and an overly congealed scoop of scrambled eggs from yet another. Good that I was hungry. It was hard to imagine Dagleish and Walker tucking into such fare. But there was a tray of fruits and thinly sliced cheese for those concerned about cholesterol intake levels. Such healthy fare would certainly suit Vhanna, I reflected gloomily. It struck me that I should not have come here, should have gone instead to one of the restaurants near the dock and partaken of a solitary breakfast in a booth with a window that looked out on the fishing boats tied up at the dock. Instead I had pursued Vhanna and now felt a fool.

Scarborough and I found a corner at a table where we could sit across from each other and tucked into our breakfasts. Between mouthfuls, he said, "Saw you fraternizing with the enemy. Don't know that I care to live in a town that's nothing but the personal fiefdom of Darren Dagleish and his damned development company. Might be time to start thinking about selling up and moving on, partner." Usually a carefree, live-and-let-live person, Scarborough's serious tone took me by surprise.

I countered that although Dagleish was picking up a number of properties around the community, Scarborough was surely painting things darker than was justified.

"You know, Elias, you should spend less time with your head up in the clouds and more time looking at what's right in front of your feet," he said flatly. "That guy's going to sweep the last traces of Lotus Land right out from under you and wash it out to sea. Then there'll just be him and his cronies and maybe your girlfriend left here to pick up the cash and turn paradise into a fucking parking lot. No apologies to Joni Mitchell." Scarborough dug into his crusty scrambled eggs with the intensity of a miner shovelling through hardpan.

I let my eyes drift over to where Vhanna sat with her back turned toward me and her attention fixed on Dagleish. Her hands were moving with animation, like they do when she is excited and emphasizing an important point. Dagleish nodded seriously, as if thoughtfully considering her every word. Then his eyes raised as if he had sensed my gaze upon them and met mine evenly. He gave me a smile that seemed mocking, before turning his full attention back to the woman I love.

The food proved tasteless and hard to swallow. I tried vainly to dismiss what I thought had just transpired — the silently offered challenge followed by Dagleish's obvious certainty of victory. I felt strangely diminished by the man. And then the speeches began, serving only to confirm the lunacy of my decision to attend this event.

Lou Santucci, whose father owns the lumber store, introduced Tully. As one of Tofino's volunteer ambulance drivers, Santucci often works alongside the good doctor in the emergency ward. He pointed this out and added that Tully had been his family doctor since birth. Tully, Santucci assured us, worked tirelessly to ensure Tofino's well-being, whether that required employing his medical, political, or economic expertise for the community's betterment or combining all three together. Tully, Santucci declared, was selfless, sincere, and just plain decent. Which was true enough.

Tully kept his remarks simple and brief. Neither pontificating nor preaching, Tully reminded us that

Tofino was a unique refuge standing on the edge of a vast ocean and in the shadow of one of the Western Hemisphere's last great rainforests. Tofino was a young community set within an extremely fragile and precious environment. Hastily made decisions could result in devastating long-term impacts on our quality of life and on the very survival of all we held dear about Tofino and the Pacific Rim. Tully adhered to the conservative line of approach, one that emphasized cautious consideration of change, whether that entailed a proposal to log in one of Clayoquot's watersheds or string hotels along Tofino's waterfront. While believing growth generally positive and good, Tully cautioned that it could not be a community's sole goal. Maintaining quality of life and protecting the special trust that befell Tofinoites must take precedence over the desire for any immediate form of economic growth and development.

Tully stepped back from the podium to polite applause, but I sensed an air of impatience in the room that boded ill. And then Darren Dagleish rose from the table and ascended the podium. "Dr. Tully," he said in his crisp, clear voice, "does well to remind us of the things we all cherish about Tofino and the surrounding majestic, precious, and irreplaceable environment. For generations Tofino languished in a comfortable isolation from the outside world. But that isolation is fading away even as we sit here today enjoying our breakfast." I noted that where he had been sitting only a water glass stood as a sign of the quantity of breakfast the developer had enjoyed. "The number of visitors to this land increases annually by the tens of thousands, and as more people from other parts of the world discover all this land has to offer, they will come in ever greater numbers. This process is not reversible. There can be no turning back the clock. Instead we must grasp hold of the ripe opportunity that exists here to build a community that prospers from taking charge of its future rather than by shrinking from that responsibility. I believe that Monica Klassen is the person who can pilot us all through this period that offers not only great challenges but immense potential." He smiled warmly, as a chaplain might upon a favoured member of his congregation, while his mayoralty candidate rose from her chair to approach the podium.

The applause was brisk and energetic this time, as opposed to the almost lazily comfortable clapping that had first greeted Tully. A chill of disappointment slithered down my spine when I saw Vhanna's hands moving as enthusiastically as any in the room. Monica Klassen had been in Tofino just three years and ran an independent real estate agency that specialized in bringing together landowners and developers. Dagleish was rumoured to be her main customer. She was a dapper woman. Blonde hair clipped precisely to below the ear line and elegantly waved. Blue eyes that radiated drive and intelligence. A penchant for black power suits with shoulder pads so bulky they could have well served a football linebacker.

She spoke forcefully about the need for a new era in Tofino's business culture. It was not enough merely to respond to opportunity in the lackadaisical manner of the past. No, Tofino's entrepreneurs must seize the moment and shape their own future through vigorous development meant to capitalize on the untapped growth potential that lay within the grasp of our fingertips. We must do so today, not tomorrow. We must do so for the sake of our children, for the sake of the First Nations population that called this region home and needed opportunity, for the sake of all those who sought to continue calling Tofino home and must be given new opportunity to replace the dwindling fortunes of the resource development industries. Tourism and destination residential development could work in tandem to provide the economic engines of the future that would promise prosperity to all. Taking control of our destiny to get these engines working hard would require imagination and a determined council led by a mayor endowed with appropriate vision and business skill. She left no doubt whom that mayor should be. "I have the knowledge. I have the ambition to make Tofino all it can be. But to do that I need your trust and support. I humbly ask that you give me that support and that trust, so that together we can embrace a future of prosperity and security for everyone living in our wonderful community."

As Monica stepped back from the podium she was greeted with even more enthusiastic applause than had preceded her speech. Tully was sitting with Lou Santucci, Wilma Effertson, and some of the other older businesspeople, and I noted the thoughtful expression on his face as he vigorously cleaned his glasses with a checkered handkerchief. He looked suddenly old and tired. Monica Klassen was mingling amid a gathering crowd, shaking hands, talking animatedly, looking to all appearances like someone who has already been first across the finish line and is bound for the winner's circle to accept a well-earned prize. Gathering my coat and hat from the rack in the hallway I walked glumly out of the hotel.

A hand gently touched my arm as I opened the door of the Land Rover. "Elias, wait," Vhanna said. When I turned, she offered a small, almost shy smile. "This isn't the time or place, but we need to talk."

"Do we?" I said tightly.

Vhanna paled and her eyes sparked with a cold, hard glint. "It's not like you're thinking."

"Tully's a friend. That's all I know."

She brushed a long strand of hair away from her face with an angry flick of a hand. "He's my friend, too. That's not the point."

Although I wanted to put my hands on her shoulders and pull her close to me, I said instead that I had pressing business to attend to and shoved my hands deep into the Filson's pockets.

"I was sorry to hear about the girl," Vhanna said and lightly rested her hand on my arm. "Are you okay?"

"Fine." It was suddenly like Sparrow's barbed-wire-tormented corpse lay between us. There was a duty to fulfill and no time to waste on frayed personal feelings. "Would you like to come for dinner?" I blurted. My heart started to beat harder as I awaited her response.

Vhanna's face softened and she smiled tentatively. "How about my place instead?" When she suggested that Fergus come too, I dared hope the invitation might extend beyond dinner. We concluded the negotiations as awkwardly as teenagers agreeing to a first date. "I'll bring wine," I said. Vhanna agreed to that, and I assured her that my work would be unlikely to make me later than seven.

As Vhanna started to turn away, I lightly touched her cheek. She put her hand on top of mine, and we stood like that for a moment, each meeting the other's eyes uncertainly. The tenderness that passed between us in that moment was palpable and something I wished we could hang onto forever. But then Vhanna's hand slid away and she turned from me and walked to her Jeep without a backward glance.

chapter six

"Understand this, McCann, your inquiry in no way supersedes my investigation." Danchuk glared down at the form on his desk blotter. "Bloody nonsense. What do you hope to achieve?"

"Somebody tortured and killed that girl for a reason, Gary." Still wearing hat and coat, I stood across the desk from where he sat. Danchuk was obviously in no mood for civility.

"And that's for me to find out, damn it, not you. You start nosing around where you're not wanted or get in my way...."

I held up a placating hand, forced myself to respond calmly because there was nothing to be gained in a yelling match with the sergeant. "I've no intention of getting in your way, Gary. You know we can work on this together."

He leaned back in his chair and pressed his hands down so flat and hard on either side of the coroner's investigation declaration form that his knuckles whitened. "Anything you find out, you give me imme- diately. You don't, I'll stick a hand down your throat so fast your tonsils will be out on the ground before you even notice I've grabbed them."

I promised not to hold anything back and sought an assurance he would do the same. He smirked at that by way of answer.

As I walked out of Danchuk's office and stepped through the detachment's general office area Nicki glanced up from her computer screen to flash a quick smile and a wink my way. Danchuk's threats had been so loudly uttered there was no question of her not hav- ing heard. I shrugged and walked out into the fresh air.

Clearly my investigation into Sparrow's murder was off to a completely inauspicious start. Together Danchuk and I might have been able to make some progress, but I doubted that either of us working alone was going to get very far. Truthfully, I had no idea where to begin.

So I drove out to the Ashton property in the hope that having a more measured look at the crime scene might turn up something worthwhile. Simms stepped out of his trailer, wearing his blue uniform, when I pulled into the yard, and he shuffled toward the Land Rover as I climbed out of it. His face looked grey and haggard, his eyes shot through with red, and when he shook my hand his fingers trembled. "Ms. Walker's told me I have to accompany any visitors at all times. She made it clear that included any police or other officials that might show up because of this incident."

"That's fine by me, Mr. Simms."

He ran a hand over the back of his neck. "You can call me, Jed. I ain't much on formality." The man was so close to me that when he exhaled I could smell the sharp pungency of distilled juniper berries on his breath.

"Okay, Jed, why don't you just walk me through what you did and saw over the twenty-four hours before we found the girl in the woodshed."

His eyes darted toward the shed and his expression became even more haggard. "Told that already to the police sergeant and the woman constable that was with him this morning. They took me into the station and I had to go through all that on tape for them." He shifted uneasily from one foot to another. "You think I'm a suspect, Mr. McCann?"

Danchuk and Monaghan had obviously shaken him badly with their questions and formal approach. Not that I blamed them, for the bloody gash on Simms's hand certainly needed explaining. "I imagine they're just doing what they have to do, Jed," I said. Before proceeding further I also pressed the record button of the tape recorder hidden in my pocket. Although not advising the man that I was taping our conversation probably rendered whatever he said inadmissible in court, that didn't concern me, for mine was not a police investigation.

As we walked toward the woodshed, Simms described his solitary existence as the Ashton property's security guard. Water, sewage, and electric hookups were provided free for him to connect to his trailer and he received a meagre salary, but in exchange he was expected to spend most of his hours and days patrolling the grounds to keep trespassers out and to maintain the perimeter fencing. Ms. Walker was extremely particular, he said, about ensuring the security of the property.

"Why do you think that is, Jed?"

He thought on that a moment. "Because of insurance issues, she says. Someone gets hurt on Mr. Dagleish's property they might try suing. He's a wealthy man. People always looking for some leverage when there's someone with money involved."

"You get many people coming onto the property?"

"Just them damned homeless people. Particularly that girl and the older guy. I found her inside the house a few times and lurking around the woodshed here, too."

I asked what she was doing when he caught her inside the house or in the woodshed.

Simms shrugged. "Mostly just seemed to be getting out of the weather. You know, sitting on the floor of the house. Usually be in the living room. Once in a while up in one of the bedrooms. Sometimes she had all her junk with her, like she might have been sleeping there. Guess she wanted to get away from the others."

"How did you move her off?"

He laughed. "Didn't take much doing, really. I'd tell her to get and she'd call me names, but she always went. Knew if she didn't I'd phone the police and have her arrested. That's what I always told her. Told her not to come back again, either, but that never worked. A few days later, week maybe, I'd find her in the house there or sitting on the chair here in the shed."

I thought about that. There wasn't a stick of furniture in the house, yet there was a chair in the woodshed.

"Can't really say," Simms replied when I asked him why that was. "It just showed up one day about a month ago. Didn't seem worth the bother to remove it. Wasn't worth anything."

"You think the girl put it there?"

He pondered that. "First time I found her in here she was sitting on the chair and handling all the tools. Can't recall if the chair was there before that." Simms nodded his head thoughtfully. "Could be she put it there. Funny thing to do, don't you think?" I agreed. "Would think in the house would make more sense. If she wanted a dry place to sit down." Simms seemed to be warming to this line of speculation.

I stepped into the woodshed and crouched next to the bloodstained wooden chair. The white paint was peeled and chipped, revealing a kind of black shellac coating underneath. At some point the seat had split in two, and somebody had nailed a thin covering sheet of plywood overtop for reinforcement and to hold the two pieces together. It was a simple design. Four spindles fitted into a curved yoke top piece formed the backrest. One inside spindle was missing, as was the crossbar that should have run between the two right-side chair legs. The whole thing wobbled when I gave it a jiggle. "Any other furniture around here? In a crawl space under the house or somewhere?"

There was a crawl space, Simms said, but nothing down there other than rats and other varmints. "I put poison out, but it don't seem to do no good." He suddenly became more animated, plowing on relentlessly about his efforts to purge the house of pests. While he talked I tried to examine the woodshed with a fresh eye. But there was nothing new to see. Just the same tools, the bales of wire, the chair tipped on its back in the centre of the shed. The door hanging off-kilter.

"This door always been like that?"

Simms shook his head. "No, it was just like that yesterday. Would have fixed it, if it had been. I'm supposed to keep things in good repair. Didn't notice it myself until you fellows showed up."

The lower hinge was still attached to the door, but not to the doorway. Long, rusty wood screws dangled from the three holes inset in the wedge-shaped hinge that would have fit into the door jamb. There appeared to be no signs of the hinge having been pried or forced free. Instead it looked more like the screws had simply fallen free. I pulled out my Swiss Army pocketknife, flipped the wedge blade out, and gently pried the wood around one of the screw holes. The blade gouged easily into it. "Rotten," I said. But it would still have taken a bang on the door from inside to wrench the screws out of the wood. So had the door been closed when Sparrow was tortured? Had it been banged free of the hinge while the murderer struggled with her? Questions for which there seemed no way to find answers.

I asked Simms about the older man who had sometimes accompanied Sparrow. "He's a strange one, I'll tell you. Big, shaggy beard, and strong looking. Dresses like the rest of them, nothing but a bunch of rags. But he's got these creepy grey eyes that seem to look right through you when you talk to him. Never made a fuss, though. I'd tell him and her to move on and he'd just nod and whisper to her and she'd follow him quietly off. No lip then, not like when she was alone." Although he had caught the man and girl inside the house a couple of times he more often caught them cutting through the property on their way to the beach camp with food and other supplies. That was when they would cut the wire or trample it down, forcing him to make repairs. Just the two of them, usually. The others tended to stay off the property and really hadn't been much of a problem. "Except for their damned drumming late into the night and the big bonfires they'd build down there."

He chuckled. "Sometimes I'd creep down the trail to check on things. Make sure they weren't going to let that fire get out of control and burn the place up, you know." I nodded to assure him I understood. "They'd be dancing around that bonfire naked or next to it. The girls, you know. Tits bouncing all over the place and a lot more, I'll tell you." His eyes darted nervously away, as if he thought telling me this might have been a mistake. "Ms. Walker should have got that injunction," he said. "We'd moved them off, maybe this never would have happened."

I asked him again about the twenty-four hours before we found Sparrow's body. Simms replied that he had been in Port Alberni most of the day picking up supplies and parts for the truck. "Had dinner there and didn't get back until after dark. It was a dirty night. Slow drive back. Got up in the morning and started working on my truck, putting in a new air filter and hose system. Then you and the sergeant showed up."

"You never heard any noises from the woodshed or heard anyone moving around the property?"

He shook his head. "Never heard a thing. Being so late and all, I didn't bother making any rounds when I got back. Figured to do that after I finished fixing up the truck in the morning."

No sooner had I turned out onto the highway than a set of flashing lights appeared behind me. A glance in the rearview mirror confirmed that an RCMP cruiser was riding my tail. When I bumped onto a gravel shoulder overgrown with wild grass, I pondered the likely nature of my offence. Certainly not speeding — a ridiculous idea for my old Land Rover. Most likely the taillights were on the blink again. But the car pulled up in the lane beside me, and when the passenger window dropped I saw Monaghan leaning across the console of electronics and other equipment that stood next to the driver's seat. I twisted the little silver knob that serves as a window catch on the Land Rover's doors and tugged the glass to one side to open it. "Been looking all over for you," she said with a note of frustration in her voice. "There's a pullout about half a mile ahead. Meet me there."

She gunned the car and shot off without waiting for a reply, quickly vanishing around a corner. I followed at the Land Rover's best pace, engine whining fiercely.

Despite the added insulation provided by an asbestos sheet I long ago bolted on top of the aluminum floorboards, the heat given off by the exhaust pipe still radiated through my boot soles to toast my feet. Almost precisely a half-mile later I spotted a narrow dirt track that ran off into a stand of alders. Following the fresh tire tracks left by Monaghan's cruiser, I soon pulled up behind where it was parked well out of sight of the highway.

Monaghan was leaning against the driver's door. She wore a yellow and black police jacket and standard-issue watch cap. "Nobody will see us back here," she said as I walked over. "No way do I want Danchuk getting word that I'm flagging you down and passing information." She pulled a package of Player's loose tobacco from a pocket and, flicking a little square of paper out of a blue ZigZag folder, began expertly rolling herself a cigarette. "If I roll my own, I smoke less. Might stop altogether someday." A brass lighter flashed and she inhaled deeply, tipped her head back, and released a small cloud of smoke with a contented sigh.

If Sergeant Danchuk had the slightest idea how many informants I have within his ranks his blood pressure might just move into a high-risk zone. I looked around at the trees walling us in and the garbage that lay strewn on either side of the track. Empty beer cases, broken bottles, rotting pizza cartons, castoff condoms, a couch with the springs bursting out, an old cabinet-style television with a broken tube, and a couple broken porcelain toilets. "You know how to pick a rendezvous point," I said.

Monaghan laughed. "One of the less desirable make-out destinations around here on weekend nights, but still tends to be busy."

"So what's up, Anne?"

"We bagged the entire One Earth Family this morning trying to board the bus. Danchuk's questioning them one by one with Norman in support. You should be there."

"He never mentioned this."

Monaghan looked at me flatly. "The sergeant wants them all to himself. He figures that at least some of them are good for this. Fourteen people. No way the detachment lockup can hold them all. So Danchuk's got them sequestered down at the old fish packing plant. Josinder is keeping an eye on them, making sure they don't talk among themselves until Danchuk's had a chance to run each person through questioning."

"Anne, why is Danchuk being left with this? He's not a detective. Why aren't you there?"

She braced her hands on the web belt circling her waist, one hand resting on top of the pistol butt. "Whole region's short-staffed. Nickerson tried to get some detectives in from Nanaimo, but they're stretched trying to solve a string of killings between the local Hell's Angels bunch and a Vietnamese gang that's muscling in on their turf." Monaghan grimaced. "One homeless kid gets murdered out here in the boonies. It isn't going to be a priority." She pointed at the dashboard of her car where the radar gun was mounted. "He's got me on traffic detail to make sure I don't get in his way. Josinder's a good cop, but he's not going to make waves with Danchuk and jeopardize a fitness report that might get him transferred to Surrey or Delta. And Norman Tom's so fresh out of training his uniform still squeaks.

"So it's down to you, Elias. Danchuk's started with the young ones first and is working his way up toward the old guy. You don't want to miss that interview for sure. I don't like the hold that guy's got over the others. And I don't like the fact that of the fourteen, nine are young women. Numbers should be the other way around, if you ask me. Go down to Victoria or into Vancouver's East End and look at the homeless there. Lot more boys and men than girls."

"Is Danchuk going to let me in?"

"Depends on you, Elias. You're running a legal investigation. I don't think he can keep you from sitting in if you insist." She coughed on a drag from her cigarette and laughed grimly. "But it isn't going to make you any more popular with him, and for God's sake don't let on that I told you about this. There were a lot of people around when we rounded up the Family at the bus station. Just let him think that one of your other friends told you about it. He'd have me working night radar traps in Pacific Rim National Park for the next year if he knew it was me."

She stubbed her cigarette out on the heel of her clunky police shoe, then field stripped it by slicing the butt open with the nail of her long and glossily manicured index finger to scatter the few remaining threads of tobacco on the wind before letting the fragment of paper fall to the ground. "Better than filtered tubes," she said. "Breaks down in no time." Monaghan looked at me hard. "Remember how many hookers had to die on Gore and Hastings streets before anybody did anything to find the killer?" She poked me in the chest with the same finger that had opened the cigarette butt. "You're Sparrow's best chance to get justice, Elias." Then she said in almost a whisper, "She deserves that. They all do."

chapter seven

The fish packing plant where Danchuk was holding the Family was a tin-roofed relic from the local fishing industry heydays of the early 1900s. Originally owned by the Nakamura family, the plant had been confiscated and sold by the government following the forced relocation of Japanese Canadians from the west coast after Pearl Harbor and the outbreak of hostilities between the Allies and Japan. The Nakamuras and the other Japanese families in Tofino had mostly been fishermen, but the government locked them up in an abandoned mining town somewhere in the province's interior. Fishing boats, businesses, homes, and generations of dreams all confiscated and auctioned off. War over, there was no redress or compensation offered, so few could return to their former homes.

A Vancouver fishing conglomerate that bought the plant at auction ran it until the early 1960s. By then the large foreign factory boats operated by the Soviet

Union, Poland, and Japan were cutting such a large swath of fish out of the local market by buying directly from the Vancouver Island trawlers and seiners that the plant ceased being economical. It had since been slowly rotting and rusting its way towards an eventual and inevitable collapse.

The interior was damp and dark, and the smell of gutted salmon, hake, and herring lingered still, mixed with the mildew odour of rotting wood. Long ago the processing lines and other machinery had been dismantled and removed by salvagers intent on wringing the last dollar out of the place for the conglomerate, so now the large main gallery that had once been the factory floor was empty and stark. The Mounties had erected a pair of floodlights on tripods that seared one corner of this space with a glaring white light. Pinned inside these harshly illuminated pools, a large number of Family members sat on the floor with their backs against a wall.

Three girls, sitting cross-legged, tapped softly on drums while swaying slightly from side to side in cadence to the gentle rhythm. A young man with a wispy beard with beads woven into it accompanied them on a small wooden flute. In the centre of the line of youths sat an older man with shoulder-length grey hair and a beard that hung thick and full onto his chest. He was broad-shouldered and even seated it was apparent that he was unusually tall — six-foot-five or more. Seeming to sense my eyes on him, the man's head came up and he met my gaze in a manner that seemed to take my measure without offering any challenge.

Facing the Family, Josinder perched on a fold-out lawn chair. On the floor within easy reach of his right hand was a large red canister fitted with a thick spray nozzle that I suspected contained pepper spray. To one side of the homeless group, a line of backpacks had been braced against the wall. Each was tagged with a large piece of yellow paper that I figured identified its rightful owner and had been placed there by one of the police officers. On the other flank of the Family was a small room that had probably once been the plant manager's private domain. A still-intact glass window faced the now-barren plant floor, and I could imagine the manager sitting at his desk in there and using this clear view of the workers to keep tabs on their productivity. Danchuk and Norman Tom were inside this office seated on one side of a portable table. Opposite them, back to the window, sat a teenage kid with long, stringy hair. A cassette tape recorder was set square in the table's centre, and to one side a video camera on a tripod pointed at the boy.

The sounds of my shoes striking the bare concrete floor echoed through the empty building and prompted Singh to swivel in his chair. His brilliant white teeth flashed out of his dark face in a smile of recognition, but seeing that I was heading for the office door his expression became one of alarm and he started to rise from his chair. "Mr. McCann," he called, "you can't go in there."

But he was too far away, too unsure of his right to challenge my authority, and too apprehensive about leaving his guard post to successfully interdict me. I rapped on the door sharply and then stepped in without waiting for an invitation. Danchuk cut off a sentence in midstream and scowled as he punched the stop button on the tape recorder. A finger slashed across his throat told Tom to get up and shut down the video camera. "You wait outside," Danchuk snapped at the teenager. "We'll call you back if we want you."

The boy, who had a severe case of acne covering his face and dark circles under his eyes that suggested he was either exhausted or sick, or both, offered a yellow-toothed smile. Several molars were missing on the right side, as if he had once been badly beaten or the victim of a grim accident. "Sure, man," he said. "Whatever you say." He ducked out of the room with a speed that clearly indicated his relief to escape Danchuk's sights.

The sergeant stabbed a blunt finger toward where the contents of a filth-blackened red backpack spilled out on the floor. "Get that stuff out of here, Constable," he snapped at Tom. "I'll want one of the other men next. We go through them and then the women. Leave the old guy for last. Understand?"

"Sure, Sergeant," Tom said. After jumbling everything up off the floor and into the backpack he scuttled out of the room as eagerly as had the teenager.

"What are you doing here, McCann? I warned you not to get in the way of my investigation." As I was still standing across the table from him, Danchuk was forced to tip his head back and peer out from under the bill of his cap so that he could meet my eyes.

"We both have a job to do, Gary. You should have let me know that you were doing these interviews. You know that," I fired back. "Do I have to phone Dr. Harris and get him to contact your district commander?"

Danchuk slapped the palm of a hand on the table-top so hard it sounded like a pistol shot. "I've had it with your interference, damn it."

Placing both hands firmly on the table, I leaned across the table so my face was mere inches from his. Danchuk's breath was hot, sour from the meat and onion sandwich he must have eaten for lunch. "I'm going to sit down in that chair next to you, Sergeant. And we're going to bring in those people one at a time, and you and I together will pose our questions for each person until neither of us has anything worthwhile to ask, and then we'll interview the next one and the next one after that. I am not going to leave until those interviews are all completed, and when we're through here you are going to make copies of those videos and give them to me within forty-eight hours so they can become part of my investigative file. That is how this is going to work, Gary, and there's not a damned thing you can do to stop it playing out that way."

Not waiting for an answer, I stepped around the table, pulled a ring-bound notebook of the kind that journalists favour from the inside pocket of my coat, then draped my coat on the back of the chair that Constable Tom had previously occupied. I placed the notebook squarely in front of me with what I hoped Danchuk would not see were far from steady hands, flipped its cover open, snapped the nib of my pen out, removed my hat, and set it down on the table. "Ready whenever you are, Gary."

"This ain't the end of this, buster." But the Mountie's threat was mumbled and lacking in conviction. "Tom," he bellowed. "Bring the next one in here."

With Tom operating the video camera and Danchuk and I asking questions, we started sorting our way through the cast of characters that collectively comprised the Family. Each in turn denied knowledge of Sparrow's true name, and there was no agreement about where she came from. "I think she grew up in Point Grey," declared a boy called Indian because of his Mohawk-style haircut. "What the fuck brought her to the streets, who knows?" Indian seemed genuinely puzzled by this, for he came by the street life honestly. His father could have been any of the parade of tricks his mother had turned on a Hastings Street corner in front of a squalid rent-by-the-week hotel to buy the heroin she heated on a spoon before spiking it into ruined veins in front of her son.

Indian had set out on his own at the age of twelve. Now fifteen, he had the vague, disinterested expression of someone who has already abandoned hope of any better life. The boy's real name was Bill Robert Wallace, and when Danchuk later pulled his criminal record it bore a long list of personal property crimes and detentions for prostitution. Sparrow had been alive, the boy said, when the Family packed up camp and moved into town. Arriving too late to catch the bus out that day they had been preparing to sleep in an alley when the local priest offered the church basement instead. "Talk to Father Welch," I jotted on my notepad.

"Did Sparrow spend the night in the church?"

He stared at the ceiling, as if seeking an answer there. "Can't say I remember. She was there at the start. People always come and go, you know, I don't pay much mind."

"No," a young woman with hair razored to her scalp, a half-smoked cigarette tucked behind one ear, and a tattoo of a black widow with its web radiating up one arm to disappear into the sleeve of her black T-shirt confidently assured us, "Indian's wrong. Sparrow came off a farm somewhere up around Fort St. John or Prince George or somewhere up there, you know. She hated the fucking snow and the motherfucking cold and I think her dad or brother or some other fucking cocksucker raped her. So she, like, fucked off, you know."

"Mind your language, young woman," Danchuk said with the scolding tone of a schoolmaster.

"Oh, fuck, so sorry, officer," she said and grinned at him with the yellowed and chipped teeth of an old woman.

"Damn, but this is a waste of time, McCann," Danchuk muttered after the woman sauntered out of the office and Tom went off to fetch the next one. "Can't believe these people. Should be crushed under a rock or something. Do society and them a favour. Maggots."

I kept my own counsel, for it was obvious that the sergeant's effort to remain civil was hard duty. His brow glistened with sweat that returned as soon as he mopped it away with his blue-and-white-checked handkerchief, and his stubby fingers were trembling with what seemed to be barely repressed rage. "After this next one, I'm sending Tom to get us some coffee and doughnuts. Going to take the rest of the afternoon to get through everyone, and I bet we don't get a single useful lead. These people are all hiding something," he said with a hard, knowing gleam in his eyes. "I think one or all of them were involved in that girl's murder. They're all covering for each other. That's why they won't give us the girl's real name or birthplace. Can't tell me they don't know even that about her. Some family, if that were the case." He snorted contemptuously and swiped more beads of sweat off his forehead with the flat of his hand.

"What's your name?"

A girl with purple-dyed auburn hair tied off in two short pigtails that stuck out from behind her ears considered the question thoughtfully, a steel tongue stud clicking against the enamel of her teeth. "Moot." Her blue eyes flashed with mischief when they met Danchuk's, and I could see the repressed grin tugging at the corners of her mouth.

"Moot?"

She nodded at the sergeant, as if to help him along in a mental exercise. Danchuk scowled with frustration.

"As in moot point?" I asked.

"Got it in one." Her merriment was contagious. I was unable to repress a smile.

"We got a dead girl here. Someone you called family, right? And you want to play word games. For starters I want to know your real name. Where you come from. Your age. This ain't no joke, young woman."

The smile blew off Moot's face as abruptly as if Danchuk had slapped her. She declared herself of legal age in petulant voice. "You shouldn't need my name. You can't force me to go back home now."

"Listen, young lady," Danchuk said as he stood to lean across the table so his face was almost in hers, "you are a material witness to a murder. In fact, you're just a few inches from being a suspect in a murder. So I want to know your name. Your Christian names, all of them, and your surname, not any more of this street tag nonsense. Got that?"

Moot bunched her hands in her lap and stared down at the table with a resentful scowl darkening her teardrop-shaped face, the rasp of the stud sweeping back and forth against the back of her teeth the room's only sound. "Shit," she hissed. Then she stared directly at Danchuk, who still leaned intimidatingly toward her. "My," she swallowed and cleared her throat. "Meredith," she whispered. "My name is Meredith Ashley Bainsbridge-Stanton." Danchuk dropped heavily back into his chair and then made her spell each name out letter by letter for the tape recording. I looked at the slender young woman and the black wool sweater that was torn so that the hard knob of her right shoulder jutted out. Hers was the sort of androgynous name reserved for upper-class girls attending expensive private boarding schools who wore plaid kilts, knee socks, and white blouses with dark school ties tied primly about their necks.

It transpired that it was Moot, not Sparrow, who was from Point Grey. And although she claimed to be seventeen, I thought this unlikely. Fifteen, more like. "Get Bethanie down here soon," I jotted on a sheet in my notebook, tore it off, and pushed it across the table so Danchuk had to read it. He glared at me and then nodded with obvious reluctance.

Bethanie Hollinger was Tofino's social services caseworker for the provincial Ministry of Children and Families. I was beginning to think that at least half of the Family members were juveniles. And given the circumstances common with street kids, most were probably wards of the province as the result of one tragic family implosion after another. Danchuk knew he needed to include Bethanie in figuring out what to do about the Family, but he obviously was going to keep her out of the picture until his interrogation was concluded. Getting social services involved at this point might result in more formal procedural requirements, might hamper his ability to harangue people.

It suddenly struck me that Danchuk was sweating not just because he despised the Family members and what they stood for. He also feared failure, feared fouling up this investigation that should never have been left in the hands of someone more trained in the administrative operation of a small detachment than any form of detective work. No wonder he looked and acted like a man clinging to a cliff face with no life-saving rope in sight.

"Why don't you tell us about Sparrow, Moot?" I asked. "How did you meet her?" Danchuk's eyes narrowed at my asking questions without clearing them first with him, but I hoped even he could see there was little to be gained by our bickering in front of the girl.

Moot sucked in a deep breath and then, without need of interruption or coaxing, told her story in a manner I believed forthright and honest.

The girl from Point Grey had met Sparrow on the roof of a city-owned parking tower in downtown Victoria while looking for a covered lair where she might snatch a few hours of precious sleep out of the rain. Moot had stepped off a bus earlier that afternoon after a two-day ride from Calgary, where a bitter, unseasonable storm had plunged the late summer temperatures below freezing. Every shelter had immediately filled with so many crazed and addicted men and women, who were as often as not violent, that Moot no longer felt safe. So she had used the last of some panhandled cash to buy a bus ticket to Victoria.

Danchuk wanted to know if she had tried phoning her parents from the bus depot in Vancouver while waiting for the changeover from Greyhound to Pacific Coach Lines. "They have any idea where you were?"

She shook her head. "You have some weird idea in your head that they care. They don't. My dad's a freaking creep and mom should be declared legally blind for all she chooses to see going on around her. Prozac makes the world go round." Her smile was empty of humour. "Or away."

"Let's leave that for now," I said, risking another glare from Danchuk but anxious to maintain the delicately balanced and tentative rapport that had got Moot talking freely in the first place. "You arrived in Victoria and were up on the roof of a parkade."

"Yeah, that's right. It was a shitty night, pissing rain, with this wind coming off the harbour. All I owned was what I had on and a wool blanket I had found in an alley earlier. My pack and sleeping bag had been stolen off the bus. Tried to use the blanket as a cover to keep dry, but by the time I found this corner on the roof I was soaked."

"Why didn't you go to a shelter?" Danchuk asked with genuine puzzlement.

"Just got into town. Didn't know anybody yet. Girl goes into a shelter alone and nobody knows her," she gave a little shrug, "well, you're just asking to be a victim of something or other. I needed to hang a bit, get to know the kids here, get to know who was okay to pack with. It was better to just hide out for the night and then see what was what come morning. There were some dumpsters in the alley beside the parkade with no chains on the lids. I figured to do some diving when the rain eased. Seen worse."

Instead of having to slither about in the slime and filth of a dumpster, however, Moot had met Sparrow just in the nick of time. Sparrow appeared like a wraith, slithering down from the roof through an opening in the wall with a backpack slung over one shoulder. The shadowy figure propped itself against the wall across from Moot and considered the girl sitting there with legs curled up against her chest and back pressed hard against the cold, damp concrete. Moot tried to still her chattering teeth and to look cool, strong, and tough — like somebody you wouldn't mess with despite the tears shining in her eyes. The cold was pressing into her body like a knife, and a sluggish drowsiness warned Moot that she was probably becoming hypothermic and just might not survive this night. Going to a shelter had begun to seem a worthwhile risk, but she had been unable to summon the necessary strength to even move.

Moot dully realized that the person sitting across from her was a woman, but that didn't count for much, for some women on the streets were more dangerous than men. In the dim streetlight glow, Moot couldn't make out a face. Just a Medusa coil of thick ropes of hair, a stocky frame, and the curves and swellings of a woman's body not quite hidden inside rough, thickly layered clothing that included a dripping rain slicker.

"Fucking southeaster ain't going to blow through until morning," the woman said with a cheeriness that seemed at odds with her words. Then she dug around in her pack and tossed a mummy-style sleeping bag at Moot's feet. "You get out of those clothes and into that, girl. You got any dry things to put on?" Teeth rattling around inside her mouth like castanets, Moot could only shake her head. More fishing around in the pack produced an armload of clothing that was thrust Moot's way. "Wool socks, fleece pants, a sweater. You'll be swimming in them, but they're warm. Get into them and then get into that sleeping bag. I'll hang up your clothes and maybe they'll dry by morning."

Struggling to stave off her lethargy, Moot wriggled out of her clothes and into those the woman had provided. They bagged and sagged, so much so that she knew they wouldn't properly fit the other woman either. She was bigger than Moot, but not that big. Probably stuff she had picked up off the street hoping to swap for something better. But Moot didn't care. The clothes were dry, and as she rolled up inside the sleeping bag, Moot knew the woman had likely saved her life. It was then that she asked for a name and learned the woman went by Sparrow. A strange tag, she thought. Sparrows were common, and the kindness the woman was showing Moot was anything but common on the streets. "I've taken your sleeping bag," she said. "You'll get cold."

Sparrow brushed a rough palm across Moot's forehead. "I've got a blanket, too. That's good enough. We're dry and we're warm. We'll see the dawn." Moot could still feel the woman's hand on her forehead as her eyes shut and she fell asleep.

In the morning, Moot was surprised to discover that Sparrow was little older than she was. Moot had imagined Sparrow to be a seasoned street veteran. But Sparrow seemed to know what she was about. Neither Moot nor Sparrow confided their real names to each other. Moot claimed this was because neither cared about the past; there was only the future to look toward, and their street identities were all that mattered. The same went for where they came from. "I wasn't about to tell Sparrow that I was Meredith Ashley fucking Bainsbridge-Stanton from oh-so-la-ti-da Point Grey. That's just a nightmare some other person lived before I was born. Sparrow came from somewhere else and some other life and who cares?"

Despite knowing nothing of the other woman's past, Moot willingly followed in Sparrow's wake and was soon introduced to a group of about fifteen street people that had recently taken to calling themselves the One Earth Family. Sparrow said they had struck a pact to stick together, to look out for each other through good or ill. "All for one and one for all is how Devon puts it," Sparrow told Moot.

The band had formed about a month earlier when a group led by Devon Lysander erected an unofficial campground in a wooded copse next to one of the downtown cathedrals. It had been Lysander, Sparrow said, who scrounged more than a dozen tents and managed to get temporary approval from the church deacon to pitch them in the grassy shelter. The refuge lasted a month, and then the police came. The tents were torn down and the people told to get off the property. They had, the deacon said ruefully, become too numerous, and there were no hygienic facilities. Neighbours were complaining. He was sorry and the police were silently menacing. There was no arguing. So they had gathered their meagre belongings and walked out into the wilderness of the streets.

"Tell us about this Devon Lysander, Ms. Bainsbridge-Stanton. What kind of man is he?" Danchuk asked.

Perhaps Moot failed to note the mocking tone Danchuk wrapped around her regal-sounding name, for she answered him without any defensiveness. "He's the father most of us never had." She waved a dismissive hand, as if cutting off an unspoken objection. "I know, you look at him with his unkempt long hair and beard and tattered clothes and see nothing but another old bum." Moot's eyes brightened and she was suddenly even more animated than ever. "Devon is always there for us. He's ready to listen, to help however he can. He asks for nothing, but gives freely everything he has." Her eyes were fixed on a point on the wall set above our heads, as if she saw Devon Lysander standing there, gazing gently and lovingly down upon her. If this man was some sainted priest, Moot unquestionably counted herself among his acolytes.

Danchuk scowled at this revelatory image of the Family's leader and fidgeted in his chair impatiently while Moot continued to offer up a litany of Lysander's many strengths and virtues unleavened by any hint of faults. "So how on earth," Danchuk said with hands turned palm upwards, "Ms. Bainsbridge-Stanton, did Mr. Lysander come to be a homeless bum?" He jabbed a stubby index finger toward her. "Explain that."

Moot lifted her chin in a gesture of such haughty disdain that for a brief second I could see inside the ragamuffin seated before us the high-born young lady educated in private school manners and values that perhaps still lurked quiet and hidden somewhere within her. "Devon chose the life," she said flatly. "It wasn't thrust upon him. You decided to be a cop, he decided to dedicate his life to the street and the people there." Her blue eyes challenged Danchuk to dare question Lysander's integrity.

Somewhat firmly I tapped a knuckle on the table to break the mutually antagonistic standoff hardening between the girl and Danchuk. "Moot, I wonder if you could tell us how the Family ended up coming to Tofino?"

She held Danchuk's eye for a final long moment and then, with a little smirk that seemed like a claim of limited victory, directed her gaze my way. "After the camp was broken up the idea started to be kicked around that we should maybe leave the city," she said, while twirling the fingers of her right hand around the short hank of purple hair sticking out from that side of her head. "You know, get away from all the weirdness of cops and foul-mouthed store owners who don't want you sitting in front of their places, or the security guards paid by the banks or McDonald's to keep us moving, or those bylaws that make it illegal to pan for change. Just go to the country. Live in tune to the land."

A snort from Danchuk clearly indicated his opinion of this reasoning, so I carefully kept my expression neutral. But I had to agree that sleeping on the beach and panhandling around Tofino didn't seem to have much to do with living on the land or getting back to the country. "Why Tofino?" I asked.

Sparrow's idea, Moot said. She had been here the previous year with a group that had joined the seasonal coastal mushroom harvest and then wandered up to Tofino and discovered it to be a place where people were less uptight than in Victoria. "Practically everyone there is an old hippie of one sort or another, she told us. Sounded pretty good."

Devon Lysander had hesitated to have the entire Family show up in Tofino without knowing what to expect, so he had asked Sparrow and Moot to go up as a kind of advance party. "To check things out, you know, and report back if it looked workable."

"Understand him sending this Sparrow girl," Danchuk said, "but why you?"

The girl shifted her eyes down to her lap for a moment. "Sparrow and I were tight by then. She wanted me to come," Moot said in a near whisper. When she looked up her eyes were clouding.

I dug a clean tissue out of a coat pocket and handed it over. She dabbed her eyes and sniffed. "She was the best person I ever met."

"We won't keep you much longer. Just tell us how it went from when you both came up together to Tofino to yesterday."

They had ridden up on the bus, stepping out of the false fog of its diesel exhaust into air washed clean by a salt wind. The town was fine. Nobody seemed queered out by their presence. They tried a few pans in front of the liquor store and the Co-op Grocery with a modest return earned. So they could live. And then there was the beach. Moot had never seen anything like it and just wanted to run and run and run along the long sweeping expanse of pale sand. Sparrow had strolled along in her wake, looking as pleased as a genie who had just granted someone their greatest wish.

"Phone them. Tell them to come," Moot urged Sparrow. "Tell them we've found heaven."

By the time the rest of the One Earth Family stepped off a bus Sparrow and Moot had a good start on the camp in front of the Ashton property. "Why there?" Danchuk asked.

Moot shrugged. Sparrow had liked the site. It was at the end of the closest beach to town and not crowded by houses like the rest of the shoreline. "She figured we'd be less likely to get hassled and there was those creepy dark woods right behind it. So it was private."

"You didn't like the woods?"

She shook her head. "I don't like dark places. I need space around me. To see the sky."

"But Sparrow was different," I suggested. "She didn't mind the forest. Used to go there sometimes, despite the 'No Trespassing' signs."

"We don't have a lot of use for signs," Moot said with a grin. "Yeah, Sparrow liked the woods. She'd explore them for hours."

"You ever go with her?"

Once, but the forest had been dripping from a rain just passed and smelled like things rotting and dead. Then there had been the old house and the falling-down shacks around it and that scrawny but mean-looking security guard prowling the grounds. She had half dragged Sparrow back to the beach and refused to go into the woods again. While some of the others would shortcut through the forest to the road beyond to walk or hitch into town, Moot always followed the beach instead.

"Did Sparrow ever tell you why she liked the forest or what she found interesting about the house?"

Moot pursed her lower lip thoughtfully, then shook her head. "I don't think she liked it. She'd come back quiet and real thoughtful, sad like. It'd take some doing for me to cheer her up. To reclaim her for the beach and the sky." The girl smiled, remembering.

"How'd you do that?"

Moot's eyes swivelled to take aim at Danchuk. "I loved Sparrow and she loved me."

"And?" Danchuk all but shouted.

But Moot was swiping tears away from her eyes with a suddenly sodden little white tissue and then pressing her knuckles against her teeth. "And we were happy," she whispered. "We were happy. That's all. That was enough."

I reached past Danchuk and jabbed the stop button on the tape recorder. "Thank you, Moot. You can go." The sergeant started to protest but then clamped his mouth shut so hard that it formed a thin, tight line.

The girl paused and looked back over her shoulder halfway through the door when I said, "Moot, I'm sorry for your loss." She didn't reply. Just quietly, firmly closed the door behind her so that Danchuk and I were left sitting alone together behind the table next to the still tape recorder.

chapter eight

It took three more hours to interview everyone but Devon Lysander. By that time it was five-thirty and we were red-eyed, sludgy brained, and stiff of back and shoulders. Moot had been either the most forthcoming or the one who had known Sparrow best, for we garnered nothing of value from the others. Nobody admitted knowing Sparrow's real name, where she had come from, or her true age. Details offered by one generally conflicted with the vague recollection of another. As to the events that had transpired immediately prior to Sparrow's murder, none admitted any useful knowledge. Family members came and went as they liked, and Sparrow had not been gone unduly long or in a manner out of keeping with her normal patterns. They expected her to show whenever she did. Even Moot had expressed feeling no concern at her absence that night, believing they would rendezvous at the bus stop in Tofino the next day.

"I'll call Bethanie," Danchuk said when the last of the young people was escorted out the door by Constable Tom. "We can get some portable cots in here and rustle up some pizza or something for them to eat. Toilets still function and there's even hot water. Better than where they've been staying for a long time. Can't let them go off. They'd likely all hightail it out of town." These last observations were made in a distracted tone as if Danchuk was just thinking aloud to himself.

Unfortunately, I knew the sergeant was probably right in his fear that they would take flight if given the chance, and his solution seemed uncharacteristically humane. With time Bethanie would probably be able to identify the underage, the runaways from foster care, and then see that everyone was properly placed in their appropriate slot. For now, though, housing the Family in the old fish plant seemed workable.

I was relieved when Danchuk declared his intent to leave interviewing Lysander until the morning. I sensed the Family's leader would be no more forthcoming than the rest. So we would have to be in our best form to get anywhere.

"That one ain't staying here with the kids, though. He goes in lockup."

"Gary, are you sure that's wise?"

"I tell you how to do your job, McCann?" With Moot, Danchuk had held back from jabbing his finger into her chest, but that nasty little digit started thumping against my sternum as a form of punctuation that completed each sentence. "I want him isolated. I want him having nothing to do but think. Think about the lies he's going to need to tell. I want him to sweat through the night, worrying that every night for the rest of his sorry life might be spent in a place like he's going to spend tonight. I want him tired and nervous tomorrow.

I can hold him for questioning and I'm damned well going to do it."

Finally I wrapped my right hand around his smaller, pudgy one and gently, but firmly, lowered his arm to his side to stop him from poking my chest. His eyes seemed to suck back into their sockets and his face whitened, but he did not respond physically or verbally.

The sun was dropping low on the horizon as I drove the Land Rover toward Vhanna's. Fergus perched cheerfully on his haunches in the passenger seat, alertly scanning the passing surroundings. Although his vision is not as acute as when he was young, Fergus retains a puppy-like enthusiasm for going for drives at any time and to any location. But of all possible destinations none excites Fergus more than rolling down the lane that passes by the entrance to Vhanna's seaside home. When I pulled into it, he shot a bright-eyed grin my way and the little stub of his tail started wagging so vigorously that his butt rolled from side to side on the seat.

The high wrought iron gates that normally seal off Vhanna's driveway and garage stood open, which I took as a good sign. There have been times when I have scaled those same gates like a burglar to gain access, setting off the panoply of motion-detecting alarms that protect her home from some feared invasion. I have long since ceased trying to comprehend the need for someone so utterly fearless while venturing into the wildest and most remote places on the globe in pursuit of eco-adventure to live within a fortress. When the subject has arisen, Vhanna has always elusively dismissed its significance in a manner that brooks no further discussion. Jabronski, who has greatly profited by providing her with a full-service security system that includes round-the-clock immediate response to any and all alarms, chalks it up to the horrendous events experienced after a pack of blank-eyed Khmer Rouge killers broke into the family home in Phnom Penh.

Parking in an alcove to one side of the double bay garage doors, I jumped out, grabbed the chunk of flattened packing case cardboard set against the exterior wall, and slipped it beneath the Land Rover's engine. This to prevent an incurable oil leak from slowly eating into the driveway's red bricks. Vhanna is fussy about such things, for although she lives in lavish opulence, none of it is taken for granted and all is pristinely maintained and meticulously cared for.

Viewed from the front, the house appears relatively modest behind its entrance gates and eight-foot-high stone wall. No windows face the small enclosure that, other than for strategically placed shrubs planted in two halved oak wine barrels, is largely given over to driveway and a path that wends past more shrubbery to the front door. With Fergus beside me, I approached this heavy wooden entrance, pressed the doorbell, and tried to avoid looking at the lens of the surveillance camera mounted above the door. A soft chime rang within the inner sanctum and was immediately followed by an electronic clunk that indicated the locks had been released. Impatiently, Fergus bustled in ahead of me and set off toward the kitchen, while I paused to kick off my boots and hang my coat and hat.

If the front of Vhanna's home bears a distinct resemblance to a military bunker, the interior and ocean-facing rear are stunningly grand. Great slabs of glass look out across a wide wraparound deck to a long sandy beach, Templar Channel, the rocky banks of Wickanninish Island, and beyond to the endless Pacific Ocean. Underfoot is either bleached hardwood or large graphite-shaded slate tiles. Ceilings soar. In the living room, a stone fireplace occupies one wall, its mantel sparsely adorned with small brass Cambodian figurines. Hung judiciously on this or that wall are several large natural landscapes painted by Tofino artist Mark Hobson, and a selection of elegant native carvings by Roy Vickers is strategically placed so as to be visible but not intrusive. Two plush black leather couches are spaced well apart in such a way that both provide a vantage toward the ocean view and, simultaneously, to the living room's interior charms. There is an elegant minimalism about the room that money can buy, but only a discerning eye can create.

Below this main floor are two others, each as grand in its own way. The entire house hangs on a cliff plunging straight to the beach. A long cedar stairway switchbacks from the deck to the sand. The lowest floor is given over entirely to the office space from which Vhanna runs Artemis Adventures Incorporated. There are no security walls on this side of the property, just discreetly placed signs that warn off intruders. And dozens more intruder detection systems that will bring Jabronski running if someone ignores those posted warnings. It's a long climb up the stairs, so lots of time for Tofino's security czar to appear.

A small black phone set on a table by one of the couches rang. Seeing no sign of Vhanna on the main floor, I answered it. "It's me," she said. "I'm just finishing up some things. Be up in a few minutes. Beer in the fridge. Send Fergus down."

Fergus took this news happily and with hips rolling with each step sashayed down the stairs. So much for solidarity between dog and man, I thought, while envying Fergus his invitation. I comforted myself that being excluded meant that she would find my presence more distracting than that of Fergus, who could be counted on to curl up behind her chair once the formalities of greeting were concluded. If at all possible, Vhanna would never see work go uncompleted before quitting for a day. A strong entrepreneurial spirit blows through her soul and requires approaching business matters with a zeal baffling to a remittance man.

I wandered into the kitchen and opened the vast chrome and black refrigerator to fetch out one of the bottles of Spinnaker's finest brown ales that Vhanna has shipped to Tofino by special order from the brew-pub in Victoria. As Vhanna rarely drinks beer, this is something she does purely to indulge that fellow in her life blessed with a taste for good drink. Draining the bottle into a heavy glass stein, I wandered through the living room toward the deck with plans to watch the sun slide gracefully into the ocean while sprawling indolently on a chaise longue.

I was just in the process of taking a good long swallow of the nutty brew when the phone on the table by the couch rang again. Thinking it was Vhanna with further instructions, I hefted the receiver. There was a soft hissing sound as if the caller was phoning long distance on a poor connection. A fact confirmed when I glanced down at the caller identification display screen and noted that the caller's number was preceded by the 604 area code of the greater Vancouver region. As I started to say hello, a man asked, "Vhanna, are you there?"

"Sorry, no," I said. "She's downstairs in her office. Can I take a message?"

Although the voice seemed familiar I was unable to place it. "No," the man said, "I'll phone again when it is more convenient. Thank you." Whoever it was hung up before I could offer the number for Artemis Adventures.

Stepping out on the deck, I leaned against the railing and watched the last few minutes of the sun's fiery, violent red descent into the ocean. The sky was scattered with puffy clouds, the colour of old blood, that scudded on a high wind, and the ocean glittered with thousands of diamonds. Gulls swirled on wide-spread wings, their shrieks muted from normal raucous revelry to something gentler and more reflective due to the distance to where they soared high above the wave tops.

A small hand slipped under my arm as deftly as a pickpocket's, and Vhanna pressed against my shoulder. "Sunsets like that are a blessing."

Setting the beer glass on the railing so I could rest my other hand on hers, I said, "It's always a blessing to share a sunset with you."

Vhanna was wearing narrow-lensed sunglasses that made it impossible to see her eyes, but her tone was light as she scoffed, "You're such an incurable romantic."

"Do you mind?"

She gave her head a small shake. "No, but there is much risk in it for you." With a last flare of brightness the sun sunk below the horizon, and instantly the wind turned cold. "Let's go in and I'll make dinner." Arm in arm we moved inside, Fergus happily at our side. This is the way he likes it, both of us under the same roof and safe under his watchful and protective eye.

A couple hours later we adjourned from the remnants of a Cuban pork stew to the living room with the last dregs of a tart pinot grigio in our glasses. Our conversation remained light, as if we were both adhering to an unspoken resolution to not taint the pleasure of dinner. But the words exchanged that morning cast a palpable chill that neither the stew's spicy heat nor the candlelight's warmth could dispel. Now, seated at one end of a couch with Vhanna at the other, legs curled up beneath her, and Fergus stretched out on a rug before the cold fireplace, I muddled through a morass of thoughts in search of the right words. Not surprisingly, the more direct Vhanna swirled the contents of her glass thoughtfully for a moment and then pre-empted me. "I don't want to argue tonight, but I do want to talk about today. You think I was consorting with the enemy this morning by sitting at Dagleish's table, but it doesn't mean I think any less of Doc Tully or even necessarily plan on voting for Monica Klassen."

Fergus sniffed gently enough just to be heard and cast a baleful eye full of obvious suggestion at the stack of firewood on the hearth, then the fireplace's dark mouth. The thought of building a fire rather than having this discussion was appealing, but the possibility that we could avoid ending in a fight offered some promise. "I shouldn't have reproached you," I ventured cautiously. "It just seems that Tully's fighting an uphill battle and needs all the friends he can get to be out there visibly offering their support."

"It's going to take a lot more than Tully's friends to win him this election, Elias. Monica's got the lion's share of the business community behind her."

"And Dagleish."

Vhanna's mouth became a thin line and her eyes hardened, but her voice remained even. "And, yes, she's got Darren Dagleish's support and he's a powerful player now in Tofino's economy. You think just because he appeared so recently that he shouldn't have such influence. But he's pumping millions of dollars into the region, money that's softening the blows dealt by the decline of forestry and fishing. A lot of people are going to get work from his projects, in both building and running them."

I had to concede this was true. Wherever one turned these days another sign announced a Dagleish Properties development soon forthcoming on this or that site surrounded by the inevitable barbed wire security fence. One site might be proclaimed as an economy-boosting hotel, resort, or guest house, another adjacent to the highway on the edge of town a retail building, while yet another was to be transformed into a residential subdivision to house dozens of the soon to be happily employed Dagleish workers. The pace of Dagleish's acquisitions was dizzying, his appetite for development apparently unlimited, and his pockets endlessly deep.

"Jim Scarborough thinks Dagleish is going to turn Tofino into another Whistler. Destroy all we really love about the place."

"And you agree?"

I smiled weakly. Vhanna tipped her head back and stared at the ceiling. I could feel her frustration with my lack of imagination or vision. "A community can't simply stand still, remain frozen in time. That's the road to stagnation."

"So there must always be growth?"

She nodded and added heatedly, "The alternative to growth is decline."

"But shouldn't growth be moderated? If things move too fast, there's always the risk of lost control and irreversible results that could be disastrous."

"Good repartee," Vhanna said with a smile. She was warming to a debate I wanted nothing more than to close. "You're starting to sound like an economist. A conservative one, however, with an aversion to risk."

I rested a hand on her knee. "I like stability."

"You like an ordered universe in which things are predictable and routine." She laughed. "Morning walks with Fergus, a bowl of chowder at the Crab Pot Café, single malt Scotch sipped by the fire in the evening."

"The woman I love in my bed at night."

Vhanna leaned over and kissed my cheek. "That's a distinct possibility. Do you want to stay over?"

I attested to how there was nothing that would suit me better as I kissed her throat and undid a couple of her shirt buttons. "There are dishes to clean up and a conversation to conclude."

"A conversation best left behind and nothing else that can't wait until morning." I bent over and lightly kissed a nipple that had become exposed when the last shirt button had come undone.

"You offer a convincing argument," Vhanna said, and, taking my hand, led the way to her bedroom.

chapter nine

Awaking after dawn I lay in bed beside Vhanna and watched the sun cast Wickanninish Island in a yellowish glow. The sky was clear and the ocean heavy with swells edged by white horses. Tofino, it appeared, was to be blessed with some unexpectedly fine fall weather. Lying under a thick white duvet on a bed that braced its wrought iron headboard against a wall facing floor-to-ceiling windows, I stretched with lazy contentment and then turned on my side to spoon Vhanna's back against me. I softly kissed her shoulder and then lay my head on the pillow with thoughts of dozing. But rather than being able to linger happily on the remembered images of the night, my mind filled with visions of a dead young woman wrapped in vicious strands of barbed wire. *Who were you, Sparrow? And why did someone murder you?* So far I had no answers, only ever more questions. Rolling onto my back, I stared at the ceiling and thought about what little I knew of the girl.

If Devon Lysander was the Family's spiritual leader, it seemed that Sparrow had been his right hand. A woman who, despite her young age, assumed responsibility quickly and efficiently. Taking under her wing a girl who considered herself so inconsequential she adopted the street name Moot. Suggesting the move from Victoria to Tofino. Conducting the reconnaissance and then finding a base camp on the beach in front of the Ashton property. According to Moot it had been Sparrow who had initiated all of this and led the way.

The decision to move to Tofino had been based on nothing more than a previous good time. Uprooting a dozen or more people to make a long, expensive bus trip to such a remote corner of the world on so little experience was decidedly impetuous. Yet nobody in the Family appeared to have questioned the decision. Sparrow had reported positively and they had followed. So perhaps Sparrow had been the unofficial leader who took responsibility for the day-to-day affairs of the Family, leaving Lysander to attend to their spiritual well-being. It was a thought worth pursuing in the forthcoming interview.

And once here, Sparrow's behaviour had little differed from that of the other Family members. Hanging about on the beach, panhandling for change downtown, nothing to set her apart. Except perhaps for her apparent fascination with the Ashton property — its woods and the sadly empty house. What had drawn her to its rooms? And had her fascination with the place brought her to the attention of a murderer? Simms, the hard-drinking security guard? Or had it merely put her where she was vulnerable and alone, so that someone with murder in mind could strike? Lysander? Simms? Both could fit the bill. So, too, probably every other male in the Family's ranks. Or someone else entirely, someone lurking on the sidelines and watching for a chance. Torture and kill a homeless girl and what did you have to worry? Sparrow was such a nonentity that it was left to Sergeant Danchuk and a sham of a coroner to try to find her killer. Precious little to fear there.

Vhanna rolled over, propped herself on one elbow, and brushed her hair back over a shoulder. "What are you thinking about?" she said through a small yawn. Cradling her head on my shoulder, I summarized my thoughts on Sparrow and her death. Vhanna shuddered noticeably when I described in general terms the manner in which the homeless girl had been first tortured, then murdered, and I wondered if her own exposure to similar brutality made such cruelty all the more poignantly imaginable.

We lay in silence after I finished, my thoughts stumbling about in tedious circles so that I concentrated instead on massaging Vhanna's back, my hand tracing the length of her spine past where it kinked unnaturally — the result of a brutal blow by the butt of an AK-47 during the enforced march from Phnom Penh.

"I can't understand the thing about her spending so much time alone in the house and the woodshed," I said finally, and then told Vhanna about the house having been stripped of furniture and rendered nothing but an empty, depressing husk.

"Sometimes you can feel things in an empty house," Vhanna said. "Spirits. Especially if the house has been a place of tragedy." Only months before, Vhanna had returned again to her family home. When she had done this two years earlier she had found the building taken over by previously homeless Cambodians who had split the big home into tiny living spaces in which two to three families shared a single room. During this last visit, however, Vhanna had found the house abandoned. Perhaps the numerous impoverished people who had moved back to Phnom Penh had succumbed to starvation or disease or had fled the city for an uncertain opportunity to try re-establishing farms in the mine-strewn countryside.

Vhanna told me how she had wandered through the great empty rooms and weed-infested gardens. "I would turn and see my mother in the piano room, playing Stravinsky so clearly that I could hear every note. But then the image would fade and, with it, the music. Or my father would be in the garden with his white shirt-sleeves rolled up pruning the roses. He'd turn and smile at me, but as I started to reach out to touch his cheek his eyes turned grave and the image dissolved. Our maid, the family cat, the groundsman, various cousins and aunts and uncles, I saw them all in those hours, but each came only slowly. In between I waited. Sometimes walking around, but most of the time just picking a spot in a room or in the garden and trying to remember it as it had been before the madness came." I brushed the tears that trickled down Vhanna's cheeks gently aside. "It was mid-morning when I first came to the house and I didn't leave until dawn. The last few hours, sitting cross-legged on the floor of my bedroom in the deep darkness, I thought about fate and the duty of a survivor. The duty to never forget. When I left that morning the house felt more settled and at peace with itself. I wonder now if the people who had been squatting there didn't leave because of the spirits. Because they had been unable to remember them or to provide that sense of peace." Vhanna laughed dryly. "All very mystical, right?"

I didn't answer, remembered instead hours spent in Angus's house after his death. Shifting papers, reading passages from books he had loved, sitting in the big chair set so he could gather warmth from the fireplace and enjoy the views of the green fields and the mountains that rose up behind. There had been the pictures of the red-haired beauty, Lila, who had been my mother, and Angus's many letters to her all carefully stored in the precise chronological order of their writing in the lowest drawer of his desk. Never mailed because Angus had no idea of his young wife's whereabouts. The heartfelt emotion in those letters, the longing for her return, had revealed a side of my father I had never known. After reading only two of the letters I had kindled a fire in the hearth and burned them all one after the other. The photos, too. Save one, stored inside an envelope in that same bottom drawer, which now resides in the loft of my cabin. Because that same desk is now mine. During the time I was in Angus's house there were memories to be found in the papers and in the trappings of his life that filled the rooms. But I had felt nothing of his presence there, real or imagined.

Vhanna interrupted my thoughts by rolling on top of me, so we could better see each other's faces. "She knew whoever killed her." When there is a serious matter being discussed, Vhanna likes to make eye contact. "How long had she lived on the streets?"

I shrugged. We didn't know for sure. "At least a year, maybe more."

"Someone living like that's going to have been in a lot of dangerous places. I don't see her letting anyone get so close to her that they could restrain her with the wire without a struggle."

"What if it was the security guard?"

"If he tried to detain her, Sparrow would probably have bolted."

Which brought it back to Lysander. She would trust him. Why stick around if she didn't? He could probably get into a position to harm any Family member before they could react or protect themselves. And the man was big and strong enough to easily subdue someone of Sparrow's size.

A sharp sniff from the other side of the bedroom doorway, followed by a paw thumping against the floor, announced that Fergus was ready for us to begin the day. "Somebody demands his morning constitutional." I hugged Vhanna tightly and gave her a long kiss, as Fergus impatiently jangled his tags. "Okay, I'm coming, your highness," I said, as Vhanna rolled off me and we climbed out of opposite sides of the bed to face a new day and the interminable demands of beasts and humans.

As we descended the staircase to the beach, I remembered to tell Vhanna about the man who had called the evening before from a Vancouver area number. Vhanna hesitated mid-step and glanced anxiously my way, but even as our eyes met her expression became guarded and free of apparent emotion. "Probably just some telephone solicitor offering yet another credit card. They always phone right around dinnertime."

"He sounded like someone I know," I said doubtfully.

Vhanna had started trotting down the stairs with Fergus bouncing awkwardly alongside her. "Doesn't matter. Whoever it was can phone back and mystery solved," she said breezily over her shoulder. But I detected an edge of uncertainty in her voice even as I hastened to keep up with her. As we stepped onto the beach I wondered why such a bluntly honest person who is a poor dissembler would do so about a phone call.

Fergus raced off toward a thicket of brush growing against the cliff face while Vhanna strode to the centre of the beach, kicked off her running shoes, and stood barefoot on the sand with her body turned to face the ocean. Her short-waisted T-shirt didn't reach the waistband of the matching black tights, and she shivered against the morning chill. But I knew Vhanna would soon warm up performing the 108 moves of the Taoist Tai Chi ritual, which she followed every morning without fail by a vigorous round of the more ancient Tai Chi combat moves that reclaimed the martial origins of a discipline now used by millions purely for exercise and meditation.

Having attended to immediate business, Fergus had trotted down to the water's edge and was looking over his shoulder expectantly. Leaving Vhanna to her regimen, I strolled along the beach. Fergus alternated between walking beside me and rushing off to flush any birds that alighted on the beach ahead. A surprisingly warm breeze was lifting off the ocean, and soon I pulled off my jacket and slung it over one shoulder. It was tempting to carry on all the way to the opposite end of the beach, but the time for meeting Danchuk was drawing nigh. So I cut the walk short and led a grumpy and disappointed dog back toward the lone figure moving gracefully across the sand.

She looked almost childlike from that distance, and I remembered Lars Jansen's recollection of the first time he saw Vhanna practice Tai Chi. It had been a few months after he and Frieda had brought her to Tofino from the Thai refugee camp. He had stepped out of the house one morning to breathe in the fresh dawn air, and there on the old wooden boat dock fronting their waterfront property the twelve-year-old girl had been moving sinuously back and forth with slow rhythm. After watching for a few minutes Lars tugged on his gumboots and strolled out onto the dock behind her. He then moved in beside her and matched her every step as closely as possible.

In his youth Lars had left Norway to travel the globe as a merchant mariner, serving on one tramp steamer after another. Many years at sea were spent plying Asian waters alongside crews composed of Chinese, Korean, Vietnamese, and Filipino sailors. The always intensely curious Lars had learned from them how to play various exotic instruments and perform a smatter-ing of martial arts that ranged through aikido to kung fu and included scraps of Tai Chi.

Vhanna, who was still guarded and distrustful of Lars, Frieda, and the new home to which they had brought her, demonstrated neither surprise nor pleasure at Lars joining her. It was as if he was not there at all. When she finished, Vhanna had bowed toward the inlet waters and then returned to the house without a word. But the next morning she was again on the boat dock and showed no displeasure when Lars again joined her.

A couple of weeks later Lars drove Vhanna to Port Alberni, and together they began to study Tai Chi under the tutelage of a Chinese practitioner who ran a martial arts studio there. Eventually Lars learned from Vhanna that she had been taught the form by her father and from an early age had gone through the ritualistic moves each morning with him. Lars, worried now that by imposing himself into her practice each morning he had perhaps disrupted the sacred memory of a treasured family member, asked if she minded his presence. She looked at him with those serious, penetrating eyes that he found impossible to read except in terms of the great sadness that lurked deep in her soul and then gave a slight shake of her head. From then on their morning exercise together was a ritual Lars hoped enabled Vhanna to retain a happier childhood memory of her father than that of his murder.

Vhanna suddenly swung her hips and arms to the right, then snapped the right leg up in a sharp, straight-ahead kick to waist level. Just as her foot reached the kick's apex, the palm of her right hand struck the side of the foot with a sharp slap and both hands then carried past until they extended out to her left, completing the move. A visually stunning sequence that requires great physical power and coordination to correctly execute, Sweep Lotus looks deceptively simple. Watch the stylized action of the hands as they sweep through the air and you won't see the kick coming. Watch only the right leg and foot, and the delivery of the kick while balance is maintained seems impossible. For the move to succeed, arms, hips, and legs must act in seemingly opposing sequences that actually harmoniously fuse together. As Sweep Lotus is the 102nd move, Vhanna finished the set moments later and then made an immediate transition from the form's relaxed stance into a series of combat jabs, kicks, and spins executed at dizzying speed. Fergus and I appreciatively watched Vhanna's acrobatics from a safe distance until she suddenly stopped and faced us.

"Remind me to never unduly annoy you."

Vhanna grinned. "Much too late for that. Besides, knocking you around would be a misuse of Tai Chi energy that would not only injure you but also prove irreparably detrimental to my spiritual health." She walked over and circled her arms around my neck. "So give me a kiss and then off with you."

chapter ten

A few minutes later I was home pouring food in a bowl for Fergus and boiling water for coffee. By the time my Kicking Horse dark roast coffee had brewed, I had boiled an egg and toasted two inch-thick slices of Tofino bakery multigrain bread. I consumed this nourishment hurriedly, for the scheduled time of the interview approached. With apologies to Fergus, who put on a brave face to conceal how disillusioned he was at having been torn from Vhanna's company only to be abandoned at home, I started out the door, only to hesitate at the last moment.

Turning back I checked a number in the phone book, then rang up Dagleish Property Development Corporation's Tofino office and was immediately speaking to a perky and young-sounding female receptionist. When I asked for Mr. Darren Dagleish, she paused, as if consulting a schedule board, and then advised that he was out of town. "Is there another number I can reach him at? It's somewhat urgent."

Another pause before she somewhat guardedly offered that Dagleish was in Vancouver until tomorrow afternoon. I got the number of his office there and then rang off. If memory served, the number was not the one I had seen on the call display screen of Vhanna's phone. But I had not paid much attention at the time. Nor am I gifted with the ability to easily remember number sequences. They enter my brain and are as quickly forgotten. Was it then purely because Dagleish was in Vancouver and could have been the caller that I felt troubled? And a sense of disappointment in Vhanna, if that were the case.

Minutes later I pulled up in front of the single-storey red brick RCMP office, and Nicki ushered me into the windowless room used for interviews. Danchuk was there fussing impatiently with a tape recorder while Constable Tom methodically set up the video camera. I pulled up a chair next to Danchuk's. On his half of the table a lined, canary yellow notepad, three meticulously sharpened pencils, a thinly filled file folder, a steaming cup of coffee, and a glass of water had been compulsively ordered on the tabletop with military precision. "Make yourself at home, McCann." Danchuk stabbed the red record button, then clicked the pause button to freeze the tape. "Wondered if you were going to bother showing up. Police work isn't very flashy."

I chose to ignore the jibes, concentrating instead on pulling a notepad from my battered leather briefcase, hanging my coat on the back of the chair, and setting my hat off to the side of the table away from where Danchuk was going to be sitting. "How did Mr. Lysander take being locked up for the night?"

The sergeant's grin was mirthless. "Said he don't like being confined. Told him to get used to it because he's not likely to see many more free days in his life. That shut him up." Danchuk took a swallow of coffee and licked his lips like he had just eaten something tasty.

Tom stepped out of the room, returning a few minutes later with Lysander walking in front of him, and guided the man to the only unoccupied chair — a straight-backed, narrow wooden thing. Danchuk had set it several feet back from the table we sat behind in an obviously calculated move to prevent Lysander from having anywhere to rest his arms. Lysander sat on the hard seat and folded his hands in his lap so that he looked like a schoolboy serving detention. His long grey hair was dishevelled and oily, which I suspected indicated he had not been allowed to wash. There was also a green-purple bruise on his left temple.

"How did you come by the bruise, Mr. Lysander?" I asked. Danchuk leaned forward in his chair and fixed Lysander with a steady eye. The faintest trace of a smirk played at the corners of the sergeant's mouth.

Lysander smiled wearily. "People like me, we fall down a lot and bump into things."

"Why is that?"

He shrugged. "Just not careful when we should be, I guess."

"Let's get on it with it, McCann," Danchuk said. I noticed that Constable Tom was concentrating all his attention on focusing the video camera.

There had been a time in Cyprus when a Turkish man had slipped across the Green Line in Nicosia intent on seeing a Greek woman with whom he had been romantically involved before the fighting broke. Such relationships courted bloody retribution from both families. My four-man patrol had picked up the man within minutes of his slipping through the apron of concertina wire and bundled him into an armoured personnel carrier where the platoon sergeant was monitoring the night's activities over the radio. Questions were barked at the man through an interpreter, and it was soon determined that we dealt only with a lovestruck and forlorn romantic rather than a terrorist.

But the man's volatility, the loudness of his protestations of innocence combined with his frantic arm waving, proved somehow offensive to the sergeant. He hawked a wad of chewing tobacco out the back door of the APC and in the next moment slapped the man violently across one cheek with such force the Turk was knocked off the bench and tumbled to the other side of the compartment. Then the sergeant ordered the man dragged to a checkpoint and cast back over the Green Line at the feet of the Turk guards there. No thought was given to how the man would explain his having been picked up by a Canadian patrol on the enemy side of the line or what ramifications that might have for his safety. He could have been allowed to slip back through the wire the way he had come, but the sergeant thought that was too little a lesson for whatever it was he sought to teach the man. As for the rest of us, we let it happen. We said nothing and averted our eyes.

And again I averted my eyes, deciding not to pursue the issue of how Lysander had come by the bruise because it was certain the homeless man would deny the truth I suspected. "Let's get started," Danchuk declared again. Lysander met my eyes then for a brief second, and I sensed his frank acknowledgement of my knowledge and his acceptance that it mattered not a whit. In the face of abusive power the individual can do little but endure and hope to eventually cease being a subject of attention. Yet I knew Lysander had scant hope that Danchuk would soon shift the focus of his investigation and violent temper elsewhere.

Besides, there was a good chance the man was a murderer. The possibility of which Danchuk now probed, starting with the usual questions about name, age, birthplace, background. Devon Nathaniel Lysander, he replied, forty-three, Halifax, professional hobo. "Hobo?"

"Yes."

"How is being a hobo a profession?"

"I have probably been a hobo for more years than you have been a policeman."

"Yeah, how long?"

Lysander looked up at the ceiling, seemingly calculating. "Twenty-one years."

"And what were you before that?"

"A child."

Danchuk's knuckles whitened and he tapped the end of his pencil sharply against the notepad before him. "You were twenty-two. Hardly a child."

Lysander grinned, which revealed the fact that he was missing most of his upper right teeth and the others were badly stained by nicotine. "I was a philosophy major at Dalhousie University. So someone as yet unformed." For a man who had a few minutes before been looking cowed by Danchuk's threatening presence, Lysander had rallied remarkably. There was something unnerving about his responses to the sergeant's questions and how he sat with his back straight as a soldier's and his hands pressed flat against his thighs while evenly meeting the sergeant's gaze. It was as if Lysander controlled the direction of the inquiry.

"Did you graduate?"

"To being a hobo, yes. To being a philosopher, no."

Danchuk sucked in his breath and yanked some papers out of the file folder that had been lying primly next to his elbow. "I have a rather interesting criminal record here, Mr. Lysander." He lifted up the first sheet and peered at it as if seeing it for the first time. "You like knocking people around, I see. December 14, last year.

Kamloops. That ring a bell? Should, as you pulled three months for that one. Until then you had been a good boy for almost three years. No assaults after Saskatoon. Remember that one?"

Lysander nodded, but said nothing.

"A doozy. Kicked the snot out of a twenty-year-old Indian kid. Pulled a year for that one, but out in six months. Parole boards never learn. Those kids think of you as some kind of father figure. They know about these, Lysander? Or about the others? The thirteen where you were tried and convicted." More papers were shuffled to the top of Danchuk's pile. "Hell, let's look at the others from the first one. Suspended sentence in 1980, two months in 1982, a year in 1984, another year in 1987, and on it goes. Even drew federal time in 1992. Real peach that time, weren't you. Kicked a guy witless on a corner of Yonge Street in Toronto. Three years, but paroled from Kingston Pen after only half time served."

"He was selling heroin to a twelve-year-old boy," Lysander said wearily. "I warned him not to. And the one in Saskatoon was a pimp trying to recruit some of the younger girls and boys."

"That how it was with all the others? You just defended other people? Standing up for those who can't defend themselves? Being a guardian of the street? A regular Lone Ranger? Is that it?" Lysander shrugged and didn't reply. "That how it was with Sparrow? You kill her to protect her?" Danchuk's face was flushed, his eyes hard chips of blue as he scowled my way, warning me to keep my mouth shut.

"I never killed Sparrow, Sergeant. I would never have done that. Never."

Danchuk's shoulders noticeably relaxed, his voice turned suddenly solicitous. "You like a coffee, Mr.

Lysander? Would you like a break? Need to go to the bathroom or anything?"

Lysander's puzzlement was clear. "No, I'm fine. Thank you, anyway."

"Constable," Danchuk said to Tom, "get Mr. Lysander a coffee. I think he needs it. You take cream? Sugar?"

"Just black."

"Good. Bring him a coffee. Black."

Tom went out of the room and returned a moment later with a steaming Styrofoam cup. Lysander took a tentative sip and then a deeper one.

"Nicki makes the coffee pretty strong, Mr. Lysander. Too bitter for me. And then it sits there getting stronger with each passing hour."

"It's fine."

"Good. Should we continue?" When Lysander nodded agreement Danchuk leaned forward with elbows resting on the table, as if to better catch the man's every word. "Tell me why it wasn't possible for you to kill Sparrow, Mr. Lysander."

Lysander looked at the coffee in his hand and then the tabletop, but that surface was too far off, so he bent over and carefully rested the cup on the floor beside the chair. The man's fingers trembled slightly as he crossed his arms over his chest as if to ward off a cold draft. "To kill someone, Sergeant, you have to believe you are entitled to be more powerful than they are. I don't believe anyone should believe themselves superior to anybody else."

Danchuk's hands tightened into fists at this revelation. There was gravel in his voice when he said, "How about all those people you assaulted? Kind of proves you thought you were superior to them and more powerful."

"When somebody is abusing another then it is beholden on those who witness this to defend the weaker person. And only to the extent that brings about a cessation of the abuse." Lysander's voice was calm and measured. He could have been debating a philosophical point back at Dalhousie.

"Most people would call 911. Ever think of that?"

"Not those of us who live outside your social system. We sort out problems among ourselves without bringing in the police or other authorities. There's a true collective spirit on the streets."

"You sound like one of them anarchists to me. You want to tear down society, do away with social order, drag us all back into the jungle, Mr. Lysander. That it?"

"Bakunin believed that any form of political power was ultimately oppressive and that we should do away with private property and set up a system where people voluntarily cooperated with each other and were rewarded by what they contributed. I try to live like that. Most of those existing on the streets do, even if it's not a philosophical decision on their part."

"I don't care about Bakunin. I look at you and your so-called Family and see nothing but a bunch of slackers living off the backs of others by collecting welfare if you can or begging and stealing from others if you can't." Danchuk raised a pudgy hand and pointed the index finger at Lysander as if it were a pistol. "And I see before me a man with a violent history and more than ample opportunity to have murdered that girl."

Lysander shrugged. "You think as you will, Sergeant, but I did not hurt Sparrow."

"Mr. Lysander," I said, "the security guard at the Ashton property mentioned that members of the Family were often cutting the fences there and tearing down or defacing the 'No Trespassing' signs. He particularly singled out you and Sparrow as the chief culprits. Is that true?"

The man considered the question for a moment, which set Danchuk to shifting impatiently in his seat. "Yes, I suppose it was more our doing than the others'."

"And this because you opposed private property?"

Lysander smiled sadly. "More because we didn't much care for Dagleish Property and its plans for the Ashton lands."

"What the hell business of yours was it?" Danchuk snapped. "You come slinking into our town, dirty up the streets with your begging, camp illegally on our beaches, and vandalize the property of a man doing something to bring money and jobs in."

Lysander stared down at his lap, obviously determined not to take Danchuk's bait.

"What was it about Dagleish's plans that you didn't like?" I inquired.

His eyes probed mine as if seeking to divine my ulterior purpose. Then he replied softly, "Sparrow said the ground there was special, sacred somehow. There were spirits there that would be left with nowhere to be if the trees were cut and the house levelled to make way for his resort and housing development. The forest, the old house, the beach in front of it were all something to be protected in its entirety. She spent increasing amounts of time wandering about in the woods and visiting the house as the summer went on. And she started cutting the fence more often, pushing over posts, ripping down the signs. She wanted to know more about Dagleish and how he had come to control the property."

His expression became resigned. "Sparrow hadn't realized yet that people like us, people without homes or money, don't get to ask such questions. We can take direct action to send a message of our opposition to their plans, but we can't ultimately influence what they will or won't do."

"God, what a bunch of crap," Danchuk muttered.

"Had Sparrow shown much belief in spirits before this?"

"Not that I remember. But we were in the city before. The only spirits there were the ones found in a bottle." He shrugged dismissively. "We discovered a good natural place up here and I think she just fell in love with it. And wanted to save it. So she did what she could to get in Dagleish's way."

"But that was pretty much limited to tearing down signs and cutting wire, right? As you say, there wasn't much else she could do."

Lysander grinned. "Oh, she was inventive. There were survey stakes that could be relocated or removed. Tires on vehicles that could be punctured or an odd windshield broken."

"Bloody little vandal," Danchuk said, but I sensed also a note of puzzlement in his tone. During our discussions with Roberta Walker and Jeb Simms neither had mentioned this level of vandalism. I doubted any police reports had been filed. It must have been obvious that it was members of the Family who had been doing these things. So why had no complaint been made that could have resulted in their being forcibly evicted from the beach under the authority of a court injunction? Had Dagleish truly been so tolerant of the Family's presence that he had been willing to absorb the added costs of new surveys and repairs to vehicles rather than go to the bother of having a bunch of homeless people moved?

It took a further two hours for the interview with Lysander to end with nothing of apparent value having been extracted. Danchuk was certain he had his man and just needed time to prove it. But he also had no evidence to justify holding Lysander. "This investigation's going nowhere, McCann," Danchuk grumbled to me in his office. In the reception area Nicki had returned the homeless man's belt and meagre personal possessions and was having him sign the necessary paperwork confirming receipt. After that Lysander would be free to go wherever he pleased. "He'll head for Vancouver or Toronto and lose himself in the crowds. Could take years to track him down again."

"How long before the DNA analysis results come back?" Nickerson, the RCMP crime scene investigator, had collected dozens of samples for testing.

"Damned slow process," the sergeant said. "Backlog is huge. It could be months." He ran a hand over his bald pate and shrugged. "Well, not like I don't have a hundred other things that need doing. Told headquarters they needed to send a detective out. Got nothing back but excuses of being short-staffed." He started shuffling indifferently through a stack of papers on his desk that looked like time logs and shift reports. "Not that it stops them sending people up here and not telling me what for. Bother."

"So finding Sparrow's killer isn't a priority, I take it?"

Danchuk lips tightened into a hard line and his face reddened. "You know how it is, McCann," he said, even as a chill of regret for my words ran through me. "Killers in remote places sometimes get to walk because nobody can spare the resources to take a good long, hard look at the case. Worked for you."

I pulled on my coat and hat, forcing back the angry retorts that spilled through my brain. Finally I just said, "Gary, some day you're going to realize that I never killed Merriam."

"Miracles happen every day, they say. Just get out of my sight. Sometimes you make me want to puke."

chapter eleven

Lysander and I happened to depart the police detachment together, like two men with something in common. Which, both being murder suspects in the eyes of Sergeant Danchuk, perhaps we did. "Want a lift over to the fish plant?"

"That would be most kind, Mr. McCann. I want to get everyone together. We have to decide what to do next."

I released the latch lock on the passenger door for him, and Lysander climbed up into the seat, closing the door with a firm and perfectly measured thump. Passengers more accustomed to the weight of vehicle doors constructed primarily of plastic and alloy synthetics generally treat the Land Rover's doors either as if they are setting a china lid on a bowl or are ramming home the breech block of an artillery piece. The former fails to get the job done while the latter threatens the latch's finicky balance so I end up spending hours trying to get the mechanism working smoothly again.

When I commented on this, Lysander smiled. "My father was a Cape Breton circuit preacher. Sundays were spent driving a hundred or more miles of backcountry roads to get from one church to another and back home again. He drove a 1958 long box with a two-litre diesel engine. Bought it new and was still driving it when he retired. As a kid, I rode with him every Sunday. Mom up front here like I'm sitting, me in the back on whichever side bench I pleased. The benefit of being an only child. Bundled up like an Eskimo in the winter and sweating buckets in the summer. Nothing comfortable about that vehicle, but it was sure dependable. Got us through no matter what weather came our way. Don't believe he ever missed a service."

"You in touch with your family, Mr. Lysander?"

He tugged his beard, staring straight ahead at the wiper slapping ineffectively at the big sloppy raindrops that had suddenly started falling from the belly of a great dark cloud that had erased the sun from the sky. I was beginning to think Lysander was ignoring my question. "He hanged himself in the barn out back of the house in 1980," the man said softly. "Two weeks after my mother died of ovarian cancer."

I pulled up in front of the packing plant to park beside a police cruiser and Bethanie Hollinger's shiny yellow Volkswagen Beetle. Realizing that was the same year Lysander had faced his first assault charge, I asked him if there might be any connection. He was stepping out of the Land Rover when he turned back and looked across at me. "I got drunk in a bar down on the Halifax waterfront the night after we buried her. Staggered against some stevedore on my way to the john. He took exception and there were words. Then some punches thrown. I was twenty-two, but for some reason the police phoned my father to advise him I was in the drunk tank and facing an assault charge. He didn't come down from Cape Breton and I didn't call him when I got out. Then the police phoned to say he had hanged himself in the barn. Last time I had seen him he was a tired, defeated old man standing in front of his wife's gravestone. But he had his God. He had his unshakeable faith. Or so I thought. So why would he take his own life?" Lysander shut the door firmly and correctly, and walked purposefully toward the fish plant.

I followed Lysander inside and found Bethanie perched on a chair behind the table in the office. Standing no more than five-foot-two and blessed with elfin looks and long blonde hair so straight it looks ironed, Bethanie could easily be mistaken for many of her charges. Until she opens her mouth. For the fates have cursed Bethanie with a husky alto that evokes images of chain-smoked cigarillos and glasses of tequila tossed back by hard-faced women in roadside bars. Bethanie's personality, however, is more in accord with her looks. She is a gentle, caring woman who takes her social service caseworker duties seriously and whose only vice is a passion for philately. Of late the focus of her studies in this regard has gravitated toward the collection of a complete set of butterfly postage stamps issued by tropical nations. Since Bethanie is afraid to fly, I suspect this is her way of taking a vacation to somewhere warm and sunny.

Outside the office the Family members were gathering their packs and drums under the watchful eye of Constable Singh. But the pepper spray canister was gone and none of the hostile tension of the previous day hung in the air. From where he stood at a virtual parade rest with his back to a wall, Singh gave me a friendly grin and nod. I sensed his relief that this duty was soon to be completed and he could return to the normal small-town duties of catching speeders and defusing domestic disputes.

Looking up from some half-completed forms as I entered the office, Bethanie smiled and asked what had brought me there. "Still trying to learn what I can about the woman called Sparrow. It would be good to identify her, at least."

"I asked every one of them about that, too," she said. "I don't think they're lying about not knowing her name. Most of them, anyway." Bethanie glanced out of the office toward where the collection of young men and women had dropped what they were doing to gather around Lysander. Many hugs and lighthearted laughs ensued. Only Moot, I noticed, failed to join the small celebration. She stood beside a green backpack that seemed ridiculously big for her slender frame, chewing with grim thoughtfulness on her lower lip. Meredith Ashley Bainsbridge-Stanton looked utterly lost and alone.

"She knows something, Elias. The one by herself."

And even as Bethanie spoke, Moot looked up and met my eye for a moment, holding the gaze as if passing on some knowledge that only I could comprehend. Then suddenly she bounced across the room on her toes to circle her arms around Lysander's neck and join in the laughter with a gaiety of manner totally at odds with her anguished countenance of only a moment before.

"I think she knows more than just Sparrow's name," Bethanie said in a low voice, "but Meredith is one tough cookie under the cheery little girl veneer."

"She professed to love the girl. Why wouldn't she give us her name if she knew it?"

Bethanie stood up and smoothed imaginary wrinkles out of her short black cotton skirt. Her high heels clicked sharply as she paced back and forth behind the table. "Meredith doesn't trust any of us. She has no reason to, either. I can't go into details, but take it from me that our precious system of childcare failed her completely. Best decision she made was hitting the streets. And that's bloody tragic." Bethanie sat back down and peered at her papers. "I'm putting the two youngest into a foster home in Ucluelet. We've got these kids out of the cities right now, so might as well see if being isolated from the lifestyle can help break the cycle." Her smile was more forlorn than hopeful. "Not much else to try."

"And Moot?"

"Meredith. Her name is Meredith," Bethanie said softly. "I don't like how these kids strip themselves of their identity." She raised a hand as if to ward off my unspoken protest. "I know most of them have been through hell and would like nothing better than to be somebody else. But you can't just recreate yourself and thereby escape your past or your present. They have to learn to embrace their past and process it into something that can form a steady base out of which they can build a better future. That's their only hope." She shrugged. "I'll get off my soapbox now."

"No worries. But what becomes of Meredith?"

"She and the rest of them do what they like. I suspect they'll make their way back to Victoria or go over to Vancouver. Maybe they'll stick together, but after the reality of what's happened here sinks in I imagine the group will fall apart and everyone will drift off in their own direction." Bethanie looked at me levelly. "Don't start thinking there's anything you can do for her, Elias. Just as she won't tell us what she knows, she's not going to trust someone like you to be offering her help."

Father Allan Welch lives in a small whitewashed ranch-
er a few hundred yards from the church where he and
his disparate Tofino flock gather to worship. His Volvo
station wagon filled the muddy driveway, so I dropped
the wheels on the passenger side of the Land Rover into
the ditch to get somewhat off the street and hurried
through the increasingly hard falling rain to bang on his
front door. "My word," Welch said with a gruff laugh,
"the wayfaring stranger cometh calling."

I stepped into his foyer and shook water from my
hat and coat onto the floor and his bedroom slippers.
"Offer me lunch, Allan."

Minutes later I was seated across a much nicked and
scarred pine table in the kitchen biting into a tuna sandwich laced with diced onion and red chili peppers. A
stein of Guinness sat by my elbow. The good Father was
similarly equipped across from me. "Times must be lean
indeed for a remittance man blessed with ill-gotten
wealth to barge into the quarters of a mere servant of
God seeking sustenance."

"I needed the food to stave off collapse from
hunger. The beer to slake my thirst. But I come primarily seeking information."

My host drained off half his stein and licked the
foam from his lips with satisfaction. Father Welch does
not fit the stereotypical image of an Irish Catholic
priest. He keeps his large skull clean-shaven, boasts a
flourishing Mexican bandit-style black moustache, and
his large body has been transformed into hard muscle
through years of dedicated weightlifting. "What is it
you seek, my son?"

"Your personal wisdom, Father. Nothing more," I
replied with equal scorn. Over the years Allan Welch
and I have whiled away many an hour playing chess,
drinking beer and whiskey, and talking of subjects lofty

and banal. Today I said what I sought was knowledge of serious import.

He downed the rest of his beer as I finished explaining and plucked a couple more bottles from the fridge even though my own stein was still half full. "There is precious little I can tell you, Elias. Over the summer I took the time to speak with most of the drifters who showed up on the streets. It is a duty that I rather enjoy. Most are interesting people with a tale or two to tell. Occasionally I can offer some small service or provide modest physical or spiritual counsel. A warm pair of socks here, a blessing there. Nothing that will change their lives, but possibly a help nonetheless."

I popped the cap off the second bottle and slowly drained half the contents down the side of the stein to bring it up to full, carefully angling the stein so as to avoid building too great a head. "And as regards the ones who call themselves the Family?"

Welch swallowed the last of his sandwich, delicately dabbed up the few crumbs on his plate and popped them into his mouth. "During the summer no more contact with them than with any of the others. A couple nights ago, however, I opened the church and let them sleep on the floor there. Dirty night. They were going to catch the bus out in the morning. Given the way the weather's turning I thought this wise. It was sometime the next morning I learned about the murder. Damnable thing."

I asked the father if any of the Family had said or done anything during his time with them that night that might have seemed unusual.

"Not really. They were wet and cold. The older fellow expressed suitable gratitude for my charitable treatment on behalf of them all. About what I would have expected." He closed his eyes for a moment as if bringing the memory of events more clearly into focus.

"There was the little waif with short purple hair gathered up in those tiny knots at the sides of her head that some of the girls fancy these days. She was upset, teary and very red-eyed. Like she had been crying a good long while. Asked her what was wrong, but she just turned away. Went and sat on a pew at the front of the church with her back to us all and started heaving with these great wracking sobs. I was going to go to her, but the older man, Devon, I think it is." I nodded that Devon was correct. "Yes, well, he said, 'It's okay, Father. She's just had a spat with a friend. We'll take care of her.' These groups are pretty close-knit in a sort of anarchistic kind of way. So I didn't want to further interfere.

"And that's about it. When I went around in the morning they were already gone. They had swept the place so that it was spotless. I would have gone and checked on them at the bus stop, but it was my day to take the boat over to Opitsat and I was running late. Sorry, Elias, precious little there. I gather things are not going well in finding the killer if you are having to follow a thread as flimsy as this to try and glean some useful clues."

I confirmed that indeed the chances of snaring a murderer or even the identity of the woman killed appeared ever slighter, declined another beer, and took my leave.

chapter twelve

The rain was sheeting down as I drove toward my cabin. Raindrops big as quarters smacked against the windshield. A driving wind off the ocean buffeted the Land Rover with such force it was hard to steer a straight course. I wondered where the Family had gone and hoped Constable Singh had got permission from Danchuk to allow them to wait out the storm at the fish plant.

It was just as I stopped and signalled for the turn into the lane leading to my cabin that I saw someone who seemed familiar somehow walking up the shoulder of the main road. Cancelling my turn, I drove up alongside the person, whose face was turned away in a probably futile attempt to avoid staring head-on into the slanting rain. Wrapped in a yellow rubber poncho with the hood up, it was impossible to tell the individual's identity. But I realized that what had struck me as familiar was the green backpack strapped onto the person's back. For whatever reason, Moot was out in the storm and alone.

I beeped my horn to get her attention and then gestured toward the passenger door. She hesitated only a moment before running over and pulling the door open. She shoved her backpack in ahead of her and I pushed it over the back of the seat. The pack landed on the rear compartment floor with a thump, as Moot wriggled up onto the passenger seat and banged the door shut. She threw the poncho hood back and shook water out of her purple hair like a puppy. "Sorry, I'm getting water all over your interior."

"It'll dry. What are you doing out here?" Water squelched out of her cracked black leather high-top boots and dribbled across the floorboards.

"You're the guy who was with the cop."

"That's right. I'm the community coroner. It's my job to look into the circumstances of Sparrow's death."

She regarded me with sudden suspicion. "You were at the fish plant. You following me?"

I gestured over my shoulder. "I live back there a way. Saw you on the road just before I turned into the lane to home. Where you headed?"

Moot looked at me hard for a moment, as if weighing the pros and cons of staying in the Land Rover with this strange man who might be following her versus taking her chances out in the storm again. Finally she settled back and shuddered with cold. "I was going back to the beach. The others are leaving on the bus." It sounded like she was trying to stifle a sob, but her sinuses were also running. "I can't leave yet." Moot suddenly folded in on herself, hands covering her face, weeping as if there was no tomorrow. "I can't believe she's dead."

Digging behind me, I found a box of tissue on the jump seat and handed it to her. She tore out a clump of tissue and noisily wiped away at her nose and face for a few minutes, gathering each sodden tissue together with those that preceded it into her lap to form a tidy little bundle.

"It's no day for camping on the beach, Moot."

She shivered hard and released another sob. "There's nowhere else to go."

I thought of taking her back to the cabin, but dismissed that idea as a formula for trouble. A single man, a homeless teenager. Even I had more sense than that. Bethanie could arrange some kind of emergency shelter, but I sensed that Moot would brave the storm rather than entangle herself in the social safety net's dubious services. Because she was clearly still a teenager, Father Welch would surely want to call Bethanie if I appealed to him to put her up in the church.

"There's a friend of mine. Maybe you can stay with her for the night. Want to give that a try?"

Moot shrugged noncommittally, which I took as guarded agreement to consider the idea depending on the person and nature of the shelter. That was good enough. I put the Land Rover into gear and turned toward Vhanna's.

"I was talking to Father Welch, the priest who put you all up two nights ago." Moot's eyes darted warily my direction. "He mentioned that you were really upset. Can you tell me why?"

"I'm tired of answering questions. It doesn't matter."

The rain rattled hard on the Land Rover's aluminum roof. I let the silence hang.

"Look, it was nothing."

"Tell me, Moot."

She grabbed one of the little stubs of hair sticking out from the top of her head and gave it a sharp twist. "Just leave me alone, okay." Another twist of purple hair, so hard she winced. "I wanted to stay with her," she said. It had been late afternoon and the others were

packing up, everyone heading for town to spend the
night because it was too far to walk in from the beach
in the morning and still catch the bus. They had decided to leave during a meeting the day before. It was too
cold and wet to stay longer, Lysander had counselled
them, and everyone had agreed. They were damp or
soaked all the time now. Even on the days when there
was no rain, the sun was too weak to dry their clothes,
sleeping bags, and shelters. The driftwood so sodden it
was almost impossible to get fires going.

They would go back to Victoria. Find someplace to
stay there for the winter. All together, if possible, or
break up into small groups if not. But come back together during the days. Keep the Family together. Make sure
everyone watched out for each other. All for one, one
for all. Their motto.

Moot had been standing next to the tent she shared
with Sparrow, pushing her sleeping bag into the bottom
of her pack, when she noticed that the blonde girl was
doing nothing to get ready. Just sitting on a log in front
of the camp, staring out at the waves rolling in and
occasionally jotting some lines down in her notebook.
Moot knew her friend didn't want to leave. This had
come to be home for her. She thought the place special.
There were the spirits she talked about. Up in the dark
woods that Moot found creepy, and in the creepier dark
house. Moot had sat on the log next to Sparrow,
watched the ocean with her in silence. Behind them the
tents were coming down, packs were being hefted and
tested for how they fit against backs. Stuff was shifted
from one pack to another to balance loads, make them
more endurable. Odds and sods were jettisoned.

One slender arm over Sparrow's broad back, Moot
kissed her cheek. "You're coming, aren't you?" The question whispered in the other girl's ear. Moot was trembling,

holding back the dread growing in the pit of her stomach. The fear of being alone again. Because she would be alone and empty if Sparrow were not at her side. Even with the Family. "Please come." Moot realized that her pleading tone might seem pathetic but didn't care.

Sparrow put her arms around Moot and pulled the girl's head in against her shoulder. Then brushed away Moot's first tears with gentle fingers, stilling the release of the rest. "I have to stay, sweet. But I'll come later. I'll come and find you. I promise."

"Why?" Moot clung to Sparrow. Wanting to press her friend into her heart so that they would always be together.

"I still don't understand it all," Sparrow said. "But I will soon. Even tonight, maybe."

"I'll stay with you then."

Sparrow shook her head. "No, I have to do this alone. And you have to go with Devon and the others."

"Please, don't make me leave you," Moot whispered. She felt her heart breaking. Felt a terrible deep fear that if she left Sparrow here they would never meet up. On the streets a friend could walk around a corner for any number of reasons and disappear forever. You woke up one morning and everyone you knew was gone. As if carried off. Sparrow would never find her. And Moot would never know what happened to her or where she had gone. That was the way it was. The way it always was.

"Please," she said again, even as she resigned herself to losing Sparrow and tried to harden her heart. Sparrow was too strong, too determined. And Moot couldn't defy her, couldn't insist on staying or refuse to leave. She knew that when Sparrow told her to go she would.

And she had. Trudged off along the beach behind the others, tears streaming down her face and choking back her sobs so the rest wouldn't realize how distraught she was and offer comfort. Every few steps Moot cast a look back to the campsite, hoping to see Sparrow hurrying across the sand to catch up. But the girl had remained on the log, her gaze fixed on the ocean. Even when Moot had given a little farewell wave Sparrow had shown no sign of having noticed. Soon Sparrow had been only a small speck far down the beach. Then Moot had turned up the access road and lost sight of her altogether.

"I should have stayed," Moot said sadly. "If I had she'd be alive now." She looked at me miserably. "Wouldn't she?"

Moot finished her story just moments before we approached Vhanna's house, so there was no time for me to ask her then if she knew anything of what Sparrow might have written in the notebook. As we rounded the corner I saw an American model sedan parked next to the wall fronting Vhanna's place. There was a telltale short antenna fitted alongside the trunk lid of the black car. Through the wrought iron bars of the gate, I saw Vhanna standing in the door-way talking to a man wearing a long black raincoat. The light over the door caught him in profile. Instead of stopping, I slowly continued down the lane and fol-lowed it to the end of the beach where it turned to run back inland toward an intersection with Highway 4. As I turned away from the oceanside homes, Moot shifted restlessly and looked over her shoulder at the receding lights.

Ahead the road was dark and no house lights shone on either side. "Hey, where are we going?"

Suddenly, the absurdity of showing up unannounced on Vhanna's doorstep seeking a refuge for Moot struck me. And there was the question of the police officer and his purpose in visiting Vhanna. For I knew the man well.

A few years earlier he had been the Tofino detachment commander and had stood in my living room looking down on Merriam's body. "What happened here, Elias?" Sergeant Ray Bellows had asked in his courteous manner. There had been my over-and-under shotgun on the floor, the massive hole in her chest, me arrived only minutes earlier with Vhanna's scent still on my skin, and Merriam's ever-more tormented mind and soul perhaps finally at rest.

But Bellows was no longer stationed in Tofino. He was a detective in Vancouver serving on the RCMP anti-gang squad with a special interest in the doings of the Asian gangs, such as the Chinese Triads and Snake Heads.

"What the fuck's going on, man?" Moot yelled. "I want out. I want to get out right now."

I slowed, but kept driving. "Sorry, Moot, I just realized my idea wasn't going to work. Look, I'll take you back to town. We'll go to a café and get some dinner. I'll make some calls and find somewhere safe for you to stay, okay?"

Moot had her back pressed against the passenger door so she was turned in her seat facing me. "No. I'm getting out." She grabbed at the door handle, yanking up awkwardly on the unfamiliar mechanism to try to open it. Fearing she would fall out, I braked hard and brought the Land Rover to a halt.

"Please, Moot," I said, "calm down."

The door flew open and she bailed out. "Give me my pack. Just give it to me."

"Look, it's not safe out there. You'll get drenched and freeze or make yourself sick."

Moot bent down and jerked something out of her boot. A knife with a long inch-wide blade that had a serrated edge jutted out of her hand toward me. "I said I want my pack, fucker. I'll cut you if I have to."

Carefully, I raised both hands in front of me in a gesture of surrender. "Okay, Moot. We'll do it your way." I reached behind me very slowly to allow her to follow my moves and see that I wasn't reaching for any weapon, hoisted the pack, and rested it on the passenger's seat before her. She tumbled the pack out onto the ground with her free hand, keeping the knife pointed my way. "Okay, take off." Moot gestured with the knife toward the highway.

Realizing that further argument was futile I shifted into gear and drove off. In the rearview mirror I saw Moot pull up the hood of her poncho, shoulder the pack, and tromp off toward the beach. There was an access there and then a rough trail that led around the headland to the second beach where the Family had set up camp at the far end in front of the Ashton property. I cursed myself for fumbling things so badly that a young girl was now forced out into a cold, bitter rain to spend the night on a grim storm-battered stretch of sand.

chapter thirteen

Rather than cut a U-turn I spent fifteen minutes looping around via the highway in order to avoid the risk of passing Moot and convincing her even more that she was being stalked. The unmarked police car was gone and the light over the front door was out. Seeing Ray Bellows on Vhanna's doorstep, I had realized that the voice on the phone had not been Darren Dagleish's, but that of the police officer.

"It's late and I've work to do yet," Vhanna said when I buzzed her on the intercom fixed to her entrance gate.

"I know, but it's urgent."

A long silence followed before the gate opened. Vhanna stood in the shadows of the living room with her hands thrust into the back pockets of her black denims and her shoulders back in an entirely unwelcoming manner. I could hardly blame her, for she is not fond of being barged in on. Knowing it was foolish to do so, I pulled her into my arms. When her back remained as straight as a gun barrel and her hands stayed in her pockets I reluctantly released her and stepped back. We faced each other like gunfighters.

"What's going on, Vhanna?" I asked after telling her that I had seen Bellows on her step and knew it was he who had phoned the night before.

Her eyes dropped toward the floor and her arms crossed over her chest defensively. At first I thought she was embarrassed, but when Vhanna looked up it was with plain anger in her eyes. "This is urgent? The fact that I've been talking to Ray?"

"So why pretend it was somebody else? A telephone solicitor?"

"It was none of your business. It wasn't then and it isn't now, Elias. You should go," she said flatly.

"A girl's been murdered and Danchuk says no investigators can be spared to help him with the investigation. Yet here's Ray chatting with you and doing nothing to find her killer." Suddenly I recalled Danchuk's words as he had shuffled through the stack of duty sheets and other paperwork. So he had known Bellows was in town, but not why. "Vhanna, are you in trouble?"

She gave a little shake of her head by way of denial, but her eyes glittered as if she held back tears. "I can't tell you about this." Vhanna suddenly brushed her fingers lightly down my cheek and rested her palm on my shoulder. "Just leave it for now, okay? Later, I'll be able to explain. It's nothing to worry about."

This time when I put my arms around her, Vhanna returned my embrace. We stood for a long time with her cheek pressed against my chest, the scent of her hair rising around me as I gently kissed the crown of her head. "I don't like secrets between us," I whispered.

Her hands pressed more tightly into my back. "It has to be this way for now. I made a promise."

Promises are sacred to Vhanna, breaking one the height of dishonour. "You won't understand now, but it is best that you don't know about this." Vhanna stepped back, holding my elbows as she looked up at me. "Go home now, okay?" She smiled sadly. "And don't fret. There is nothing risky about this. And soon you'll understand."

Although I accepted her assurances and allowed myself to be ushered into the rain, in my heart I knew Vhanna lied. There was grave danger in whatever was going on.

Toward midnight the squall ratcheted up into a full-blown storm. Shrieking wind rattled the windows, the big cedars around the cabin swayed and groaned, and there was the crack of heavy branches breaking free of the trunks. Rain slashed against the glass and thrummed on the shake roof. Sitting in the big chair next to a blazing fire with a tumbler of single malt Scotch at hand, I tried not to think of Moot huddled in a rain-drenched shelter on a wind-battered beach. But I found myself repeatedly rereading sentences as I tried to focus instead on the snobbery, incompetence, and occasional heroism of Evelyn Waugh's British *Officers and Gentlemen* in their Pyrrhic defence of Crete from German paratroopers in 1941. Lying on the floor, one paw resting across my foot as if to hold me in my chair, Fergus shifted nervously each time the great wind shuddered the cabin or a branch banged against the roof. At heart he is a fair-weather dog, preferring gentle breezes and sunny skies over dark tempests.

Intermittently I would put the book down on the end table beside the chair and rise to stare out the windows at the fury of the storm and wonder if I should drive to the beach and try to persuade Moot to let me find her safe shelter. But I knew she would not trust me. Father Welch would have accompanied me in such a mission, of course, but I feared we would not even be able to find her. That the girl would hide and we would end up just stumbling around in the dark and get soaking wet to no better purpose than to probably drive her into fleeing whatever protective shelter she might have found. So I did nothing, and upon returning again to my chair, book, and Scotch, Fergus would give a little snuffle to register his displeasure at having been disrupted and again try to pin me in place with paw over foot.

Just as I was considering abandoning the book for bed, a heavy-handed hammering started up on the cabin door. I looked out on an apparition — beach flotsam dressed up to resemble a man. A large head jutted through a hole slashed in a large square of orange nylon tarp that draped all the way down to the man's ankles. Wrapped about his head in such a manner that his face was obscured by it was a tattered black garbage bag. From within the folds of the tarp a big hand suddenly appeared to pull back some of the plastic and I recognized Devon Lysander. Despite the improvised raingear, his scraggly beard and hair were dripping wet. There was a wild gleam in his eyes, and beside me Fergus emitted a low, sustained defensive growl.

"Is Moot here? I've been trying to find her all night."

Telling Fergus that Lysander was a friend, I stepped back and invited the man into the kitchen. He pulled the plastic bag off his head and dropped it gratefully in a corner by the door as I told him that Moot was not with me. "I feared as much," he said. "But the attendant at the gas station on the road saw you stop for a woman in a yellow slicker hours ago."

When I told him that Moot had been headed for the beach in front of the Ashton property, Lysander became deeply upset. "That's where I've come from. There was no sign of her or her stuff there. So I walked back along the highway hoping to find her trying to hitch a ride or something."

I was already grabbing my hat and coat and jamming my feet into gumboots before he finished. Lysander dashed to follow as I grabbed a heavy flashlight off a shelf above the coat rack and ran toward the Land Rover. Seconds later we lumbered toward Highway 4. Even with my foot mashed to the floor, the Land Rover's 2.25-litre engine was churning out only 90 kilometres per hour with no prospect of yielding anything more. "I thought you had gone," I yelled over the racket of the rain and the straining engine.

"The others went. I was going to, but then Moot disappeared. I couldn't leave her here alone. Searched all over town and then went out to the beach."

"You walk it?"

He grunted acknowledgement. Several miles both ways in the middle of a raging storm. Any suspicions I had that Lysander was a murderer washed away in the face of his stoically determined search for Moot. For had he sought the girl with intention to cause harm, I was certain he would not have ventured to my door.

Vast pools of water flooded every dip in the road, and as we ploughed through them spray shot over the front fenders to splatter against the windshield with blinding force. In some of the dips, creeks running in full spate replaced the pools and blindsided the Land Rover with such force of current I could barely keep it from being swept sideways off the road. We passed a car that had slewed into the ditch and, ignoring the attempt of its driver to wave us down, rounded a corner and almost plunged head-on into a semi tractor and trailer rig that had jackknifed across the highway. The driver was throwing out flares that emanated a pale pink glare as I wallowed past on the mud-choked shoulder.

Finally I turned off the highway and followed the narrow road that led to the Ashton property. But the chaos there was even worse than what had reigned on the highway. Tree branches littered the path ahead with more spinning down every moment. Flood water had overwhelmed culverts, and the resulting lakes on the road sloshed against the sill of the doors as the Land Rover slowly chugged through. When we topped a low rise, three fallen trees blocked the road ahead. I zig-zagged around the first one and crunched over the second's thin trunk, but the third was the crown of a mature hemlock snapped off like a twig by the force of the wind and now lying across the width of the road. The way its long branches shot out every which way, the tree presented a natural abatis that barred our path.

"Can you get around it?" Lysander asked. Opening the door, I leaned out and flashed the beam of the flash-light over the roadsides only to discover that the banks were steep and the ditches running like rivers.

"Your father's Land Rover have a winch?"

Lysander laughed. "Yeah, and I learned how to use it." He bailed out and started dragging cable out of the winch, which was mounted to the front bumper. By the time I had thrown in the hubs to engage the four-wheel drive, Lysander had strung the line around a stout fir beside the road and then brought it back to loop around the fallen trunk. I turned the Land Rover so that the hood almost touched the fir tree while Lysander took up the slack on the cable, locked the winch, and then stepped well clear. Dropping the transmission into bull low I reversed slowly. The cable groaned and I could hear the steel slice through the skin of bark on the fir to cut deeply into the meat of the wood beneath. But the tree took the strain, providing an effective fulcrum that enabled the Land Rover to tug the fallen hemlock around and over to the side of the road. In a few minutes we had the winch cable stowed again and were on our way. But I prayed there would be no further delays. I feared that every minute lost fighting our way through to the Ashton property boded ill for Moot's safety.

Except for a few large branches easily driven around or over the road remained passable, and soon the barbed wire fencing and meticulously spaced "No Trespassing" signs glittered in the glow of the headlights. The entrance gate was a high, sturdy thing made out of interlocked vertical and horizontal iron bars topped with a coiled snarl of concertina wire. It was a good quarter-mile from the gate to the house and the security guard's trailer. There was no sign of any kind of intercom system, and I knew trying to make our presence known by honking the Land Rover's sad little horn was unlikely to awaken Jed Simms from what was probably a drunken slumber.

"Forget about the gate," Lysander said. "About two hundred yards on there's a spot where Sparrow cut the wire. Simms may not have fixed it yet."

By the light of the flashlight Lysander and I scrambled down a bank, crossed a ditch, and climbed through a thicket of beaten-down brush to the fenceline. I stared at the stout eight-foot poles and the crisscrossed strands of wicked-looking barbed wire, but could see no opening. "Give me the light," Lysander said. I handed it over and he started creeping along the fence, examining it with careful thoroughness. "Here," he said with a laugh. "Bugger hasn't found it yet." Lysander started untwining strands that had been wound lightly together to give the appearance that the fence was uncut. "He was too quick to fix things, and it was damn hard work cutting new holes, so Sparrow thought of weaving the wire back together. She was a hell of an operator, you know. Knew this place like a native in no time. Watch this." A second later Lysander jumped down into a muddy pool of water, pulled back only the first few lower wires he had undone, and then dragged a roped bundle of brush and branches out from under the fence. Suddenly there was a four-foot-high opening running under the fence through which Lysander ducked. I hurried to follow. "She cut other gaps in the wire just to piss Simms off, but this was the one we normally used."

I started stumbling over rotting trunks of fallen trees and tripping on the tangled undergrowth. "Do you know how to get to the house from here?"

"Sure, old deer trail just over here." Keeping the flashlight beam fixed on the ground before him, Lysander led us along a weaving path that was almost impossible to distinguish even with the light.

Suddenly Lysander halted, and I bumped into his back as he doused the flashlight. When he crouched down, I pushed up beside him and did the same. Before us the shadow of the house was visible. No light shone in the windows of the aluminum travel trailer, but Simms's truck was parked beside it. "The bugger's got a shotgun he would bang off into the air at night if he heard us moving around. Bad time to go up and knock on his door. You're the guy with authority here. How you want to play it?"

I scanned the ground and buildings, looking for some sign of life or a trace of light. But there was only darkness. "Woodshed first, then the house. No sense waking Simms if there's no need."

Lysander offered me the flashlight butt-end first as if it were some kind of weapon. I took the light but left it off. Moving slowly to avoid falling over any of the bits and pieces of old equipment scattered about the yard, I approached the woodshed from the back. Peering around the corner of the shed, I saw that the door was shut. Before I stepped out in front of the door I thumbed the flashlight's switch with the beam directed on the ground. A line of footprints, both coming and going, was visible in the mud. And beside them a shallow gouged line that ran directly to the side of the entrance door as if whoever had left the footprints had dragged something to the shed and pulled it inside.

A frantic, desperate fear drove me to yank the shed door open, directing the flashlight beam into the darkness within. "Oh no," I said softly, as the light shone upon Moot's naked body lying on its side. Barbed wire encircled her, and with sickening horror I realized that one cruel strand coiled her throat and then ran down her back to bind her ankles together, pulling them up so that Moot's body was violently bowed. So long as she kept her body unnaturally curved the wire would be slack enough to allow her to breathe. But as her muscles tired, her legs and throat would move further apart, resulting in her being inescapably and very slowly garrotted. Moot could do nothing to save herself, for her wrists had been bound with more barbed wire to opposing elbows behind her back. What looked like her underwear had been shoved into her mouth as a gag.

Even as I realized what Moot's assailant had done, I was on my knees beside her and clawing at the wire around her ankles. Barbs slashed my palms, fingers, and wrists as I twisted the strands loose. Lysander was down on his knees by her head, trying to find a way to free the strand from where it circled her throat. "Can't get at it," he shouted. "It's inside her flesh."

Suddenly the wire around her ankles started loosening. "It's coming," I yelled. "Hold her." Lysander just got his arms around her chest and lightly pressed her head against his shoulder in time to prevent her body snapping forward as her ankles were freed. Gently we rolled her over on her back.

"McCann," Lysander said with disbelief, "she's got a pulse. Faint, but there." His fingers pressed against her throat just above where the wire had cut a bloody groove.

I splashed and slipped across the muddy ground to the trailer and pounded hard on the door, twisting the handle only to find it locked. "Simms, wake up. Open the door. We need an ambulance." But there was no response, no movement inside. Stepping back, I raised one big boot and smashed it with all my strength at a point just above the doorknob. There was a cracking sound as something structural gave inside the door, but it didn't budge. Hinged to swing outwards rather than inwards like a normal door, I realized. Could kick away at it all day and get nowhere.

I ran to Simms's truck and looked in the open box. There was a long steel tamping rod he probably used for working on fence posts. Snatching it up, I returned to the trailer and swung it like a baseball bat to shatter the window in the door. Several quick swipes swept away enough glass so that I could reach in and release the catch on the lock. I pulled the door open and stepped in, shouting my identity to Simms and hoping not to be hit by a shotgun blast. I fumbled a light switch. A fluorescent overhead light came on and I found myself in the trailer's tiny kitchen. Just ahead of it was a shadowed living room area.

Simms sprawled fully dressed on a couch with a gin bottle embraced in his arms like a lover. Spilled liquor had soaked his shirtfront.

His head moved slightly as I knocked some ketchup-smeared plates to the floor in my haste to get at the phone on the counter. I dialed 911. The dispatcher wanted me to stay by the phone but I refused. Moot clung to life and perhaps I could help. As I left the trailer, Simms released a long rattling snore.

Halfway across the yard I saw something move on the old house's verandah, like a shadow. As I turned to get a better look, the shadow shot to the end facing the beach, vaulted over the railing, and sprinted toward the trees. I could clearly make out the form of a man now, but no sense of size. By the time I rounded the verandah he was plunging into the darkness of the woods. I crashed after him, then stopped, trying to detect any sound that would betray the direction of his flight. But there was only the moaning of the wind in the trees, the patter of rain shaking out of the branches, and the creaking of timber. I realized that tracking anyone in this darkness would be futile. In the distance a siren wailed.

chapter fourteen

I walked out of the hospital at dawn. The storm had subsided to a gentle rain carried on a cool ocean breeze. Out past Wickanninish Island scattered pockets of blue sky opened gaps in the greyish cloud cover. A sporadic carpet of branches torn from the surrounding woods by the storm's earlier fury lay scattered across the parking lot among the many puddles.

Wearing a soft felt fedora to protect his glasses from the raindrops, Doc Tully stood by my shoulder. Wrapped in a businessman's raincoat he looked more a mayor this morning than a doctor, but through the long night he had struggled skillfully to stabilize Moot's condition and won. "I'd move her to Port Alberni or Nanaimo, but the highway's closed just past Ucluelet. Say it's practically a disaster area out there. Trees and power lines down, sections of the road washed out. Be days getting it cleaned up and restoring power to everyone." He rubbed his nose with a weary hand. "Might be for the best really to keep her here for now." Tully's hand rested on my shoulder. "You got to her just in time, I think. Fifteen minutes more and I doubt she could have survived the depth of injury. Fractures of the hyoid bone and thyroid cartilage even still."

"Does she really have a chance, Reginald?"

Tully tightened the belt of his raincoat and looked at me directly through his thick lenses. "I can't offer a prognosis on whether she will or won't come out of the coma. How long was her brain starved of oxygen? How severe was her degree of physical, psychological, even spiritual shock? What combination of all those injuries induced a comatose state? Could be she'll wake up in a few days, or a month, or a year with little or no recollection of the trauma she's suffered."

He sighed by way of stating the other alternative and then his voice grew hard, angry. "That girl was brutally raped and then systematically tortured. The bruises and contusions on the side of her head suggest repeated blows with the intention of keeping her in a semi-conscious state where she would be aware of what was being done to her but incapable of resisting. Remember when I said the other girl's killer was cruel and sadistic? Well, he's more than that, Elias. This is the work of a monster."

Tully was right, but this monster was coldly calculating in his actions. There had been a rape but no semen left behind. So a condom used. Heavy gloves worn again to ensure the barbs produced no cuts that left behind telltale blood that could be sampled. Some pubic hair picked out of Moot's own and a few tiny samples that might yield DNA evidence. But without a suspect to compare this evidence against it was of little or no value. Simms had been incoherent and virtually comatose himself due to a binge drunk that he was still sleeping off in a hospital bed. Lysander had been with the girl trying to save her life when the shadowy figure escaped into the woods. He remained by her side now, a ragged and beaten-looking man blaming himself for the death of one girl and the violence done to another. "All for one and one for all," he had said softly as we looked down on the bandaged form lying so still and silent in the bed. "All an illusion."

"If you hadn't come to my house, Mr. Lysander, we wouldn't have gone looking for her. You can't blame yourself." But I knew that he did, for he had been to the beach and had not thought to go searching for Moot in the Ashton house. It had never occurred to him that Moot, so afraid of the woods and that dark house, would venture there alone in the middle of a black storm-torn night. The fact that she had done so remained an anomaly to me. Had she gone looking for something or someone? Or just to be close to the memory of Sparrow? But, of course, she couldn't tell us now and might never be able to do so.

Danchuk, Monaghan, and I had found Moot's pack and sodden sleeping bag in the upstairs bedroom that was decorated with Winnie the Pooh characters. There had been a shredded T-shirt and wool sweater and torn pants. Blood on the sleeping bag and floor in patterns that indicated heavy flows from both a scalp wound and sexual assault injuries. A heavy coil of wire and a pair of wire cutters had lain next to the sleeping bag, and a spray of smaller blood stains suggested that Moot's attacker had coiled her in the wire there in the room and then carried her out to the woodshed. In that grim little space he had fashioned the barbed wire noose around her throat and linked it to her ankles so that the girl was forced to bring about her own death. And know it. Yes, a monster, and one still free to kill.

"I need to go home and get some sleep," Tully said. "Far too old for these kinds of all-night emergencies. At least I'll have less call on my time a week from now."

"You still have a chance," I reassured him with more conviction than I felt.

He laughed mirthlessly. "No. Unless there's some miracle, Monica Klassen's going to easily carry the vote. Hell, signs on every corner and a mailing every second day to every household in town. Dagleish is pulling out all the stops to buy the vote and it's working. I can't begin to match him dollar for dollar."

"I don't understand what's in it for him. It wasn't like you opposed many of his development schemes."

Tully smiled sadly at me. "You don't understand people like Darren Dagleish, Elias. It's about power and control. He owns Monica. She's sold herself to him in order to win the mayoralty, her first big leg up the political ladder. Two years from now she'll be the provincial Liberal candidate. Or three years hence the federal Conservative candidate. Chase the big bucks right out of here. But Tofino will never be the same. Dagleish will see to that."

Suddenly Tully looked very tired and worn. "I've been a Chamber of Commerce booster like nobody else in this town for decades. Through all the little booms and the inevitable busts that followed. This place has grown, and mostly that's been for the better. But that's because the pace has been slow, measured, and the result of people working together to make things happen. People who consider Tofino home. Dagleish is just like the construction developer who gets an exemption on a lot so he can put in a bigger house on the pretext that he's building it for himself and not to sell. Seen that one enough times. Neighbours complain, but a gullible town council gives him the exemptions. Unreasonable not to. Six months later there's a 'For Sale' sign out front and he's back before council applying to do the same thing on another street. And we never learn. I give the man five years. After that he'll sell everything and move on. And we'll be left picking through the wreckage."

Steering a course for home, I was confronted with evidence that Monica Klassen's campaign was steamrollering toward inevitable victory. Every significant patch of weed-choked lawn in Tofino's downtown seemed to sport two or three small signs or a miniature billboard proclaiming its pro-Monica stance. Sporadically a small placard supporting Tully peeked out shyly from behind the Klassen chorus line. A billboard at either end of the Crab Pot Café's parking lot and a dozen smaller signs forming a picket line along the verge of the road made James Scarborough's business look like an isolated bunker of Tullyism in the land of Monica.

Especially as just a few hundred yards past his grey, cedar-sided café a forest of Klassen billboards crawled up the slope of a long drive that led to a black iron-slab gate fitted into a high granite wall. Beyond the gate, a great swath of perfectly manicured lawn wound like a golf fairway past wide beds of meticulous flowerbeds where each specimen, whether pansy or tulip, was regimented into precise and ordered rows. Braced on the crest of the hill was a vast mansion constructed out of cedar logs as big and round as the columns of some ancient Grecian temple. From this lofty perch, Darren Dagleish was able to survey his domain while remaining aloof from its lesser inhabitants.

As the Land Rover rattled down the muddy lane toward my cabin, a cold, defeated gloom washed over me. It seemed a battle had been lost without the losing side having ever learned that it was at war.

The sight of a grime-spattered white RCMP cruiser parked beside the cabin only deepened my grim state of mind. But my spirits did lift slightly when, instead of Sergeant Danchuk, Constable Anne Monaghan climbed out of the driver's side. Her hair, normally pinned up into a bun covered by her cap, straggled toward her shoulders, and her face was pale. Exhaustion rimmed Monaghan's eyes in red. As I approached she shook one of her hand-rolled cigarettes out of a crumpled pack, lit it with her lighter, and inhaled deeply. A slow stream of smoke drifted out of her nostrils. "I had Simms figured for it, you know," she said. "And the Sarge was ready to slam the door on Lysander. Now we've nothing. Just another girl hurt."

"Come in and I'll fix some coffee and breakfast. We can both use it."

After another hard drag on the cigarette, Monaghan shook her head. "No, there's a report to write. Might be something I'll see then that I'm missing now." She pulled thoughtfully on a strand of blonde hair grazing across her cheek. "There's got to be something. Some clue. Nobody lives in a town this small and does this kind of thing without leaving a trace."

She looked at me uncertainly. "Look, Elias, that's not why I'm here." Monaghan sucked the cigarette down to where it flared close to her fingers and then stubbed it out on her heel, put the butt in a little plastic bag and shoved it into her pocket. "There's something going on that I think you should know about."

"Is it about Ray Bellows?" I told Monaghan about seeing him outside Vhanna's house and her claim that it was nothing of importance and nothing she could tell me about.

"He's got a surveillance team with him, all kitted out with an electronic-monitoring van and every other

Mission Impossible high-tech gizmo you could ask for. But nobody from the team or Ray is talking to us. They're holed up in a hotel outside Ucluelet and driving from there to here each day to do their work. Keeping it tight, so nobody knows they're around. We've got a girl dead and another in a coma and no detective squad help. Yet the place is crawling with assets."

"How do you think Vhanna fits into this?"

Monaghan had no idea. "Could be nothing. She knows Ray, right?"

I agreed she did.

"Doesn't seem like he'd be making social calls right now, though, does it?" Monaghan asked and looked off through the trees toward the water, as if considering whether to voice a thought. When she turned back her hands were braced on the web belt holding her gun, radio, and other gear. "About your girl, Elias. Would there be anything that someone could use to make her do something for them?"

I felt a rising anxiety. "What are you saying?" The hardness in my voice surprised me and caused Monaghan to noticeably pale.

She chewed her lip for a moment, obviously uncertain whether to continue. "These surveillance squads. Sometimes they recruit others, you know, civilians, to work for them. If they have some leverage to use to make it worth the person's while."

Images of Cyprus slipped through my mind. A Turkish teenager trying to smuggle banned black-market goods across the Green Line and being snagged at our checkpoint. Released and promised easier passage in the future in exchange for that most valuable commodity of all — intelligence on the strength of the military forces arrayed among the houses facing our line.

Vhanna was scrupulously cautious about legal matters. She would never fudge even the slightest expense on her tax returns. And her records were meticulously kept, whereas mine ended up a hodgepodge stuffed into an old coffee tin that caused our accountant's eyebrows to rise in alarm whenever I was directed by Vhanna to put in an attendance with my yearly records. What Anne suggested was impossible, and I brusquely told her that while walking her back to the cruiser.

At the car, she leaned back against the doorframe. "I told Danchuk we should take a hard look at Dagleish and that lady security director. Find out if there's anything we should know about there. He vetoed even a routine record check. Said it's coincidence this stuff happened on Dagleish's land. That with the election just five days away we have to be careful to not start any rumours. I was trained to check everything, consider anything possible. I don't remember being told to stay away from people bankrolling an election candidate or people who were powerful."

"You think Dagleish could be a murderer?" I asked skeptically.

Her eyes flattened, hardening like dimes. "I don't think anything, Elias. I just think it's my job to ask hard questions when people are getting murdered."

"I'm sorry, Anne. I spoke out of turn."

She rested a hand on my arm. "This thing's got me right on edge." Monaghan slipped behind the wheel of the cruiser, shut the door after her, and then buzzed the window down. "We should both get some sleep. You look like hell, Elias. How's Tully?"

I told her he was worn out and expecting to be voted out as mayor come Saturday. "He'll have your vote, right?" she said.

"Bet on it. And you?"

Monaghan smiled again in a way that seemed sadly resigned to something. "There's no future in this town for me, Elias. I'm looking for a transfer to another posting. Maybe somewhere out on the Prairies. Back closer to home. Sometimes I just think it would be nice to go home, back to where things are familiar and known."

She fired up the engine and slipped the transmission into reverse. "Sure about the breakfast?" I asked. Monaghan just waved and turned the car toward the road.

As I watched the cruiser disappear up the lane, I thought about her desire to go home. Remembered the farm that stood on the fertile shelf of the Comox Valley cradled between the towering Strathcona Mountains and the waters of Georgia Strait. My memories of the farmhouse were mostly melancholic — images of Angus growing ever older and frailer even as he clung to the memory of those brief, happy days he had shared with Lila before my birth and her unexplained disappearance.

And what of Vhanna and a house in a ruined city to which she could return but never feel at home. Wandering through those great empty rooms, where the ghosts of an entire family that had been brutally destroyed still lurked, and she unable to put them to rest within her heart and soul. Moot had fled a Point Grey mansion for the mean streets for reasons she had little revealed. And Sparrow? Who knew where her home had been? Unlike for Monaghan, home held no renewed sense of security or belonging for some of us.

chapter fifteen

After a shave and shower I went into the kitchen, dressed still in my old housecoat. I fried some bacon and eggs and served them up with brown toast, hot coffee, and a tall glass of freshly squeezed orange juice. Fergus had made known his dim view of my wild departure the night before in the company of a stranger known through a series of long, intent stares and grumpy snuffles. Even a proffered crispy slice of bacon failed to elicit the usual buoyant response. Although he did swallow the morsel in a brusquely workmanlike fashion. After following suit with my own breakfast, I pulled on some clean jeans and a denim shirt, gathered my coat and hat, and accompanied Fergus on a long stroll through the woods that greatly improved his mood.

When I topped this off by asking whether he wanted to go for a ride in the Land Rover all seemed forgiven. The clouds that had lingered after the storm's passage earlier in the morning had dissipated and it was a balmy, sunny fall day by the time I rolled into the Jansons' place.

Lars and Frieda's home is unfinished inside and out. The exterior cedar siding is unpainted, the windows unframed, and the shake roof overgrown with moss. Jutting out into Duffin Passage a narrow wharf lists to the right on posts suffering various degrees of decay. From Lars and Frieda's perspective the house is entirely fine. There is no need for the siding to be painted or stained because the natural fading is preferable. A roof should be replaced or repaired only when it leaks, and this one has yet to do so despite the thick moss coating. The plank flooring that runs throughout the house also needs no glossy coat because it has slowly assumed a darkened patina that is its own natural finish. The same holds true for the cedar board tongue-and-groove walls. As large cedars surround the house and render it invisible from the road, curtains are completely unnecessary and would only gather dust and cobwebs. Not that spiders are swept away. They are useful household animals, keeping various insect pests under control.

The furniture is simple and plain. In the big, airy kitchen are tables and chairs that Lars fashioned by hand. These are rough-hewn from fir and protected by nothing more than a light coat of linseed oil so that over the years the entire set has faded to a soft grey that blends with the darkening floor and walls. The cabinets are also handmade and brightened with a simple whitewash. The living room is lined with bookcases crammed to overflowing with books, magazines, photo albums, and innumerable binders containing various documents that Lars and Frieda have decided to hoard. Lars made the wood frames and arms of the living room couches and chairs, and Frieda sewed the back and seat cushions. Colourful rag rugs are scattered throughout the house wherever softness under feet is desirable.

Their home reflects simple tastes and needs. To make ends meet, Lars runs a water taxi. For a few bucks, Lars runs people and supplies in his fourteen-foot steel-hulled, open-bodied boat to the outer islands. It's not a service he actively advertises, and all his customers find him through the recommendation of others. He is discriminating about the fares he charges, basing these largely on the degree of bother he suspects the work will entail. Not the difficulty of the work itself, though. No, Lars thinks nothing of steering into high seas and sleet to fetch people from a rocky shoreline or to drop off needed food and fuel. He is a master with his boat and a strong worker. But he expects resilience and toughness from his clientele as well. Don't complain if you have to jump into waist-deep seas and wade to shore because the tide is low and too many rocks are exposed for a safe landing closer in. And if there are supplies to shift, you had best carry your own weight of it rather than acting like some pasha that Lars is to serve. Suspected pasha tendencies result in a quote likely to be triple or quadruple the normal fare. Pull your own weight, with a light heart, and a few dollars for the gas accompanied by a thank you for the company might settle the bill.

I found Lars on his front porch looking the sailor in rubber boots and a wool sweater, with a pipe stuck in the corner of his mouth. "There you are," he said, although I had not phoned to say I was coming and so could not be expected. "I was thinking of you just this minute."

Fergus jumped up to put his front paws on Lars's oil-grimed yellow rubber pants, and the man bent over to nuzzle the dog's nose with his own. "Good fellow," he murmured to Fergus, who licked his cheek in response. After a moment, Lars gently pushed Fergus down to the deck and turned his attention back to me. "Yes, I was thinking of how there's this girl here who needs visiting by you, you see." He grinned to take the sting out of the rebuke I knew was deserved, for it had been several weeks since last I called. "But I was thinking, too, of how I have a run of groceries and propane to make up to Old Man Schmidt at Whitepine Cove and how there's also the crabs to bring in and not enough hours in the day for a man to do both. So I thought of how a man who should visit this girl should also take the rowboat and check the pots. Taking this girl, who loves being out there on the chuck, along with him, of course."

Although I had intended only a quick visit, I could see this was a proposition that was not open for debate. "Okay, I'll take Hui crabbing. But first I need to talk with you for a moment."

Lars nodded and led me down to the wharf. "What is it?" he asked as he started pulling the nylon cover off the white-painted wooden rowboat.

"Have you spoken with Vhanna lately?"

"Just late yesterday afternoon." He grinned. "My daughter is better about visiting my new daughter than are some others."

"You know I'm not good with children," I protested.

Lars snorted, which caused Fergus to echo him accordingly. "I know there's a child who needs some sense of family. That's what I know." He pulled his pipe out and started stuffing the bowl full of tobacco. "You're a good man, Elias, but you have problems with responsibility."

This was not the conversation I sought, so I turned it back to Vhanna by asking him if she had told him anything that caused him concern. He looked at me carefully after that as if weighing the gravity of this question and not liking the feel of it. "Did she happen to mention having met with or talked with Ray Bellows?"

"The policeman? No. Is there something I should know, Elias?"

I told him about Bellows and the surveillance team. Of seeing the detective speaking with Vhanna and of her assurances there was nothing to worry about even as she insisted she couldn't tell me why Bellows had called on her. Lars puffed on his pipe thoughtfully as I spoke, then tapped the ash out of the bowl onto the sand at his feet and started fetching oars and life jackets from the wharf's storage locker while thinking my words over. "If Vhanna is keeping this close to her chest then nobody is going to get anything about it. You know that."

Yes, I knew. But there had been the scant hope that she might confide in Lars, whom she trusted more than anyone. "Let's go up to the house and fetch Hui," Lars said. "She'll be happy to see you and Fergus. Teacher's Day at the school, whatever that is, so she was just moping around the kitchen because I said it was too far for her to come with me on the delivery run. Don't trust this weather. One storm track after another and damned close together this year."

We rode the last surge of a flooding tide toward the narrow gap between Beck and Arnet islands on a glassy sea. Lars had constructed the eleven-and-a-half-foot hull with hand-laid fibreglass and four-ply mat laminates. Years of use had bleached the oil-free teak floorboards, gunwales, and frame-end spacers a buttery colour. The long sweep of the Sitka spruce oars made rowing a delight, and the boat's lightweight construction prevented any noticeable drag. The day had turned unseasonably warm, and I had stripped off my coat and rolled up my shirtsleeves.

Although usually a nervous sailor, I am inexplicably comfortable being at sea in a rowboat. Normally even more anxious mucking about in boats, Fergus sat calmly with hip pressed against Hui on the bench in the squared stern. He alternated his attention between watching my handling of the oars with a critical eye and inspecting the passing beds of kelp or cormorants and gulls flying overhead.

Hui's thin arm was wrapped around Fergus, and every once in a while she nuzzled against him, receiving in turn a delicate lick of affection. Although Fergus had always been, and remains, wary of children, the moment Hui appeared in his life he accorded her the protective guardianship that before had been extended only to Vhanna and myself. For her part, Hui appears to have no more greatly loved friend than this aged and dour spaniel.

Since her rescue and eventual welcome into the lives of the Jansons, Hui has evolved from a gaunt and fearful refugee into a vibrant, self-confident Canadian girl. She is still lean as a rake, but it's a natural condition now, rather than one born of the malnutrition she and the other migrants had suffered as a result of mistreatment at the hands of the Snake Heads during the long trip in the ship's cargo hold from China to our coast. Today she wore a dark navy kangaroo sweater and faded denims stuffed into bright red knee-high rubber boots. Her hair was tied back in a ponytail and a shockingly pink ball cap shaded her eyes from the sun's glare.

The sky directly over Tofino and the passage was clear, and the sunlight sparked dazzling diamonds on the water's surface. A heavy grey coat of mist draping over the summit of Meares Island unspooled in thin threads that trailed down through the old growth stands to pool along the shoreline. I kept a wary eye on the western horizon for signs of building clouds or rising winds while listening to Hui chatter on about school, her recent enthusiasm for needlepoint and for charcoal sketching, and playing the sprite's role in a favourite computer game. There was no hint of reproach for the infrequency of my visits.

Hui seems to live entirely in the moment, and perhaps that is best. She has never mentioned and won't discuss her life in China before washing up on our shores. So we have no information about her parents or extended family, whether they were dead or alive or if it was they who sold her to the Snake Heads. Nor will she talk about the experiences on board the ship. It is all a closed book. Attempts to open it just make her anxious, troubled, and tormented by nightmares, and after a time Lars and Frieda decided it should not be further pursued. It is not surprising to me that she is close to Vhanna; they can spend hours in silence walking a beach or a muddy forest trail.

Occasionally I pointed Hui toward a flock of buffleheads diving near a rocky shoreline or the sudden surfacing of a seal's head close to the boat. She absorbed these sights with a child's disregard for things that are routine, reminding me of how, with each passing year, it is those things that are most familiar and common that most hold my attention. The way seeing a bufflehead raise its body until it is nearly standing upon the surface, nervously fluttering its wings, before arcing into a deep plunging dive after prey seems more of interest to me than the sights found walking an ancient, foreign city.

"Steer a little to the left," Hui instructed.

Glancing over my shoulder, I spotted the red float that marked the presence of a crab pot. As we drifted alongside I shipped the oars and Hui bent over to snag the float and pull it in. The Jansons' name and phone number was painted on it in heavy black lettering. I stood in the centre of the boat, braced my feet carefully to get balanced, and started hauling. For a moment I sensed the pot's resistance to lift free of the muddy sea bottom, but then it gave and started rising sluggishly toward the surface as I reeled in the line. When it broke the surface, Hui grabbed the wire pot on one side and held it secure until I dropped the line and came to her aid. We hoisted the pot aboard, tripped the latch to open the door, and dumped the half-dozen or more crabs trapped inside into the water-filled bucket in front of the stern seat.

While I recharged the bait box with a couple of chicken backs, Hui culled the undersized crabs — grabbing them from behind to avoid being snipped by their defensively waving claws and dumping them overboard. Where their size was in question, she quickly measured them with a set of calipers and jettisoned the runts with a careless overboard toss. Closing up the pot lid, I sent it diving back to the sea bottom. It was a good catch of four Dungeness adults that we added to the two keepers that we had earlier harvested from another pot. Fergus watched the entire process from the safety of his seat, eyes wide with apprehension as Hui handled each crab.

Putting the oars out, I turned the boat homeward as Hui and I congratulated each other on a job well done. There would be a good feed in the Janson house tonight. Back ashore, we pulled the boat up and then carefully dried the teak with soft cloths before covering the boat with the tarp. I carried the bucket of crabs in one hand and held Hui's small hand in the other as we walked up to the house. Fergus padded along at her side, little stub of a tail twitching in his best imitation of a puppy-like wag.

Frieda came out on the porch to welcome us and inspect the catch. She is a tall, strong-boned woman with thick, curly steel grey hair worn loose. "You'll stay for lunch, Elias." I noted that this was not a question. "There's chowder and some fresh-baked buns and a bit of beef stew from last night for Fergus."

"Oh, yeah," Hui said enthusiastically. Tightening her grip on my hand, she pulled me toward the porch steps with Fergus happily leading the parade.

chapter sixteen

After an hour of being fed and fussed over, Fergus and I left the Jansons feeling full and drowsy. The previous night was catching up to me, so I drove homeward with a mind to taking a short, restorative nap. An idea that would certainly appeal to Fergus, who had curled up on the passenger seat and shut his eyes the moment he climbed into the Land Rover. Driving past the Crab Pot Café, I noticed a hydro company van with red plastic marker cones set fore and aft parked next to a utility control box at the point where Darren Dagleish's driveway met the highway. The utility box doors were open, but nobody was working on the array of exposed wires. Passing the vehicle, I noted the plume of exhaust from the tailpipe and the absence of any workmen in the front seat.

Stepping hard on the brake I turned into Dagleish's driveway. The tires squealed a sharp complaint, and Fergus fixed me with a disturbed glare. I ignored both, but noted with interest that a shadowy figure could suddenly be seen peering out of the passenger window at the front of the van. Somebody was home and marking my movements. As quickly as it had appeared, the figure pulled back. The van's side door was tightly shut, its smoked glass window impenetrable to the eye.

When I pulled up in front of the heavy closed gates a man dressed identically to Simms emerged from a small guard booth, stepped through a little portal in the gate, and approached the Land Rover. His eyes were hidden behind aviator sunglasses and his expression was grave. A peaked, snap-brimmed cap was tugged down low on his forehead, and he carried a clipboard in one hand and had a radio fitted to his web belt with a handset on a shoulder strap.

Sliding the side window open, I offered him a good day that went unreturned. Before coming around to the side of the Land Rover he studiously noted my licence plate number on his clipboard and then compared it against a list on a sheet of paper clipped below the top page. "I'm sorry, sir, but you don't seem to be expected," he said with the officiously polite tone favoured by police and soldiers manning checkpoints.

I invoked my position as community coroner and said that I had some questions for Mr. Dagleish if he was home. "I'm sorry, Mr. Dagleish is not to be disturbed. You will have to phone the office for an appointment and come back at a more appropriate time." The trace of a smirk touched the corners of the guard's mouth as he said this. It was clear he enjoyed possessing the power to deny access to supplicants such as myself.

"Sorry," I said. "I'm investigating the circumstances of a murder on one of Mr. Dagleish's properties and must insist on seeing him now. I'm sure he would want to be cooperative."

A scowl replaced the smirk, but he grudgingly agreed to call the house to see if Dagleish would assent to an interview. Pulling the handset free, the guard turned his back on me and walked over to stand by the gate as he talked softly into the microphone. I could hear a crackling reply but was unable to make out any words, for he had deliberately thumbed down the volume on the radio at his belt before calling in. After a few back and forth comments he acknowledged some instruction and then walked back to the side of the Land Rover. "Mr. Dagleish will see you, sir. If you'll pass through the gate and wait just on the other side someone will be with you in a moment to take you up."

Fergus by this time was sitting up with his back braced against the passenger seat, watching the proceedings in the manner of a general slightly irked at being forced to go through official procedures to which someone of his stature should not be submitted. When the gates slid open, I rolled through and paused just inside the grounds as instructed. We sat with the engine idling roughly for several minutes until another security guard descended from the mansion aboard a white-roofed golf cart, cut a tight U-turn, and signalled with his arm for us to follow him up the hill. He directed me to a small parking lot in which several humble cars and trucks probably owned by servants and other staff stood and then pointed out a rank of stalls marked with "Visitor Only" signs. Presumably more favoured guests parked somewhere closer to the main part of the house and my being brought here was to reinforce the fact that my presence was an intrusion. I slotted the Land Rover in the appropriately marked space, told Fergus that I would be back soon, and walked over to where the guard was dismounting from the golf cart.

"If you will follow me, sir, I will take you to Mr. Dagleish," the guard said in precisely the same formal, falsely polite tone the guard at the gate had used. Eyes hidden behind sunglasses identical to the other guard's, this one could be the other man's clone.

When I beckoned grandly with one arm and said, "Lead on," he fixed me with an expressionless stare, then turned briskly on one heel and led the way up a set of stone stairs toward the main level of Dagleish's home.

A massive verandah made of copper-tinged slates laid with such perfection of craftsmanship that each stone stood precisely level with the rest ran the length of the building's front. The main-floor wall was glass from ground to ceiling, and a shake roof covered the verandah. Sumptuous rattan chairs and couches were elegantly spaced along the verandah's length, giving the impression that one walked through the outdoor lounge of some posh resort. In fact the entire structure emanated a resort-like atmosphere. It was as if Dagleish had built the mansion with the thought that one day he might transform it into another source of income. I recalled Tully's assertion that the millionaire developer's commitment to Tofino was fleeting at best and thought the nature of this house supported this premise.

"How many rooms does this place have?" I asked the guard as we trekked toward the far end of the verandah.

"Couldn't say, sir. I've never been inside. Inside security is provided by a different detail. I'm with the grounds security squad."

At the end of the verandah a path made of the same slate curved past flowerbeds to the entrance of a large, two-storey building also constructed of huge cedar logs and tall sheets of glass. Set in an orderly row behind this and the main building was a group of log cottages that presumably served as guest accommodation and would work well as rental units when the place was turned into a resort. We entered a foyer floored with marble tiles, and I followed the guard to a desk remarkably akin to that found in any good hotel lobby. A young woman dressed in a black blazer and white blouse with neatly trimmed, shoulder-length blonde hair nodded to the guard and smiled at me in a manner that exuded the friendly charm of a hotel desk clerk or restaurant hostess.

"When you're ready, sir, I'll escort you back to the main gate," the guard said and marched toward the exit.

"Mr. McCann, I'll take you through to the mineral pool. Mr. Dagleish is expecting you there." She stepped around the counter, insisted on taking my hat and coat and hanging them in a closet, and then led me through a glass door. We walked down a long hall that passed several rooms fitted with various tables and types of beds that looked like they would be used for giving manicures and massages.

"I feel like I'm in a resort," I said.

Over her shoulder, the woman offered her professional smile. "Mr. Dagleish sometimes has as many as a hundred guests here at a time. Usually people with whom he is doing business. We offer as comfortable and relaxing a setting as possible for them."

We came to a point where there were two entrance-ways on either side of the hall, one marked for men and one for women. Another closed door faced us. The woman extracted a key from a pocket and started unlocking this door. "Normally visitors enter through the change rooms, but I'll take you in this way."

Following her through the door, I walked into the middle of what at first appeared to be a limestone grotto over which a high roof had been thrown and a glass wall erected to screen it from the weather. The other walls seemed to be limestone cliff faces surrounding a grey stone shelf. Low arbutus trees grew where the cliffs failed to meet the ceiling, and delicate maidenhair ferns dangled fronds out of cracks and notches on the walls themselves. In the centre of the chamber a pale blue mineral pool shimmered and was fed by several water-falls rushing down the cliff faces or falling from over-hanging ledges. Beyond the pool, the glass windows that reached from pool level to the ceiling provided a breath-taking view of the inlets fronting Tofino, Meares Island, and the dark lush forests and mountains of Clayoquot Sound beyond.

Thrusting out of the centre of the pool was a large, flat white stone upon which a woman in a skimpy white bikini lolled like a siren beckoning ships to sail toward her and disaster. It was a second before I realized that the woman was none other than mayoralty candidate Monica Klassen. Equally surprising was the discovery that the red-headed woman in a jade green bikini who was vigorously applying some kind of oil to the back of a man lying face down on a fully reclined rattan chaise longue was Roberta Walker. Darren Dagleish rested one cheek on folded arms and gazed out at the lovely image of the woman on the rock. Lolling in a cushioned deck chair with a frosted glass containing a lime-coloured drink was Jack Ashton, who was wearing red trunks that wrapped tightly around his groin. The heavy mus-cles of his chest and shoulders glistened with sweat, and I suddenly became aware of how the humid warmth in the room was causing pearls of moisture to bead against my skin and soak through my long-sleeved denim shirt. Ashton fixed me with that blank, slightly puzzled expression of his, opened and closed one hand in a man-ner that caused his bicep to rise and harden alarmingly, and then delicately sucked some of the liquid in his glass past his fleshy lips with a tiny straw.

"Sir," the young woman said to the reclining Darren Dagleish, "I've brought Mr. McCann as directed." Dagleish grunted by way of an answer, and the woman beat a hasty retreat, her heels clicking sharply against the stone floor as she departed. Walker continued massaging Dagleish's back, working along the base of his spine just above the top of his black boxer-style bathing trunks. Her hands and fingers were slender and strong-looking. She kept her head down, attention concentrated on rubbing the oil into Dagleish's well-bronzed flesh. Her lean and muscular body was equally tanned.

So, too, for that matter was the flesh of both Ashton and Klassen. But it was the uniform bronze acquired by lying cocooned in a coffin-like tanning bed rather than walking naked under a hard, hot sun across a stone-strewn desert. Their tans were as artificial as the cliffs, which I could now see were nothing more than concrete upon which a coarse granular coating had been applied to simulate the surface of limestone. The grooves and crannies in the concrete had been artfully added to create a convincing illusion of a typical limestone formation, as false as the silk arbutus shrubs and ferns.

Dagleish slipped one arm from under his head, thrust it out, and pointed with his index finger to a spot between where he lay and the edge of the mineral pool. "Come over here, Mr. McCann, so we can see each other."

Stepping into the designated spot, I looked down on Dagleish. "Among Roberta's many talents is her training as a massage therapist, something I often like to take advantage of, so you'll understand if I don't rise to shake your hand." He offered a glimpse of his perfect white teeth and then gestured with a hand toward Ashton. "Jack, rustle up a drink for Mr. McCann, will you?"

Before Ashton could respond, I announced my intention to be only a few minutes and not in need of a drink or anything else. There were, I noted, five glasses on the small table beside Ashton's chair. Each filled with what I assumed to be gin and lime juice on shaved ice. Having arranged this audience, I was no longer certain what purpose I pursued and wondered about the wisdom of having come at all.

"I just have a few questions, sir, that might help with my investigation regarding the woman who was killed on the Ashton property." Out of the corner of my eye, I saw Jack Ashton's grip on the glass tighten, and Roberta Walker paused in mid-stroke to glare up at me with her catlike green eyes.

"I don't see that there's anything —," she started, but Dagleish cut her off.

"It's okay, Roberta." Then to me he said, "Anything we can do to help regarding that terrible tragedy we will certainly do. But you appreciate that there is probably nothing we can add that you haven't already learned from Roberta and Mr. Simms, the guard stationed there."

"Did you ever have the opportunity to speak to her or any of the people she was camping out with?"

Ashton gave a little snort of amusement and Dagleish smiled good-humouredly. "I generally make it a point to avoid interactions with people like that. I prefer the company of people with ambition and ability, people who realize their potential and make a success of it. Roberta had some dealings with them, as you know. How about you, Jack? You ever talk to them?"

"No. But we should have kicked their asses out of there right at the get-go. Best thing to do with people like that is to keep them moving along. This plight of the homeless shit is just that, a bunch of bullshit." Ashton squeezed his hand into a fist again and grunted with satisfaction at the effect the action had at hardening the bicep.

"You will have to forgive, Jack, Mr. McCann. He is prone to being rather blunt."

"I call a spade a spade," Ashton growled. He locked his eyes with mine in the manner of a man in a bar challenging someone to a fight.

"Is there anything else, Mr. McCann?" Dagleish asked politely. But it was also clear from his tone that I was close to being dismissed.

In truth there was nothing else. For what would this powerful man have to do with a pack of homeless people other than that they had opted to camp on the beach fronting one of his many development properties? And their choice of that location over others apparently nothing more than coincidence. But there was one thing that I found puzzling, and I said as much now.

He gave a little sigh to indicate that he was granting me an undeserved indulgence and swivelled to sit up on the bench with his feet flat on the floor. Roberta Walker braced her hands on her bare hips and looked at me like she was considering whether to call some of her guards to toss me over the perimeter fence. "Why didn't you get a court injunction to clear them off the Ashton beachfront? After all, some of them, particularly the woman who was murdered, were trespassing at will and causing minor property damage."

Dagleish slipped off the bench and walked over to stand next to me, looking out across the pool to the view beyond. When I turned to look the same way, Monica Klassen was dog paddling away from the rock toward a point where a small waterfall gushed off a shelf about three feet above the pool's surface. "We are in the process of developing fourteen separate properties here in Tofino and another four around Ucluelet, Mr. McCann." He swept an arm out to indicate the small clutch of buildings visible from this vantage as if they symbolized his holdings. "This is the biggest, most expensive development program that the Pacific Rim has ever seen, and it may well never experience anything like this again. I spend long, hard, and, might I say, rewarding days engaged in the planning of all of this. Mr. Ashton is here right now working with me on the development plan for his family's property, and Roberta spends many hours ensuring that this significant investment is physically protected. Next Saturday, when Monica is elected mayor, as she should be elected mayor, she will provide the political leadership and vision necessary at the local level to ensure that progress toward completion of these projects proceeds without undue bureaucratic delays."

He lightly gripped my arm above the elbow and started walking with me toward the other end of the pool and the door that waited there. It was obvious my audience with Darren Dagleish was being personally brought to conclusion. "Those people were a nuisance, Mr. McCann, but they were nothing more than that, and sometimes the best way to deal with a nuisance is to just leave it to work itself out. That's what we did. And, despite the tragedies that then befell those two young women, the nuisance did work itself out, did it not? They all finally packed up and moved on, just as we knew they would." Dagleish turned the doorknob and opened the door for me. "When you get to the front desk just ask Eleanor to call security and have them come over to escort you out." The developer extended a hand to me and offered a brisk, businesslike shake.

Just as I started through the door a woman emerged from the adjacent change room. I turned to find myself face to face with Vhanna. She wore a one-piece black bathing suit that looked made for serious racing, but fit like a second skin. Her eyes widened like a startled deer's might. "Elias?" she said, as if unable to bring me into focus. When Dagleish settled a hand casually on her bare shoulder, Vhanna noticeably winced. But she also gave him a weak smile and made no effort to shake free of his light grasp. Over their shoulders I noticed Walker standing by the pool with her hands on her hips and shoulders squared. Her eyes were locked onto Vhanna and her face was drawn tight with what seemed a simmering rage.

"Mr. McCann," Dagleish said, "was just here to ask a few official questions and he's on his way out now." The expression he turned my way seemed almost pitying, but it also contained a glint of barely concealed triumph. A point he reinforced by slipping his arm around Vhanna's shoulder so that she was pulled more tightly against his hip.

Without so much as a word, I stepped through the door and pulled it shut behind me. Then I walked quickly down the hall.

Telling Eleanor I would wait for the security detail outside, I stepped out in front of the building and sucked in the fresh air. My coat was over one arm, hat in my hand, but still I sweated and told myself that it was the result of the humid heat of the spa and had nothing at all to do with how Vhanna had let Dagleish touch her. A door banged and Jack Ashton suddenly stood by my side. He had pulled on grey jogging pants and a matching sweatshirt. "Man like Dagleish gets what he wants every time, McCann," he said with a taunting grin. "That's just something to get used to."

"Is there a point to that comment, Jack? Or are you just passing wind."

Ashton guffawed and swore. "You're a funny man, McCann. And, yeah, there's a point all right. Point is that if Dagleish wants your lady, he goddamned well will have her and she'll be grateful for it."

"Vhanna's her own woman. But I'm not worried," I said weakly, while suppressing the urge to plant a fist in the middle of his thick lips.

Ashton slapped a powerful hand on my shoulder and gave it a gentle, consoling little pat. "Good to hear. A man should always trust his lady. Even when she wants something bad from someone who can make anything happen or just as easily make sure it doesn't."

I shrugged his hand away. "That how it is with you, Jack? Dagleish had the money and ability to bail you out of your software company debts? All you had to do was sell up your family home, right?"

"That's right," Ashton said. "But I'm a full partner. Man like Dagleish isn't going to stick around a place like this longer than it takes to get the developments up and running. So he needs someone to manage operations here. And that someone is going to be me. Darren awards ability when he sees it."

I tried to imagine Dagleish entrusting the care and management of his Tofino empire to someone as crass as Ashton. It didn't seem likely. But what did I really know of either man? What did I know of anyone?

A security guard was walking briskly toward us from the main house, obviously anxious to intercept and see me off. I started down the path toward him, equally eager to be done with this place. But after a few steps, I turned back to Ashton. "One more question, if I may."

"Go ahead, coroner."

"You ever see your sister since your mother's death?"

Ashton darted his tongue across his fleshy lips and the skin under his eyes tightened. "No, McCann, I haven't seen her in years."

"But you looked for her, right? To let her know her mother was dead? And to settle the estate?"

Ashton took a step toward me as if I had touched some hot spot, but then pulled himself up abruptly. "It's none of your fucking business, man, but, yeah, a private detective tried to find her. But she was just gone. Could be anywhere or nowhere. Didn't matter, really. She wasn't in the will. My mother left everything to me. She knew that was the thing to do."

The guard was standing behind me, keeping a respectful but watchful distance. "You show Mr. McCann out, Bill. He's kind of outstayed his welcome." As the guard and I started down the path, however, Ashton called out. "Hey, McCann, Dagleish tires of things and people fairly quickly when they aren't of use anymore. Sometimes he hands off the better pickings to others who have served him well. Think I'd like that, if you know what I mean." Turning quickly on one heel, Ashton strode back into the spa building. But his laughter continued to echo off the outside walls.

chapter seventeen

Had the entrance gate not already been open to hasten my departure, I would have probably tried smashing the Land Rover right through. There was nothing I wanted more than to be gone from Dagleish's estate and to escape the searing image of the man's hands touching Vhanna's skin. Most of all, I wanted her in the seat beside me being carried to safety. But she had sought no aid from me, and perhaps the flickering expression that I had taken as repulsion at his touching her had been something else entirely.

When I roared out onto the main road with barely a glance to check for oncoming traffic, the tightness and speed of the turn almost threw Fergus out of the passenger seat. He shot a dirty look my way and snorted a loud protest. Normally I would have offered an immediate apology, but such was my mood that I met his scowl with one of my own. And in doing so noticed the hydro company van still idling next to the power pole just back of Dagleish's property.

Without a moment's further thought, I stomped on the brakes, slammed the transmission into reverse, and careened backwards to bring the Land Rover to an abrupt halt just inches from the van's front bumper. "Back in a minute," I growled at Fergus. Through the van's windshield several shadowy images were visible moving furtively about in the vehicle's bowels. I hammered the side door with a fist. "Get out here, Ray."

There came a series of scuttling sounds, and what seemed to be three voices conducted a frantic and whispered exchange. I slammed the van's metal hide again. "I'm not going anywhere, Ray. So get out here and talk."

More whispers were followed a moment later by the van door opening a few inches on its slide. Dressed in a pair of coveralls with a BC Hydro logo over his heart, Ray Bellows peeked out. He was down on one knee, so had to look up to meet my eye. "Elias, what the hell are you playing at?" he hissed.

Jamming my boot into the crack to prevent his closing the door, I thrust an index finger almost into his left eye. "You're the one who's playing games, Ray. I want to know what's going on."

"It's none of your business," Bellows snapped. "Now get out of here before you compromise us."

Tempted to grab the detective by his collar and physically drag him from the van, I instead took a deep, calming breath. I needed answers, not confrontation. "Think you need a coffee, Ray. So let's both get in the Land Rover and go for a little drive."

"Damn it, Elias." Then Bellows glanced back over his shoulder. "Stay with it. I'll be back in just a few minutes." He wrenched the door back on its slider, stepped out, and then quietly slid it closed. Before the door shut,

I had a brief glimpse of two men in coveralls that matched Bellows's sitting cross-legged on the floor. They wore headphones and faced what looked like a type of radio transmitter, alongside which several tape recorders stood. "Drive down to the government dock," he said. "We'll talk there."

Bellows said not a word during the short run, but the detective had won a friend in Fergus by gently scratching his ears for the entire ride. When we climbed out of the Land Rover, Fergus jumped out too and I let him accompany us onto the long, wooden dock. With the fishing industry in ruins no more than six working boats were tied into slips, and four of these sported "For Sale" signs. A couple men in green rubber bib overalls and heavy rubber boots scraped rust off the hull of one seiner that wasn't for sale.

We walked in silence to the end of the dock and stood facing Meares Island. A cool north wind lifted the salt smell off the chuck. Gulls swirled overhead, eyeing the boats for some sign of easy fish pickings. Just beyond the dock, a cormorant perched on a post heavily spattered with guano and raised its wings toward the watery sunlight to dry them. Stretching out on his stomach, Fergus rested his chin on his paws and gazed tranquilly at the scenery as the wind riffled his fur.

"Vhanna's spying on Dagleish for you, isn't she?"

"It's really none of your concern, Elias."

"You know better than that."

"Okay," he said as if a decision had been made. "You've been into Dagleish's mansion now. You've seen the guards. They're just the visible part of a security system that's multi-layered and virtually impenetrable. Motion sensors all along the walls, jamming devices to prevent long-range eavesdropping, regular sweeps for planted bugs. We needed someone to get inside and close to Dagleish with a few toys that could be put in place that wouldn't be detected. Vhanna's doing that. And she's doing it well." He smiled. "Of course, she's always a perfectionist. Which made her perfect for this."

"Why the interest in Dagleish? He's just a rich developer." But even as I said this I knew it was likely untrue, that the developer persona was probably a lie. A fact that Bellows immediately confirmed with a story of an Asian gang based in Vancouver that dealt in drugs, prostitution, car thefts, protection, and a host of other criminal rackets that raked in a fortune every month in profits. Money that needed to be cleaned before the kingpins could use it. Originally there had been a land developer with a resort deal on a ski mountain in the B.C. interior that had faltered and left him several million in debt. The developer should have gone bankrupt, but suddenly there was money from silent investors and the deal was back on track and successfully completed. When the developer sold the resort some months after it opened he walked away a rich man. Darren Dagleish had been on a roll ever since, moving from one development to another. There was always money to buy property, always money to carry out the construction, and never, ever a need to go to a bank for a conventional mortgage or loan.

"Dagleish is a launderer," Bellows said. "He cleans the gang's money. They run it back through Dagleish Property Development Corporation. Being partners and corporate directors, they just pull what they need out as profit. Pay the taxes and everything. The surprising thing is how much profit there always is to report, considering that many of his developments are never completed." Bellows recited a list of two ski resorts standing empty on barren mountaintops where lifts no longer ran, a subdivision in Prince George that four years later remained only a series of paved streets running past lots bulldozed clear but never sold, a waterfront hotel in Kelowna where nothing but concrete footings had been poured. "Some projects get completed and are then shortly sold, but most remain under development interminably. Yet Dagleish has a magic touch. There's always a profit and generous payouts to the directors."

"Why don't you just audit the company?"

Bellows grimaced. "We did. Couldn't prove anything. No law says Dagleish has to complete developments or make them profitable, and somehow the financial records always seemed in order. Every tally tallied. The forensic auditors said they couldn't find a bloody thing."

"So you put Vhanna up to helping you eavesdrop on Dagleish, to plant bugs in there for you."

Bellows nodded. "More than that, Elias. More than that."

"Like what?" I demanded.

"That, my friend, is none of your business."

His expression said I would get nothing more. "Why Vhanna?"

He shrugged. "We needed someone Dagleish would have no reason to be suspicious of and who would also interest him. Someone already a part of the business community who could give him some instant legitimacy by association. He looks for that. We also needed someone smart enough and brave enough."

"Vhanna wouldn't have done this if you didn't have some leverage on her."

The detective started walking back down the dock toward land. "It's time to get back, Elias. I've already told you more than I should have."

I hurried after, grabbed him by the shoulder and spun him around. Bellows put his hand on my chest and shoved me back a step, an action that elicited a warning growl from Fergus, who had padded up behind us. "We don't threaten people. Vhanna and I had a discussion. She understood the problem we faced, understood that she was uniquely positioned to help us. That's all there is. Understand."

Bellows lied, I was certain. "If anything happens to her."

He put a reassuring hand on my arm that I shook off. "I won't let anything happen to her, Elias. She's on the side of the good guys here."

On the way back Bellows had me stop the Land Rover well down the road from the van. "You drive right on by without slowing or anything. We don't want anyone up at Dagleish's place to see you stopping by the van a second time."

Bellows stepped out on the grassy verge alongside the road and then leaned back into the Land Rover. "You getting anywhere with the inquiry into the girl's death?"

I shook my head. "I think Danchuk should take a hard look at Dagleish, but he refuses."

"He's probably right, Elias. Dagleish is a criminal, but he's no psychopathic murderer. People like Dagleish kill only when they're seriously threatened. And that girl couldn't have posed any threat." When Bellows put out his hand to shake mine, I kept my grip on the steering wheel and just looked at him. After a moment he let the hand drop. "So be it," he said in a resigned voice and gently shut the door.

Instead of going home, I drove out to the Ashton property again — snaking slowly around fallen trees that had yet to be cleared by highway crews and wallowing through pools of water that still flooded the road in places. For Fergus it had been a long afternoon in the car, and he registered his displeasure that we were not returning to hearth and home with a series of sniffs and shakes of his head. Despite my anxiety over Vhanna, I couldn't shake the uneasy feeling that there was something I was overlooking at the site of the attacks on the two girls. That we had all been looking at things from the wrong perspective and so had missed an important piece of the puzzle.

To my surprise the heavy gate stood wide open, so I drove down the muddy path and pulled up next to the house. A gaunt Jeb Simms was busy hooking his trailer to a hitch mounted on the back of his pickup truck. He wore an old pair of green canvas workpants stuffed into scuffed cowboy boots and a pale pink shirt with pearl buttons.

"You're like a bad coin, Mr. McCann," he grunted as Fergus and I walked over to where he was cranking the trailer hitch down to fit onto the truck's ball mount. I commented that he seemed to be leaving. "Yeah, I wake up in the hospital and there's Ms. Walker and Jack Ashton staring down at me. Cold as a fish, she says, 'You have until sundown to get yourself off the Ashton property.' Just tosses an envelope on my chest. Outstanding pay and two weeks severance in cash. That's that. Good riddance, I say. Nothing good here. Those poor girls. How could I have known? What was I supposed to do? Hell, think that sergeant in town still thinks I hurt them." He looked balefully at the still healing cuts on his hands. "Going home. Up to Williams Lake. Used to have a little ranch up there. Some good grazing acres. Economy up there's in the toilet, they say. Should be able to lease something cheap. Park the trailer on it and run a little livestock."

"Is there anything you didn't tell me before, Jeb? Something that would help?"

He pulled a chewing tobacco tin out of his hip pocket, cut off a little chunk with the blade of a short jackknife, and slipped the plug into the corner of his mouth. "Don't reckon so, sir." Simms turned his head and spit a stream of brown juice on the ground. His hands were shaking and he was deathly pale still from the effects of all the booze from the night before. "I better be going. Ms. Walker, she was serious about my being gone by sundown. And I don't want to see any of them ever again."

"Why's that?"

He fumbled the plugs that linked the trailer lights and brakes to those of the truck together and avoided my eye.

"I asked you a question, Mr. Simms."

"Yeah, you did alright," he muttered. He straightened up. The whites of his eyes were webbed with blood. "Ms. Walker likes her power. One of the guards up at Mr. Dagleish's estate was caught poking his nose in places he shouldn't have been. Something to do with those computers that Mr. Ashton's always fussing with. They locked him up in a shed down on one of the other properties and then Ms. Walker, she gathered up a bunch of us in her truck and we went down there. It was a property near the dock. Dragged him out and stripped off the Dagleish uniform. We put him on his knees in nothing but his jockeys and tied his ankles to his wrists. Then she took that damned riding whip of hers and struck him so hard it split his face open. When she finished getting her message across we cut the ropes and dumped him down the bank face first into the sea mud there. He was mewling and barely conscious, but we left him like that. I don't think she cared if he dragged himself up out of there before the tide came in and drowned him or not."

Simms spat another stream of tobacco. His hands were shaking harder. "So, I'm on my way, sir. You asked me though if there was anything I didn't tell you before. Might be something, might be nothing. That first girl, the one called Sparrow." He pointed towards the house. "Used to hear her sometimes up in that bedroom singing to herself." He paused, considering. "She was often singing to herself, that and that damned drumming they all did. So I didn't think much of it. But, sometimes the song would carry, you know, like it was picked up on a breeze. That girl was up there in the room singing the same song over and over. God, it was strange. Most of the time her voice sounded like a handful of gravel being swirled around in a pan of water, but there she'd be those nights singing soft and sweet like a little girl. Barely could make out the words, just the tune."

Then in a wavering falsetto, Simms sang ever so quietly and with a slightly wistful expression, "Hush, little darling don't you cry, mommy's going to sing you a lullaby." He shook his head and laughed weakly. "She knew the whole thing, sang it all right through. Growing quieter and quieter with each line, like she was becoming sadder by the second. Never heard her cry, though. Normally, she was up there in the house, I'd go in and shoo her out. Never could bring myself to do it those nights. Just let her be."

He looked at his watch and out west to check on the sun's descent. "Best be going, sir. You know, Mr. McCann, I liked that girl."

He looked hard at the woodshed and his eyes misted over. "Can't believe she was murdered that way just there and I didn't hear. Keep telling myself she was dead before I got back from Port Alberni. That must be it. Only answer. You think so?"

Although I knew better, I nodded. "Travel safe, Mr. Simms. I hope you find that land you want."

He spat out the rest of the tobacco and smiled ruefully. "Hope you find who did it. And if you need someone to kill the bastard, just let me know." Simms climbed into his truck, fired it up, gave the engine a few hard revs, and then rolled his rig down the lane and off on a long run to the high Chilcotin grassland ranges. I watched the truck disappear, put a reluctant Fergus into the Land Rover, and walked into the Ashton house.

The dark stains of Moot's blood still blackened the bedroom floor and spattered up one wall to freckle Pooh's face and arms. I stared at the stains and thought of a girl lying in a hospital bed from which she might never rise and a murderer who still roamed free. Ray Bellows had said Dagleish would turn to violence only if threatened. Had Sparrow and then Moot somehow become threats? It seemed unlikely. At any time he could have secured a court injunction and had Roberta Walker and her men remove the Family or even got Danchuk and his Mounties to do the dirty work for them. I found myself softly humming Sparrow's lullaby and trying to make some sense of what would have drawn her here to this room to sing it on those sad nights. From what I had learned of Sparrow, it was hard to imagine the scene Simms had described.

Hearing a vehicle pulling into the yard, I looked out the window to see Roberta Walker climbing out of her Toyota Forerunner. She wore the same Gore-Tex jacket and matching rain pants as when we first met. The riding quirt that had seemed a mere eccentricity and now seemed laden with threat was tucked under her arm. The woman strode purposefully toward the house.

I was on the way downstairs when Walker appeared at the bottom and glared up at me with her hands on hips. Her expression was the same as that I had seen on her face when she had fixed her eyes upon Vhanna in Dagleish's spa. "This is private property, Mr. McCann. You would do well to remember that." Her voice was flat and cold. Hair pulled back into a tight ponytail, she looked like a grouchy schoolmarm.

"And this is still a crime scene, Ms. Walker, even if the yellow tape has been removed. And I'm carrying out a legal coroner's inquiry. Perhaps I should have notified you that I was going to revisit the scene, but Mr. Simms was still here and it wasn't at first clear that he had been released from his position with Dagleish Development Corporation. Difficult business, that."

Walker tapped the quirt against the side of her leg and regarded me coldly. "Simms was a drunk and an incompetent. I gave him a chance and he failed me. I don't suffer fools gladly. And neither does Mr. Dagleish."

I descended the stairs slowly and we faced each other, as close as lovers. I noticed her lips glistened with some kind of gloss and a web of lines around her eyes had been smoothed out with makeup. From a distance Roberta Walker looked healthy and beautiful, but up close the mask started to crack so that she looked hard.

"Simms told me you had one of your other employees who failed you stripped to his underwear, bound his arms to his legs, and then you whipped him until his face was a bloody mess. That you had him dumped unconscious below the tide line where he could have drowned. What kind of person does something like that, Ms. Walker?"

The quirt was rapping sharply against her pant leg now and she stepped even closer to me so that her breasts brushed against the front of my coat. I held my ground, sensing she wanted to force my retreat. Sensing, too, that she wanted nothing more than to lash my face the way she had that other man. "You should know better than to believe the stories of drunks. They exaggerate. They lie. It's just how they are. Darren is a powerful man and it's my job to protect him and his possessions. It's a job I do well. And nobody, man or woman, is going to catch me out. That's the kind of person I am, Mr. McCann. The kind of woman I am."

She brought the quirt up and pressed its braided length against my chest lightly. "You bear that in mind. And you might like to remind someone else of that, too."

I closed my hand on hers and lowered the quirt to her side as I stepped past her like a partner in a waltz. "You have in mind anyone in particular, Ms. Walker?"

She tugged her hand free and fixed me with a hard stare. "You're a smart man. You'll figure it out, I'm sure. And if you don't, well, some people just refuse to do what's best for themselves and there's nothing that can be done for them."

Tapping the index and middle finger of my right hand against my hat brim, I offered Roberta Walker a good day and walked out of the barren and lifeless Ashton house into the day's fading light. My heart was beating and sweat dampened my palms. I thought of Sparrow and Moot. Of the injuries the barbed wire had carved into their flesh. As I climbed into the Land Rover and gave Fergus a reassuring pat in response to his concerned expression, I whispered Vhanna's name.

chapter eighteen

Neither Moot nor Devon Lysander showed signs of having moved since I had left them at dawn. The straight-backed chair upon which Lysander sat looked rickety to the point of collapsing under the man's solid weight. Moot's hand was small and ghostly white in his weathered palm. "I told the nurse that her eyelid fluttered once, but she didn't believe me. They keep suggesting I leave. Not just go somewhere and get some rest. The hint is strong that it would be preferred if I were to permanently disappear." He scratched his long beard. "What do you think, Mr. McCann?"

"I think you should stay. You're the only person Moot knows. It'd be good if you were here when she wakes up."

"Nobody seems to think that's likely." His face looked like it was about to break. "I swear her eyelid moved. Just a little. A little flutter." Lysander's voice choked off.

I put a hand on his shoulder. "They're right about the fact you should get some rest, Devon. Can I call you that?"

He tugged his beard and nodded. "You and me been through a bit together now. No need to stand on formality, Elias. Good name, that. You know I never quite took to this street name stuff. Although I understand the need to get past the burden a name can be sometimes. But Meredith is a good name, don't you think?"

I agreed it was. "Your Sergeant Danchuk, he called the Bainsbridge-Stantons. He told that social service woman that the father said there was no point in their coming if Meredith was unconscious. She wouldn't know they were there anyway. Can you countenance that? I've asked permission to put my bedroll on the floor here, but the nurse said she'd have to check with her supervisor and doubted I'd be allowed to do that." He looked entirely miserable, defeated. "But what if she wakes up and there's nobody here she can trust? It ain't right. Her eyelid fluttered, Elias, it really did."

It was not my habit to give money to the homeless, for it seemed a poor band-aid to apply to such a grave situation. Now, however, I pulled out my wallet and lay a twenty-dollar bill on the bed by Lysander's hand. "Take that and get yourself a dinner. Might be enough there for breakfast tomorrow, too. And if you need a place to sleep, you know where I live."

Lysander looked at the money thoughtfully before reaching over with the hand that didn't hold Moot's and tucking it in his pant's pocket. "Your house is a bit far from here, Elias, but I'm grateful for the offer." He grinned. "But I seem a man suddenly blessed, for your friend Father Welch offered me a bunk as well. And it's not far away."

I paused on the way out the door and looked back at Lysander. His attention was fixed on Moot's pale face. "I believe her eyelid moved," I told him. "Stick by her. She'll know you're there."

"One more stop, old boy," I advised Fergus as we drove past the Co-op Grocery toward the waterfront. Fergus yawned wearily but offered no serious complaint. I parked in front of Reginald Tully's two-bedroom condominium, which stands behind one of Tofino's wharves and overlooks the single remaining semi-viable fish packing plant. These days it's closed as often as not, generally opening only when there is hake to pack for export to Asian markets or farmed Atlantic salmon brought in from one of the big pen operations that clutter many of the sheltered inlets of Clayoquot Sound.

Right now the plant was dormant, doors firmly shut and nothing but stacks of wooden pallets crowding the concrete landing and loading docks. I looked up to the third-floor unit on the corner of the condominium complex that faced out to the channels running between the native community of Opitsat on the western end of Meares Island and Tofino. There were lights on, so I knew the good doctor and mayoralty candidate was home.

"You've come at the right moment, Elias," he said, ushering me through the door and insisting on taking my hat and coat despite my protestation that I could not stay long. He was dressed in his version of casual clothing — grey dress slacks, a starched white shirt, grey silk tie, and a wine-coloured wool vest that was pilled with age. Suffering perpetually cold feet, Tully's favoured household footwear is a pair of knee-high wool-lined buckskin slippers with fluffy rabbit fur tassels and intricate beadwork that the Haida in the Queen Charlottes had once given him during a potlatch. It greatly amused Tully that the moccasins had been made by the Peigan people living on the eastern edge of the Crowsnest Pass in Alberta. He was convinced that one of the Haida elders had received them as a gift and, deciding he must give something to this mayor from somewhere as inconsequential to him as Tofino, passed them on to Tully.

I watched the gathering clouds out over the ocean while Tully poured us each a stiff helping of Jamieson's Irish. "There's another storm coming. Be raining by midnight, I bet," Tully said as he handed me a brimming glass. It wasn't a bet I was going to take. A great ring of cirrus clouds surrounded the rising full moon and a southeasterly was blowing whitecaps hard enough against the wharf fronting the condominium that spray was sloshing up onto the wooden decking.

Tully settled in one of his Nordic black leather recliner chairs and gestured for me to take the matching one set across from him. It was possible for us to sit facing each other this way and both still enjoy the view. So we sat like a couple old duffers on a rest home porch and enjoyed our drinks in companionable silence for a few minutes while the sky darkened and the clouds lumbered toward us. "Rumour is that the advance polls were a landslide for Monica," Tully said after a time. He pushed his glasses up on his forehead and rubbed his eyes tiredly. "Be lucky if this election isn't a terrible embarrassment. Should probably have stepped down and faded gracefully away."

"Then she would have won by acclamation," I said. "Nobody else around who could have run against her and had even a fighting chance."

Tully gave a dismissive little chuckle. "You know, it's not so much losing to Monica Klassen that gets in my craw. It's the fact that she's fronting for Darren

Dagleish. That man's nothing but trouble for this community and nobody seems to see that."

I thought for a moment of telling Tully about my discussion with Ray Bellows, of the suspicions the Mountie had and the evidence he was trying to gather. But that would only heighten Tully's anxiety about the consequences of losing to Klassen and there was nothing he could do at this late stage to turn the political tide in his favour. So instead I got to the point of my visit.

"Reginald, I'm still trying to get somewhere on this inquiry into the girl's death."

Tully's expression grew grave and he took a long, measured drink. "The other girl. I checked on her earlier. The older fellow, he said her eyelid fluttered for a moment." He shrugged. "Might have. But it doesn't necessarily mean anything. Sometimes coma victims speak out loud or move around without being any closer to regaining consciousness. The terrible truth is that we can treat the physical wounds she's suffered, but right now the psychological trauma is beyond our reach. She has to fight that alone, poor soul."

"You mentioned that Moot had been sexually assaulted."

Tully nodded.

"Do you know if the assailant was necessarily a man?"

The doctor's eyes widened with surprise, but then grew thoughtful. Again, he pushed his glasses up to rub his eyes. "Never did get any sleep today. Couldn't keep myself from thinking about these girls and what was done to them." He drained his glass and then looked with disappointment at my still half full one. "To answer your question, no, it's entirely possible that the assailant could have been a woman. There was forced entry, but there was no trace of semen. One would assume the use of a condom, but it could also have been that someone, man or woman, used an instrument of some kind to achieve penetration."

Tully got up, fetched the whiskey bottle from the kitchen, and put it on the stand beside his chair. Then he methodically poured himself a stiff second and offered the bottle toward me. With a shake of my head, I declined. "Still a bit of work to do tonight."

He shrugged. "I was going to suggest we get some oysters and mussels at Scarborough's, but this business isn't good for the appetite. Think I'll settle for a sandwich and call it an early night." He sipped his drink. "If it was a woman, she had to be strong. Same goes for any man. You don't garrotte people with barbed wire easily. Not when the victims are young and capable of struggling. And it's hard to imagine that even with gloves they wouldn't have suffered some kind of cut with all those barbs flying around. That kind of wire is hard to handle, I would think."

I allowed that from my time in the army I knew this to be true. The thought deflated me. Earlier today Roberta Walker had stood before me in a bikini that left very little not on show. Her strength had been apparent, but so had been the fact that her body was unmarred by even the slightest scratch. The same for Dagleish, I realized, and Jack Ashton. But there was the incident Simms had told me of the security guard and how the others had obediently helped Walker brutally punish the man and then leave him in a situation that could have resulted in his death. Was that how it had been with Sparrow and Moot? Did Walker have some of her hired goons in their narrow Ray Ban sunglasses do the dirty work? Did she watch? I thought it likely that she would enjoy that.

"You have a suspect in mind, I think."

Tully's words brought me back into his home.

"Maybe, but no proof. Suspicions really, nothing more. Nothing that I could take to Danchuk."

"Can't say as Danchuk is showing much initiative on this," Tully offered.

Finishing my drink, I gathered my coat and hat from the hall closet while Tully hovered by the door with his glass in one hand. "One of the great shames in this," he allowed, "is that we don't know the first girl's identity. I hate the thought that she'll end up buried in some modern version of a paupers' field."

That image haunted me as I walked out into the night to where the Land Rover was parked. And even as I summoned up visions of a meanly cut headstone in the local cemetery that was absent a name and engraved merely with the date of her tragic death, another image filtered into my mind. A possibility, perhaps, but one that would have to hold until morning to pursue.

chapter nineteen

It had been a long, wearying day with too many unfolding events and revelations to encourage restful sleep. Consequently at midnight I still brooded before the fire with a glass of Bowmore single malt Scotch by my side, listening to the storm that had blown in earlier slap rain against the windows and the shakes overhead with a heavy hand. Fergus had long abandoned me, ascending on heavy paws to the loft shortly after the first rain started falling. A few creaks and groans from his wicker basket as he circled about to find an ideal position and then only silence. One of us had gained a contented rest.

I was just debating the disparate merits of pouring another shot of Scotch or trudging upstairs to bed when a car pulled into the yard and the engine stopped. Through the kitchen door window I recognized the lines of Vhanna's dark green Miata sports car standing under the tree next to the Land Rover. As she stepped onto the covered porch, I switched on the outside light and opened the door. Rain streamed out of her long hair and beaded her face like tears. Caught in the light's glow behind her, rain swirled in sheets, and the racket kicked up by its pounding on the roof made speech impossible. Instinctively I reached out and gently brushed the water from her cheeks and forehead. Then I bent over and kissed her, my arms enfolding her dripping body against my chest.

We stayed like that for a long time. Her black wool sweater was sodden. My shirt grew damper by the second and the growing puddle on the porch planks crept out to encircle my leather slippers. Finally I released her, stepped aside, and waved her into the shelter of my home. I passed her a clean towel hung by the door.

"You're soaked through," I said.

Vhanna was bent over at the waist, working the towel through her hair, which hung down almost to the toes of her black leather boots. "I was walking on the beach. The tide was out so I walked out on the tombolo to the islet. That's when it started to rain. Didn't have my rain jacket." She straightened up and her eyes were full of shadows. "I didn't know whether to come or not. So I stayed there a long time thinking and letting the rain wash over me." Her voice dropped to a reflective whisper, as if she spoke only to herself. "Wash me clean." She shivered hard, but whether from the cold or some inner chill I didn't know. "But you deserve an explanation for today. I —"

My fingers touched her lips, silencing her. "I spoke to Bellows. He told me a little of it." I took her hand in mine. "You need to get into something dry."

From behind me there came the sound of a dog padding quickly across a tile floor, and then Fergus brushed past my leg to stand looking up at Vhanna, his stub tail wagging. When she bent to scratch behind his ears, Fergus released a mighty yawn and then shook his head.

"A hot shower would be good," Vhanna said.

While she went into the bathroom to strip off and get into the shower, I fetched the white terry-cloth hotel robe she had stored in the bedroom closet some time ago and a pair of white rabbit-fur-lined moccasin slippers. After exchanging my damp shirt for a dry one, I carried the robe and slippers downstairs. The bathroom door was ajar, so I stepped in and hung the robe on a door hook. Through the shower curtain, I could see the outline of Vhanna's slender form. Her hands were scrubbing her scalp and her back was arched sensuously. I let my gaze linger on the swell of her small breasts and follow the line of her flat stomach down to her thighs.

Her sweater, black jeans, socks, and underwear were all dumped in an untidy, sodden pile on the floor. I gathered them up and took them into the living room. Back in the kitchen, I put the kettle on to boil and then went into the living room and stoked the fire by putting two thinly split pieces of cedar on the still glowing coals and setting a couple more piecces on top of them. Once the cedar started to crackle, I added a wedge of hemlock. I stood watching the flames roll up around the hemlock, but saw instead the image of Vhanna walking on the sandy spit of the tombolo to the edge of the islet off Chesterman Beach and then standing there facing the blackness of the sea as the rain lashed down at her from a sky black as charcoal. When the fire was well underway, I fetched a couple kitchen chairs and draped Vhanna's clothes over them so that they were close to the fire. Within seconds a light hazy steam started rising off them. There was a slight chance that all but the sweater might dry by morning. But it didn't really matter. Along with the robe, Vhanna has some clothes also in my closet.

By the time she emerged from the bathroom wrapped in the heavy robe I had a pot of cinnamon and apple spice tea brewing, with slices of carrot loaf baked a few days before spread out on a dish. Fergus took up his position on the rug before the fire and Vhanna sank gratefully into my overstuffed chair next to him while I poured tea and set things out on the stand beside her. I took a place on the hearth next to the chair, and we sipped our tea and ate slices of the loaf in silence. There was no hurry. Vhanna was here. She was safe. And if she was here, it was to be with me. I told myself that was all that mattered. We could just linger here in a cocoon of comfort.

"What did Ray tell you?" she asked finally, and the grim reality that existed beyond the walls of the cabin mocked my earlier thoughts that it could be escaped or ignored for more than the briefest of moments. I told her what I knew of the policeman's suspicions about Dagleish and how he had said that Vhanna had volunteered to help.

She smiled wanly. "I wouldn't call it volunteering, exactly. Better to say that I was persuaded it would be in my best interests and those also of a young girl we both are acquainted with if I did what Ray needed."

"Hui?"

Vhanna nodded. "Her refugee status is tenuous at best. Ray hinted that if I cooperated with him he could facilitate her being granted landed immigrant status."

"And if you didn't?"

"It might go the other way."

"Bastard."

Vhanna put a hand on my knee and squeezed lightly. She had related this all matter-of-factly and without a trace of anger and continued to do so. Her calm was infuriating. I wanted to find Ray Bellows and bang his head hard against a wall. "Ray isn't being deliberately cruel," she said after I expressed this desire. "He was out of options. And I was positioned to help."

Vhanna told me about an undercover RCMP officer who had managed to infiltrate Dagleish's manor by getting hired on as a security guard only to be found out. He had been badly beaten and left for dead below the tide line. After that Bellows knew he could never get another agent in place by conventional means. He had to find someone who was already involved with Dagleish and shrewd enough to do what Bellows needed without getting caught.

"Darren Dagleish and I were already pretty far along in negotiations that would see Artemis run eco-tourist adventure packages out of the hotels and resorts that he's planning to establish all over the island and up the mainland coast. Day- and week-long kayaking expeditions, surfing instruction, heli-hiking excursions into the backcountry mountain ranges, cliff and mountain climbing packages. Artemis would be able to base all of this right from the front step of a series of first-class hotels. Dagleish Development gets the adventure services his target clientele will want and Artemis gets an assured customer base to enable it to grow exponentially into the nation's biggest adventure company." Vhanna's eyes gleamed with enthusiasm.

"What of the women-only concept behind Artemis?"

She shrugged. "I was going to split the company. Artemis would remain as it is. But there would be a new entity that offered the services through Dagleish's resorts and would be open to anyone with the money and necessary skills for whatever level of adventure being offered. Opportunities like this don't come along very often."

"And are usually too good to be true."

The gleam that had been in Vhanna's eyes dimmed. "Yes, too good to be true. But Dagleish doesn't know that. He thinks I still believe it's possible and want it badly."

I thought of Vhanna standing in the spa and of Dagleish's possessive hands on her body. Harsh words formed in my mind, words full of jealousy and betrayed anger. But I quelled them, knowing they were unfair. Vhanna was not letting Dagleish touch her in order to win the right to operate Artemis from his hotels and build her already profitable business into an even greater powerhouse of commercial enterprise. She did so to gain entry into his inner sanctum, to gather information for Bellows that could be used to bring the man to justice. "It's too dangerous. He's no fool. And neither is Roberta Walker. If they get suspicious —"

Vhanna fixed me with that flat cautionary gaze that warns her patience at my protectiveness is wearing thin. "I'm no fool either, Elias. And neither is Ray. Tomorrow it's done." She smiled grimly. "Most people have a fatal flaw. Darren has two. First, he likes to surround himself with women, but he doesn't respect their intelligence. Second, he has a poor memory. So he is always jotting little notes on scraps of paper when he's on the phone around us and doesn't bother concealing them. Yesterday he took several calls while we were by the pool." A shiver ran through her and she tugged the front of the robe more tightly over her breasts. "For a while he and I were alone together. He decided to swim a few laps and with each stroke that carried his head under the water, I had a moment to read part of the notes. There were some interesting numbers."

Vhanna has always had a steel-trap memory, particularly for numbers. She could retain a string of numerals with only a quick glance and rattle them back to you with uncannily accurate recall. It was a skill tragically learned. When Vhanna and her mother began the long march from Phnom Penh into the Cambodian killing fields, Lin had patiently and repetitively forced the ten-year-old girl to memorize a seemingly random series of numbers and an address. Also given into her care were the Cambodian passports and other papers that would prove her identity as the child of Yuan and Lin Chan.

Months later she had recited those numbers and the address to Lars Janson in a Thai refugee camp. The address proved to be that of a Hong Kong bank and the numbers matched those of an account established there by Yuan Chan. When the political situation in Cambodia had begun deteriorating, Yuan had quietly liquidated most of his property holdings into gold and U.S. dollars and transferred that wealth out of the country. He had probably intended for the family to flee as well, but the collapse of the Cambodian army in the face of the Khmer Rouge offensive came so rapidly that the city fell before many wealthy citizens could make good their escape. And so they were swept up in the bloody mayhem that followed.

But Vhanna had escaped. And her facility with number retention ultimately brought the reward of a small fortune upon which she has built with a steady attention and enthusiasm that is puzzling. Whereas I have more than enough and seek to limit further gains through investment, Vhanna's desire for the accumulation of wealth seems insatiable.

"What kind of numbers?" I asked.

She looked as pleased as a cat with a bird between its paws. "Verification numbers for the transfer of funds from one offshore account to another, complete with initials of the various banks and countries in which they are located. Just two transfers, but Ray says that's enough because one is for the transfer from the source account to the account of a blind company in Bermuda and the second to an account of Dagleish Properties in the Caymans. The blind in the middle is a company on which Darren is listed as a director of the board. So he's implicated right down the chain."

"And the source account?"

"Hong Kong. Ray says the police there have identified this bank as providing a central laundry point for the Triads. And the particular Triad controlling the source account is running major operations in Vancouver and every other major city on the Pacific coast. Darren Dagleish is a funnel through which the profits from their operations are being washed back into the legitimate economy."

Vhanna's eyes were hard as flint. "It'll be a pleasure to have been a part in bringing him down."

He had handled her like one of his possessions in front of me. It was easy to imagine the suggestions that probably had been made during the past days. Vhanna was a beautiful woman with an independent spirit. Dagleish would want to possess her completely, to diminish her into being one of his servants. I thought of Roberta Walker in the skimpy bikini, massaging oil into his back. The way she had kept her head down and eyes averted as if ashamed. That was the kind of grip Dagleish liked to have on the women around him.

"Do you have to go back there?"

Vhanna stood up and took my hands in hers, pulled me up from the hearth so that we stood facing each other. Delicately she traced her fingers down my cheeks. "We're supposed to finalize the deal for the Ashton resort tomorrow morning and then have a celebratory lunch. We've always conducted our business either in the spa or in the manor house office. But tomorrow I'm meeting Darren in the office where he really does his business. It's in the upstairs above the spa."

In the unmarked van two men had been hunched over a bank of what had seemed to be radio receivers. "Bellows wants you to leave a bug." I gripped her shoulders hard. "It's too dangerous, Vhanna. You can't do it."

Her arms came up inside of mine and swiftly swept my hands from her shoulders with the surprising strength and gentleness of a Tai Chi Chen adept. Vhanna grinned and poked an index finger against my chest. "You see, I can take care of myself. And Ray and the others are nearby. It'll be okay. Darren doesn't see me as a threat. He trusts me as much as anyone, I think."

She undid the knot on the belt of her robe and let it fall open. Took my hands and settled the palms on her hips. "It's late." Vhanna stood on tiptoe and brushed her lips against mine. "Let's go to bed."

Vhanna held my hand as she went up the stairs ahead of me. She slowly undid my shirt. Soon my clothes were scattered across the floor. I reached out and slipped the robe off her shoulders, and it fell free of her arms to pool at her feet. We wrapped our arms around each other and gave ourselves over to the feel of flesh against flesh and hearts beating together.

Ever the prude, Fergus allowed one snort and then shuffled off downstairs to find refuge on the couch. Vhanna pushed me down onto the bed and knelt to straddle my hips. Her hair was like a cloak draping down from her shoulders to veil her breasts and stomach. I moved to brush it aside, but she lightly restrained me by pushing my forearms down onto the mattress with strong hands. She rode me slowly at first, then ever faster until I came with a great shuddering groan.

We lay in each other's arms after, just listening to the soft sound of our mixed breathing. Eventually Vhanna rolled over on her side. I pressed myself in against her back with one arm lightly draped across her, and we both surrendered to sleep.

Vhanna still slept when I woke in the morning. I quietly slipped from under the covers and dressed in a natural-coloured cotton shirt and beige khakis that I hoped would make me appear dressed somewhat formally for the task ahead. Fergus had returned to his bed sometime during the night, but followed me downstairs and sat on his haunches looking purposefully at the kitchen door. I let him out and then put on some coffee to brew. Gathering green onions, a tomato, a link of Portuguese hot sausage, a square of Edam cheese, and some eggs from the fridge, I proceeded to chop the other ingredients into the whipped eggs to make a simple hash. There were some leftover roasted potatoes that I sliced thin and put on to fry in a dash of extra virgin olive oil, while thick slices of multigrain bread from the Tofino bakery toasted.

A scratching at the door reminded me that Fergus had finished with his urgent mission outside, and as I let him back in Vhanna appeared at the foot of the stairs wrapped in the white robe. She rubbed her eyes with the backs of her hands, an almost childlike gesture, before walking across the room to give me a hug and kiss. "Sex, sleep, and now food. What more could a man give a girl?" she said with a sleepy smile.

"Hearth and home," I suggested.

She tipped her head to one side as if actually considering the proposition. "Is the coffee ready?"

Having learned long ago not to press the subject, I turned my attention to pressing coffee instead and then poured the strong brew into mugs. Soon we were seated at the table tucking into our food like two just-rescued castaways. When the plates were polished off and wiped clean with the last of the toast, I refilled our mugs and we sat looking at each other.

I told her of my plans for the day, but offered to set them aside if she wanted me to be near Dagleish's estate in case she needed help. As I knew she would, Vhanna told me that was unnecessary. "What you've got to do is important, Elias." She reached across the table and rested her hand on top of mine. "It's a question that needs to be answered. Nobody should go unidentified."

Her eyes darkened, and I knew she thought of her mother and father, of all her family, and of the 1.8 million others who lay in unmarked graves and pits throughout Cambodia. In places like Choeung Ek, where a twenty-metre-high glass tower filled with human skulls now stands as a grim tribute to the twenty thousand or more people murdered in that one field alone. In her travels to Cambodia in recent years Vhanna has visited virtually every known site of the murders, as if in search of some meaning or to at least honour those who died while she managed to live. She does not talk of the things she sees or of the thoughts or feelings she experiences on revisiting these horrors, and I know not to ask of them.

"You will be careful today?" I said as we put the dishes into the sink.

"We both will," she replied and gave me a brief hug before going upstairs to dress. Outside the rain still fell. In the living room her sweater and other clothes were still sodden and hanging on the chairs in front of the cold fireplace.

chapter twenty

Beyond the wide swath of Pacific Rim National Park's sandy beaches gunmetal clouds pressed hard upon a sea churning with dark white-frothed waves crashing toward shore. A hard westerly whipped across the dunes that fell back from the beach to the highway, plastering down the dense clumps of European beachgrass and the occasional surviving remnants of the tougher and coarser native dunegrass not yet displaced by the foreign invader. I clung to the wheel of the Land Rover and banked the little vehicle windward slightly in order to keep bearing true. Rain slathered the windshield and the wind moaned and whistled through the many gaps where the door and window gaskets had rotted away with age. Head hunkered down into his shoulders like some old mariner contemplating the merits of launching a boat into the very teeth of the storm, Fergus stared toward the passing beach through the spattered and misted passenger window.

There was little traffic moving in either direction. Occasionally I glimpsed in the rear-view mirror the silhouette of a blue or black SUV, but its driver was either in no hurry or being very cautious, for it never overtook us. In the beach access parking lots only a few vehicles were parked, these undoubtedly attached to the scatter of brave or plain crazy young people in wetsuits who were perilously riding the wild waves on surfboards. They were members of a new clan making its presence felt in Tofino: the surf gypsies with bronzed skin and sun-bleached hair who pursued the great waves from here to Costa Rica and back again.

Finally I passed through the southern gates of the park and rumbled along a stretch of highway where steep banks fell away on both flanks. On the landward side the rain had transformed the customary swale into a virtual lake, while oceanward dense thickets blocked any view of the water. It was a bleak, grim place, and I was happy to reach the intersection that leads from the highway down to Ucluelet.

Soon I pulled into a "Visitor Parking" slot at Ucluelet Secondary School, the Pacific Rim's only such institution of higher learning. Inside, I presented myself to a bustling middle-aged secretary who manned a counter guarding the entrance to the principal's office. She looked dubiously at the rain dripping off my Filson hat and coat before inviting me to have a seat on a narrow bench running along the wall opposite the counter.

I perched there next to two teenage girls who had their hair twisted into messy ponytails held tight with brightly coloured elastics. Their midriffs between their short tops and low-rise jeans were bare, and each had a small piece of glass jewelry shaped like a hummingbird dangling on a little glass bead chain from the centre of their navels. They alternated between snapping the green chewing gum in their mouths and giggling as if at some shared secret. They both had their legs crossed, and the foot of the leg thrown over the other fidgeted constantly. Around their necks were small headphones linked by an umbilical cord to a CD player that each had set in her lap.

"Tanya, Heather," Mrs. Officious snapped authoritatively, "Ms. Beal will see you now."

The one girl rolled her eyes dramatically toward her friend, who paled noticeably and followed the other hesitantly through the door bearing the name of the vice-principal. Even as I wondered what offence the girls might have committed and what their punishment would be, the woman summoned me to go into Mr. Jackson's office on the left.

"I'm Principal Jackson," said the man, who wore a yellow V-necked cotton sweater pulled over a pale blue oxford-style shirt, as he rose from behind his desk to shake my hand. He stood a head taller than I and had a long, bony beak of a nose that he inclined toward me as a hand thin as a claw took mine. He was perhaps fifty-five, hair gone to grey, bifocals dangling from a cord around his neck.

Handshake over, he quickly reclaimed his seat in the manner of a man self-conscious about his height and given to hiding it. I took the proffered straight-backed plastic chair across from him and explained my purpose. Jackson's lips compressed into a thin line that bordered on a grimace.

"Janet Ashton. Dropped out when she was about sixteen. That would have been approximately five or six years ago. It'll mean pulling files. I just took this position last year, you understand." He told me to wait and walked from the room with his head out front of his long body like a blue heron. My eyes wandered, finally settling on a series of narrow volumes occupying a bookshelf under the window. On closer examination they proved to be the school's yearbooks, and I quickly pulled out the one that was five years old.

Inside, I found a series of group photographs for each of the school's grades. Janet had been sixteen when she quit school, so I guessed grade eleven or twelve. Scanning the list of names beneath each photo, however, produced no listing for her. But when I tried the volume from the previous year I found Janet standing in the second row from the front of the grade eleven photograph. She was a chunky but pretty girl with blonde hair hanging down to her shoulders and a thoughtful, closed expression on her face. She stood at the outside edge of the row, slightly farther from the girl beside her than was true for any of the other kids in the photograph. The fingers of her hands were shoved into the front pockets of her faded jeans and she wore a flat black T-shirt. Both looked well worn, but were neatly pressed. Tempest's work, I imagined. By this time there had likely been precious little money. Yet the clothes were not much plainer than those worn by many of the others. The economies of Tofino and Ucluelet were not conducive to financing stylish attire for children or anyone else.

"Ah," Jackson said as he came back into the office, "good idea, that. Grade eleven, right? Six years ago."

I nodded. He set down a file that contained her school report cards and attendance records. The principal riffled through the pages quickly, his head turning from one side of the page to another as he scanned the lines. "Well, not exactly a stellar student. Good enough marks in her first years here, but nothing extraordinary. Then in grade ten there's a sharp decline in grades coincident with a matching increase in truancy days. Same pattern through grade eleven, but it becomes even more pronounced. And she didn't return for grade twelve."

He poked a long digit down on another page. "Counsellor report. Completed after her first suspension for prolonged truancy and then another toward the end of grade eleven." He thumbed through a couple pages, nodding his head as if finding nothing but further confirmation of the girl's failings as an individual. "Uncooperative, defensive, sullen, quick to anger, flirtatious, and possibly promiscuous would sum up the counsellor's findings. No promising traits that could be nurtured in order to improve her behaviour and chances of achieving academic success. The outcome, although regrettable, seemed inevitable."

It was a moment before I realized he was referring to Janet's dropping out of school and not the conclusion I had reached that had brought me here in quest of a photograph. "Can I get copies of her file?"

Principal Jackson pursed his lips as if the thought was unpleasant but then agreed. "If it will do any good," he added skeptically. When he returned with the photocopied documents I fetched my coat from the back of the plastic chair and hat from the top of his desk and thanked him for his time. "For her sake I hope you're wrong about this, Mr. McCann," he said as he settled back behind his desk.

"I hope so too," I murmured on my way out of the office. But I was certain that the young woman who had used the alias of Sparrow and returned to Tofino only to end up dead on a beach had been Janet Ashton.

From the coffee shop payphone in a downtown Ucluelet hotel I phoned Tully's office. He was with a patient, so, saying I would call back in fifteen minutes, I took a stool at the counter. A waitress splashed thick and bitter brew into a chipped china cup, then returned to the other end of the counter and a conversation with a couple of unshaven locals dressed in flannel shirts, work pants held up by wide suspenders bearing the Stihl logo, and worn work boots. A haze of cigarette smoke lingered over their heads as they told their stories and kept the waitress laughing. I dumped the contents of three cream containers into the black liquid, managing to taint it only to the colour of grey mud.

When fifteen minutes had finally passed, I happily abandoned the cup, leaving a two-dollar coin on the Formica counter. Tully heard me out in silence. "I fear you're right," he said morosely. Then he had me wait while he retrieved Janet Ashton's medical records from his patient archives in the office basement. This time I forewent the coffee, instead standing outside on the hotel's covered front verandah to watch the fishermen and whale-watching operators batten down their vessels for a long, idle winter.

The rain had eased to drizzle, but the wind remained fresh and cold. When I stepped back inside the hotel ten minutes later, Tully answered right on cue. "Nothing in the files regarding distinguishing marks or symptoms that I could use to confirm her identity. She was a healthy girl, it seems. Last physical was when she was ten, and after that nothing more than occasional treatment for flu, strep throat, usual afflictions of childhood." An uncomfortable silence ensued, as if Tully was embarrassed. Finally he said, "No gynecological exams, so no indication about the scarring that seemed to date back to when she would have been still living with her mother. My understanding is that it's not uncommon for adolescent sexual assault victims who want to keep their experience secret to avoid such examinations. Might be the case here."

Tully said her dentist was recorded as Jim Walters, who had retired a year ago and failed to find a buyer for the practice. "But he's as much a packrat as I am, so I bet his files are stored away at his home." It was coming up to noon, and Tully promised to call him once he finished with his next patient. "All goes well I should be able to get over to the hospital and check the dental X-rays and bite moulds I took during the autopsy against Janet's records and have the results for you by about one o'clock. Come by the hospital."

My next call was to the Tofino RCMP detachment. "Sugar, where've you been? I've been sitting here pining for a call," Nicki said with a throaty laugh.

"I've been thinking about you constantly, but, alas, business must always come before pleasure."

Nicki snorted disbelievingly. "I think work ethic and, you know, somehow your name just doesn't pop up on the screen as a match. Polar opposites be more like it."

"I'm misunderstood."

"Yeah, just like me. That's why I'm always having to fight off those German males at the hotel on Friday nights." On Friday evenings Nicki teaches line dancing at the hotel bar. She once confided deriving a perverse pleasure from spurning the endless come-ons. For several years now Nicki has lived with a slender Haitian woman named Lacy, who works the counter at the bakery and is rumoured to be her lover. "Anyway," she said, "I expect you seek my lord and master rather than to simply while away the hours in discourse with yours truly."

"Elegantly put."

"Unfortunately, dear heart, he is off on matters to which I am not privy. And he has with him constables Singh and Tom. All most hush-hush, but I suspect it has something to do with the fact that Ray Bellows is in town and yesterday indicated he might require the services of the department as backup to something that he's got afoot."

Until now I had been telling myself that the anxiety growing in my gut as I absorbed the probable identity of the dead girl was misguided and of no immediate concern. But knowing that Bellows had assembled a team of Mounties on the morning Vhanna was to penetrate Dagleish's inner sanctum made my blood chill. I asked where Anne Monaghan was. "You know how to make a girl jealous. Always wanting to know where our favorite tomboy is," Nicki said with a laugh, for the two women were fast friends and general allies in the low-intensity war that existed between both of them and their commanding sergeant. "She's right here, as it happens. You wish to confer?"

Most definitely, I said. Monaghan groaned in the same kind of disgruntled tone that Fergus often directs my way when he is displeased with my intentions after I briefed her on Sparrow's possible identity and what I wanted to do next. "I'm not sure about doing this without Sergeant Danchuk's go ahead. And we really should have a warrant."

"If we find anything we'll leave it there, report to Danchuk, and then get the warrant." When I explained my real concern, she reluctantly agreed to meet me in an hour.

Traffic on Highway 14 was still surprisingly light as I drove north toward Pacific Rim National Park. I pushed the Land Rover hard, keeping the accelerator glued to the floor and working the gears mercilessly to claw a path up and down the various hills at the best possible speed. The engine growled, the transmission whined, and various body parts rattled as if the entire vehicle might shake apart. How fast I was actually going was a mystery, for the speedometer needle had long ago developed a habit of bouncing nervously back and forth across a range of about twenty miles per hour. Currently it offered the estimate that I was driving somewhere between fifty and seventy, but I seriously doubted the Land Rover was capable of anything over sixty.

When I rounded a curve and the Land Rover listed over into the opposite lane I eased off on the gas a little, recognizing that getting into an accident would be worse than arriving late. As I broke out onto the section of raised highway bordered by the flooded ground next to my lane a dark SUV appeared in the rear-view mirror. It was travelling fast, throwing up a wake of spray. There was a corner coming up marked with a speed reduction sign, so I slowed to allow the driver a chance to pass before the curve. As the SUV closed I saw it was a dark blue Nissan Pathfinder and resembled the silhouette of the vehicle that had never overtaken me on the trip down to Ucluelet.

I glanced over at Fergus, who was rolled into a small ball and snoring gently. Suddenly metal shrieked against metal. The steering wheel tore out of my hands and I was thrown hard toward Fergus just as the front wheel on the passenger side dropped off the asphalt onto the grassy verge. I flung myself back behind the wheel and tried to steer back onto the pavement. The Pathfinder was suddenly alongside veering hard toward me. There was a deep scour in the paint on its front bumper, and I had the sickening realization that the driver had sideswiped the Land Rover and was about to do so again.

Its windows were smoked, making it impossible to see the driver. As the big machine crossed the line, I jammed on the brakes, hoping to cause it to overshoot. But the driver anticipated my action and also braked. There was another hard crash as its bumper smashed into the Land Rover's front fender with terrific force. I tried to hold a straight path, but the weight and power of the other vehicle was too great. The Land Rover yawed off the road, slewed across the grassy verge, and pitched headfirst over the edge of the steep embankment and down toward a rain-flooded pool.

Fergus let out a sharp frightened yelp that turned into a yowl of pain as he rocketed off the seat and slammed into the dashboard with a hard thud before being pitched onto the floorboards. I clung to the wheel, feet jammed on the brake as if I could somehow stop the Land Rover's crazed descent. My stomach lifted into my chest and then the Land Rover's nose struck the water with a mighty crash and the world turned upside down.

chapter twenty-one

I regained my senses to feel something cold and wet rising around my head. Forepaws on my chest, Fergus barked urgently into my face. I patted him weakly on the head while the world slowly ceased spinning. Reaching up, my hand gripped the steering wheel, and I struggled upright to find myself staring up at the Land Rover's floorboards. Dully I realized that the vehicle was upside down and rapidly flooding with water squirting in through the gaps in the doors and windows. On the other side of every window there was only the blackness of water. A few minutes more and the Land Rover would be our watery coffin.

When I tried to wipe a gummy substance that was blocking the vision of my right eye, my hand came away red with blood. A wave of nausea washed over me and I desperately wanted to vomit. Pain knifed so violently through my skull that I could barely continue sitting upright and wanted nothing more than to curl into a fetal ball with my hands pressed against temples. But each of Fergus's sharp barks spiked painfully through my brain and prevented a slide back into unconsciousness.

Then a jet of water shot through the air vent at the top of the dashboard and splashed icily against my face, helping to clear some of the numbness from my brain. Suddenly frantic, I clawed at the driver's door and tried to heave it open. But the outside pressure of the water pinned it shut. With a moan of despair, I realized the other doors would be similarly sealed. That route of escape was closed, and the windshield and side door windows were too small to crawl through. The back compartment windows were both covered with racks for holding hunting rifles and fishing rods. That left only the window of the rear door.

"Come on, Fergus," I said, and floundered on my stomach into the back compartment. The water was up to my waist now, and the rear door window was completely submerged. Fergus was dog-paddling beside me, eyes wide with fear. It suddenly occurred to me that I was able to see quite well despite the Land Rover being submerged. Traces of light filtered through various holes in the floorboards, meaning the vehicle might not be entirely underwater. But we still either got out or died. The water pouring in was shockingly cold, so even if the inside should fail to completely fill and a small pocket of air remained we would both succumb to hypothermia in little more than a few minutes. Already my teeth were clattering and my fingers felt like they had gone to sleep.

Desperately I groped around for the tool box, only to find it had torn free of its fittings. That meant it was somewhere underwater. I ran a hand carefully along the roof and finally managed to feel the steel box. Its lid was open and tools were spilled everywhere around. I came up with a screwdriver — too little for the job. Water chest deep now. Running out of time.

"Damn, of course," I gasped. Twisting back toward the front of the vehicle, I frantically released the clips that held the driver's seat in place, cast it aside, and saw that the heavy cranking bar was still secured in a bracket anchored to the body. Used to manually turn the engine should the starter button fail, the crank was the kind of backup technology that could keep a person alive in the middle of an African desert or the high passes of Pakistan. Or now, when drowning in a stinking pool of water. I yanked the steel crank free of its bracket. It was thirty inches long, a good inch around, and heavy as a small sledgehammer. Holding my breath, I ducked under the surface and slammed the crank against the back door window. Water rushed in through the hole I had punched in the glass and increased in velocity as I swiped the crank crossways and up and down in frantic circles to clear away the glass all the way over to the metal frame. Finally I could reach out and feel a hole large enough to crawl through.

I broke the surface to find the cabin now so filled with water that I could just suck in a breath by tipping my head right back with my nose brushing the floorboards. All of Fergus I could see was his snout. I wrapped my arms around his body and then dragged him down. Surprisingly he didn't fight, just went limp in my arms and let me take him where I would. I shoved him through the window and released him. Then I pressed the middle of the crank handle down onto the metal rim and used it as a brace along which I crawled to avoid slashing my stomach and chest on any glass shards that might still be fitted into the framework.

Once through the window, I swivelled around and grabbed up the crank before standing up and breaking the surface. I stood neck deep in water, sucking in air while swaying unsteadily on my feet. Fergus staggered out of the water and up the bank a few feet before collapsing onto his side. He lay there panting, eyes fixed encouragingly my way as I sloshed across the pool and crawled up alongside him.

Only when I was safely free of the water did I think to scan the top of the embankment for any sign of our assailant. But there was nobody to be seen. Presumably he imagined his mission a success and had not wanted to linger long at the scene for fear of being observed. Leaving us for dead, he had taken flight.

The Land Rover's wheels and undercarriage stuck forlornly out of the water. I wiped away more of the blood on my forehead and then wearily climbed up the embankment to the road. As Fergus stumbled up beside me, I reached down and patted him softly on the head. "Thanks, old boy," I whispered. He licked my fingers and fixed me with a look full of nothing but the greatest devotion.

From the direction of Tofino a white car was approaching, and a few moments later I made out its rack of emergency lights. Anne Monaghan pulled onto the shoulder in front of me. When she stepped out of the car, her eyes widened as she looked over the embankment and saw the overturned Land Rover. "Jesus, Elias, when you didn't show I was worried you might have broken down or something." I walked over and hugged her tightly. Then I told her what happened.

"There's an abandoned skid trail just before the bog area begins that works well for a radar trap site. Can see everything down the road without being detected. Speeders race past and you just jump out of there on their butt. Most never even figure out where we come from. He probably tailed you into town, figured out what you were up to, and then parked there to wait in ambush."

That made sense and gave a good indication of the assailant's identity. There had been the questions I had asked about Jack Ashton's sister. Enough possibly to make him suspicious. Then he would have seen me going into the school and likely guessed my purpose.

My body was shaking violently from cold and the draining off of adrenaline. "I'll take you to emergency," she said.

"No," I said through chattering teeth, "there isn't time." As I explained my fears Monaghan pulled from the cruiser's trunk a pair of blue coveralls with "Police" emblazoned in bold yellow letters across the back and tossed them over to me. Then she fished out a first-aid kit and several grey wool blankets.

I stripped and pulled on the coveralls. Although I wrung the water out of my socks and drained it from my boots as best I could the effort was largely futile. Shards of glass were embedded in the back of my old canvas coat and there were tears in my jeans where the glass had lacerated them. Monaghan meanwhile had her back turned to afford me some privacy and was using one of the blankets to vigorously dry Fergus's coat with greater success than I managed with the socks and boots. She then helped him climb into the patrol car's back seat. Fergus was staggering with exhaustion and limping badly on his right front leg. After Monaghan wrapped him in one of the dry blankets, he simply collapsed on the seat and closed his eyes.

It was tempting to follow his cue, for I was having bouts of dizziness and it felt like someone was sticking a sharp needle directly into my forehead. But I slumped down on the front seat with my legs out the passenger door instead and let Monaghan start working on the gash in my scalp. Crouching in front of me, she quickly and efficiently cleansed the cut with a Q-tip dipped in rubbing alcohol and applied a bandage. "The training guides say you should get some stitches for that within four hours or there's a good chance it'll leave a scar that mars your perfect looks. Now look me straight in the eyes." She leaned in close enough that I could feel her breath on my face and fixed me with a critical gaze.

I tried to meet her grey eyes evenly to demonstrate clear lucidity, but her pupils tended to join together at the bridge of her nose and then drift outwards fuzzily. "Jesus," she hissed, and then suddenly darted forward and lightly kissed my cheek. Monaghan was walking around to the other side of the car so quickly that I was left wondering if I had only imagined it. "Okay," she said gruffly, "let's get this done."

By the time I painfully swivelled my body into the car and shut the door she had the engine started. The constable cut a hard U-turn, turned on the emergency lights, and gunned the car up the highway. Glancing at the back seat I saw Fergus still lying in a stupor under the blanket. I picked up the spare dry blanket from where it lay at my feet, wrapped it around me, and tried to quell the shivers coursing through my body. It would have been a pure delight to shut my eyes, but I feared not being able to awaken. So I concentrated on the road racing toward us and tried not to jab for an imaginary brake pedal as Monaghan hurled the car through the corners.

The rain picked up again with such force as we barrelled out of Pacific Rim National Park that the drops striking the pavement jumped waist high. Fog swirled off the beach and out of the roadside ditches. "Last time we freelanced like this I killed a man," Monaghan said. "I should radio this in and get some backup."

"And they could be monitoring your channels. We can't take that risk."

She glared at me for a second before applying her attention back to the road. I felt the rear end drift as we careened around a corner, but Monaghan handled the car like a Grand Prix racer, and it came out of the turn tracking straight and true down the centre of her lane. "If this goes to shit, Danchuk will burn my ass and be right to do so. Christ, why do I let you get me into these things?"

The turn to the road leading to the Ashton property came up and Monaghan took it, dousing the emergency lights as she did so. She cut the speed back to where it was only a bit over the posted limit. Soon enough we reached the gate barring entrance to the driveway up to the house, and Monaghan parked in front of it. There was a chain on the gate and a heavy lock. While Monaghan unclipped the shotgun from its dashboard mount, I told her about the cut in the wire fence that Devon Lysander and I had used the night we rescued Moot. Fergus raised not even an eyelid as we climbed out of the car and set off.

I led her down the lane and then through the brush to the fence. The gap was still there. We slipped through and then moved quietly toward the house, staying in the trees and trying to use their cover to conceal our advance. The pain in my head had dulled to a hard throbbing, and I was only slightly unsteady on my feet. More than anything I wished to be carrying Monaghan's shotgun, but I knew better than to make the suggestion. There were some rules she would never bend, and arming a civilian was one of them.

Monaghan had the radio on her belt turned down to prevent any incoming messages from betraying us. Usually there was an almost steady stream of messages, mostly incidental, coming over the police radio net. Since I had got into Monaghan's cruiser, however, the radio had been ominously silent. Bellows was obviously keeping communications wired tight at his end. Monaghan and I had agreed that the silence indicated that the detective still had Danchuk and the rest of the detachment probably somewhere close to Darren Dagleish's estate. And Vhanna was somewhere inside trying to crack Dagleish's security so Bellows could catch his man.

Rainwater shook off the leaves and branches as we crept through some dense brush and ran icily down my neck. Monaghan had a regulation ball cap on with the bill turned backwards so that it directed the rain onto the back of her jacket, but I was bareheaded — my old canvas hat somewhere inside the overturned Land Rover. I parted a clump of branches and we looked out across the muddy ground toward the house. The yard was empty. No dark blue Pathfinder with what I imagined would be a crumpled or at least badly scoured front fender on the passenger side.

We crouched behind the screen of brush for several minutes, scanning the ground and the empty windows of the old house for any sign of life. I tried to think again like a soldier. "You should stay here and cover me," I whispered, "while I check it out. You've got the guns."

"No way," Monaghan murmured. "It's my hook."

I shrugged. So much for reasoned tactics. "We go together then," I said. "Woodshed first." I lumbered off before Monaghan could insist I wait in the cover of the bush. She was right on my heels by the time I reached the little building and leaned against a wall for support, bent over clutching my pulsing head in both hands. "Damned fool," Monaghan said without a trace of sympathy. I sat in the mud with my legs crossed, gasping for breath and letting the world spin. A hand settled on my knee, and after a few minutes the planet returned to a normal pace of rotation. I smiled at Monaghan weakly. "I'm okay."

"You're concussed. When we're done here I'm taking you to the hospital."

"We're going to the hospital all right, but not to get me any treatment," I said and shook my head for emphasis. An action I immediately regretted and which caused me to whimper with pain. I sucked in another hard breath and stood up by steadying myself against the wall. "Let's take a look."

Shovels, rakes, hoes, and other long-handled yard tools hung on their pegs as before. Rust covered the metal parts and the handles were cracked and grey — the result of years of neglect in a damp climate. In a back corner, leaning against the wall, I found the old splitting maul and carried it out into the grey light. Jack Ashton had been holding the maul in his hands when I first saw him standing over Tempest Ashton's body. She had been cutting wood with it when she collapsed and apparently fatally struck her forehead on the heavy cutting block. Or so we had been led to believe by a killer, and no serious investigation had been conducted to either prove or disprove that explanation. A cursory autopsy had supported such a scenario. Nobody had thought to suspect the son of killing his mother.

I turned the maul in my hand and we peered closely at the blunt end of the heavy metal head. I pointed to a tiny pattern of dark spots on the butt of the blade.

Monaghan pursed her lips. "Could be oil or grease."

"Or blood that he didn't manage to clean off."

She nodded, agreeing that it was possible. "Was Mrs. Ashton cremated?"

I told Monaghan that she was buried in the cemetery next to her husband and oldest son. "They had a small family plot there." I didn't elaborate that I knew this because it was my practice to attend the funerals of all the people whose deaths I investigated. It seemed a macabre ritual, but one I felt was necessary. A sign of respect not only to the relatives and friends but more so to the person whose life had ended violently enough to require my involvement.

"If there are blood traces, she'll have to be exhumed." Monaghan looked at me sadly. "Do you really think?"

I nodded. "Yes. And he killed Sparrow, too. His sister."

"And tried to murder the other girl." Monaghan flipped the shotgun up by its grip and leaned the barrel against her shoulder like she was contemplating firing it at someone. "Elias, I don't know about the mother. But those girls. The bastard enjoyed hurting them. If Sparrow was his sister, then he derived pleasure from murdering her that way."

I wiped the rain from my face. "Let's go, Anne." We walked back to the car, and Monaghan put the axe in a plastic bag and noted the details of where she had confiscated it from and the date and time of the seizure on a label that she attached to the bag.

Monaghan rammed the shotgun hard into its bracket and gripped the steering wheel tightly in her hands. "I swore I'd do anything possible to avoid killing again." Her eyes were flat and free of any apparent emotion when she looked over at me. "But if he gives so much as a reason," she said calmly.

chapter twenty-two

We drove past the strip of cheap motels, gas stations, and rundown houses that form Tofino's outskirts and took the narrow dirt lane to my cabin. I carried Fergus, still wrapped in the blanket, inside and lay him beside the wood stove in the kitchen. "I'll make a fire," Monaghan said. "You get changed."

Upstairs I yanked off the police coveralls and pulled on a pair of canvas pants, a denim shirt, and an old army-issue green wool sweater. When I walked back into the kitchen, Monaghan had a fire going in the stove and was stoking it up with some big pieces of split fir with one hand while hanging up my phone with the other. "I called Nicki. She's going to phone Port Alberni and ask the detachment there to put its Emergency Response Team on alert. I don't have the authority to actually request they be sent here, but at least we can have them at readiness in case things go sour."

Fergus's eyes were open, and when I filled his bowl with water he rallied from under the blanket to lap it dry.

I refilled it, poured out some food, and assured him that I would be back soon. He offered no sign of wanting to join me on another foray out into the mad world beyond the cabin and sighed with sorrowful exhaustion when I wrapped him up in a dry blanket pulled from a closet.

As we left the cabin, I pulled on a seldom worn green Gore-Tex rain jacket that Vhanna had insisted I buy once as part of a planned modernization campaign and set a navy woolen watch cap gingerly on my head to prevent disturbing the bandage. Monaghan and I drove past the entranceway to Dagleish's estate without slowing, but I scanned the surrounding ground for some sign of a police stakeout. The hydro utility van from the day before was nowhere to be seen, and I could see no other obvious sign of hovering police.

"I didn't see anything either," Monaghan said. "They must be up some side road."

A few minutes later we pulled into the hospital parking lot on the opposite side of town. Doc Tully's rusted blue Cadillac listed at an awkward angle in his designated parking slot. Monaghan fished the maul in its plastic bag from the trunk and we marched inside. The duty nurse looked warily at the axe as we asked after Tully. We proceeded down into the building's bowels to where the air was always thick and rancid, the pale green paint was flecking off the walls in long strips, and the battleship linoleum was worn through in spots to reveal the concrete foundation underneath. Tully was in the little cubicle set aside as his pathology office, and the two of us squeezed into the space across the metal desk from him. Splayed out on the desk were three white file folders — one thin and new, the other two both relatively fat but darkened with age.

Tully had the new folder open and had been jotting virtually illegible notes on a ruled sheet of paper. He finished the sentence, took off his glasses, and looked at us with watery eyes. "What happened to your head?" he asked me.

I told him briefly about being run off the road and then of what we had found at the Ashton property. Monaghan put the maul on the desk. "Really should send this to one of the crime labs right away," Tully comment-ed, "but I guess it won't hurt if we take a quick peek to see what there is to see." Grabbing the edge of the desk with one hand to provide some leverage, Tully pulled himself to his feet. "Come on. Let's go to the lab. Have some things to show you there." Monaghan picked up the axe and we followed him down the hall to the lab, which was situat-ed next to the autopsy room and morgue.

Tully clipped a series of X-rays to a viewing screen, turned on the light, and then pulled a pen from the chest pocket of his white physician's jacket. "On this side we have right and left views of the murder victim, and over here virtually identical views of Janet Ashton's dental structure as taken a few days after her sixteenth birth-day. This was the last time that Dr. Walters saw her for a routine cleaning and checkup. Not uncommonly for most teenagers she required one filling that day." He tapped a bicuspid on her upper right jaw with the pen nib. The filling showed as a white irregularity against the black solidity of the teeth.

I looked quickly over to Sparrow's X-rays and noted what seemed to be an identical filling on the same bicuspid. Tully followed my glance. "It's a perfect match," he said. "Look here." He pointed again to Janet Ashton's X-ray and traced a white line that appeared under the first incisor of her upper jaw. "When Janet was fourteen she had this incisor knocked clean out of her mouth when another girl elbowed her during a soccer match. I found the notation in my own records because between the force of the blow and the

injury to her dental structure I had to prescribe medica-
tion for the pain. Dr. Walters had to put in a crown to
replace the lost tooth. You can see it here."

He turned to then tap the X-ray on Sparrow's side of
the screen. "And you can see the same crown right here.
Plus all three of Janet Ashton's molars on the lower jaw
are filled and so are those of the other girl." He pointed to
a lower incisor on the left side of the dead girl's X-ray.
"The only difference is that this tooth had a slight chip as
if she suffered some kind of blow that cracked off the
enamel. I took a look at her again and would say that the
injury happened some time in the past year because of
how little decay there was in the dentine area exposed by
the loss of the enamel." Tully stared at us through his milk
bottle thick lenses. "Janet Ashton is no longer missing.
She's right over there in the morgue. For whatever reason,
she came home, and then someone murdered her."

Leaving the maul with Tully to examine with his micro-
scope we headed back to the car. I had refused to let him
take the time to stitch up the gash in my head. There was
a killer loose. Monaghan and I were sure we knew where
he was and that apprehending him could not wait. We
drove to the RCMP station. Monaghan ran inside and
came out a moment later looking frustrated. "Nicki did-
n't know where the others are. She tried calling them on
the radio for a situation report and was told to get off the
air. By Bellows, not Danchuk. What the hell's going on?"

All we could do was drive around and hope to trip
upon the surveillance team, which meant more time
lost. Knowing it was a futile and undoubtedly unwise
course, I proposed that we just go in alone and see how
things shook out. Monaghan laughed without a trace of
humour at that and ignored me. We drove up two dead-

end roads that bordered Dagleish's property without seeing anything. "What if they're using someone's house or a barn or something as an operational base?" I asked dispiritedly. It was already mid-afternoon. Vhanna would have been inside for four hours or more now. Anything could have happened in that time.

On the property's west side a small cul-de-sac around which houses had yet to be constructed had been pushed into the woods that bordered Dagleish's fenceline. The previous developer, who had been planning to build a series of modest bungalows on this site, had been bought out by Dagleish Development. The original nine lots were broken up into just three, and Dagleish announced that each would be home to a rambling executive property that would fetch five times the price the first developer had imagined asking for the same amount of ground. So far, however, the development remained nothing more than a scrubby patch of wood into which the short paved road ran. Weeds were breaking through the pavement and, because the drains had never been properly completed, the road was partly flooded. We drove up to the base of the cul-de-sac and Monaghan pointed to where a bulldozer had punched a gap into the densely packed stand of alder, below which thickets of salmonberry and salal grew. Just the fronts of an unmarked van and Danchuk's Blazer were visible inside a small gap in the trees.

As Monaghan pulled up in front of the vehicles Sergeant Danchuk strode out of the woods toward us. He had a ball cap pulled down hard on his brow and a yellow slicker flapped around his knees. When I got out of the cruiser he stopped abruptly. "What do you think you're doing bringing him here?" he snapped at Monaghan. It was obvious that he was trying to keep his voice down, but having a difficult time doing so. More likely he wanted to bellow in rage.

I walked toward him. "Easy, Gary, is Ray here? All of us need to talk."

"This is a police operation, McCann. Nothing to do with you." Danchuk scowled at Monaghan. "Damn it, constable, you're supposed to be out on traffic patrol, not chauffeuring McCann around. And now you show up here and possibly compromise a serious operation. I'll see you suspended for this or worse." He shook a finger in her face. "That's a promise you can take to the bank."

"Go to hell, Gary," I said and brushed past him. There was no time. I had to make Bellows understand the gravity of the situation. Ignoring Danchuk's thankfully hushed demands that I stop right where I was, I walked to the van and rapped on the back door. As had happened the time before several shadowy figures rustled about inside, and then the door opened a crack. Bellows looked out at me with a mixture of puzzlement and frustration.

"Jack Ashton murdered the homeless girl on the beach, tried to kill the other one named Meredith Ashley Bainsbridge-Stanton, and probably murdered his mother. A couple of hours ago he also tried to kill me. He's probably up there with Dagleish and Walker right now. Ray, you have to pull Vhanna out of there."

Bellows was wearing a dark jacket with "Police" written in silver reflective letters on the back and front. It was undone, and a shoulder holster was visible underneath it. Behind him two men monitored the radio receiver as they gazed up at me.

"If Vhanna's at risk, Elias," Bellows said tightly, "it's because you're here in that police cruiser and possibly alerting Dagleish's security. Jack Ashton's a go-boy for Dagleish. He's not a threat to her."

Danchuk and Monaghan were hovering close behind me. "What's this?" Danchuk demanded.

I restated Ashton's crimes and my concerns for Vhanna. Danchuk scowled and then glared over at Bellows. "I don't like the sounds of this. Have you heard anything?"

Bellows shook his head. "No, none of the bugs she planted before in the main house or the spa are picking up anything at all. And the one she had with her hasn't been activated yet because we're not picking up anything from it." He shrugged. "She's probably just being careful. Biding her time so she can place it somewhere discreet. It hasn't been that long since they finished lunch and went up to the office." Bellows glanced over his shoulder. "How long, Mike?"

"An hour and twenty-five minutes, boss," one of the men replied. "Shouldn't worry." But by the tone of his voice the man seemed to be doing exactly that. "She's good. A natural," he said without much conviction.

"One of your own people got caught in there and Walker nearly killed him," I snapped. "Ray, get her out of there." I remembered Roberta Walker's pronouncement that it was her job to protect Dagleish and that I should keep that in mind with regard to someone I knew. At the time I had thought her words provoked by jealousy, but now I wondered if she had not suspected what Vhanna was up to.

The man named Mike stepped out of the van and joined our little huddle. His eyes were ringed by greenish-yellow bruises and both cheeks were webbed with a series of still healing cuts. "Boss," he said to Bellows, "I don't like the silence. It's like a bloody tomb. We should be picking up something. Housekeeper singing or a security guard radioing in a report. I'm worried we've been tagged."

I could see the growing uncertainty in the detective's eyes. "We can't go in there without some certainty she's at risk," Bellows said.

"Anne, give me your cell phone," I said. She shot me a puzzled look but handed the little device over to me. "Ray, you have Dagleish's main phone number. Right?"

Mike recited the number from memory as I punched the digits into the phone. "Be discreet, Elias," Ray cautioned.

A woman answered. It sounded like Eleanor, who manned the reception desk in the spa. I identified myself and said it was urgent that I speak with Vhanna Chan. The woman put me on hold and then after a long pause came back on the line. "I'm sorry, Mr. McCann, but Ms. Chan is no longer on the property. It seems she left about an hour ago." The receptionist brusquely bid me good day and rang off before I could ask anything further.

"She would have seen Vhanna leave if it were true. She spoke to Walker or someone and was told what to say. Vhanna's in there and she's in trouble," I said.

Mike added that Sergeant Danchuk's two constables were watching the Dagleish driveway from the woods and would have reported in if Vhanna had driven out.

"I have the Port Alberni ERT on alert," Monaghan said. "But it'll take a couple hours for them to deploy here, even if they come by chopper."

"That's too long, Ray. We have to go in now."

Bellows glared at me. "Damn it, McCann, we could lose the entire investigation. Dagleish could end up walking right out of this. We need a warrant. We need probable cause."

"Probable cause is that a woman might be murdered, Ray," Danchuk said. He unsnapped his radio microphone and tersely told Josinder Singh and Norman Tom to rally on his position immediately. "You can do what you like, sir," Danchuk said to Bellows. "But Ms. Chan is a resident of Tofino and a civilian. It's my duty and responsibility as the local detachment commander to protect her. If you and your people want to come along, fine. But we're going to go in there, secure the place, and ensure Ms. Chan's safety." Danchuk's face was white as chalk and his fingers trembled, but his eyes were determined.

"If she's not in trouble —"

"I pray she isn't, Sir." Danchuk pointed at Monaghan. "Get the shotguns from your car. I'll get the ones from the Blazer."

Mike leaned into the back of the van. "Carl, pass me one of the shotguns and a vest." He shrugged into the bulletproof vest and then checked the action of the shotgun. I noted he was careful not to look at Bellows, who was still glaring after Danchuk.

"Carl, you'll provide radio security and backup," Bellows suddenly said. "Tell the Port Alberni ERT to get here as fast as they can and get Nicki to put the local ambulance on alert. Mike, fetch my vest, will you?"

Mike grinned. "Sure thing, boss."

chapter twenty-three

I followed close behind the six Mounties as they crept up to the edge of the high stone wall at a point directly across from the spa building where Dagleish had his second-floor office. When I had refused Bellows's order that I stay with the vehicles he had reluctantly handed me a vest and demanded that I stay well back of the police team. As we moved into the woods, I had slipped up beside Danchuk and thanked him for intervening. "I don't want your thanks, McCann," he grunted. "It's nothing to do with you."

Now we crouched in the treeline, while Bellows and Danchuk looked up at the loops of concertina wire running along the top of the wall. Danchuk held a heavy bolt cutter that he had taken from the Blazer's tool kit. Singh and Tom were slowly and quietly erecting a steel extension ladder they had brought from the van against the fence. "Doesn't look electrified," Danchuk whispered to Bellows, "but the moment we start cutting, alarms will go for sure. Take about a minute to clear the wire. Maybe we should have tried to force the front gate."

Bellows shook his head. "Mike says it's too heavy to ram open, and the guard would issue an immediate alert. This way at least we're inside before anyone can react. None of the perimeter or house guards are armed. But there's no getting to the office by surprise. That's for sure."

"McCann, you stay here with a portable radio," Bellows said. "Anything happens that you think either us or Carl should know about sing out." I nodded. Though I wanted nothing more than to take one of the shotguns and join in the action, I knew there was no way that was going to happen. To the others, he said, "Gary cuts the wire. Then I go over." He pointed to each officer in turn, numbering the order in which they would follow. Danchuk would go last. There was to be nothing fancy about the operation. The six Mounties would simply cross the open ground at a run, bust through the front door of the spa, and sweep the building clear. "We want Dagleish, Ashton, Walker, and Ms. Chan. Take down anyone else who puts up resistance, but if they run for it let them go until we have the four targets secured. Right?"

The others nodded. Monaghan's face was pale, her expression grave, as she tightly gripped the shotgun. Everyone else looked equally apprehensive. There was no knowing what opposition Dagleish's people might offer. They could have an arsenal of automatic weapons at their disposal and be willing to use them.

"Let's go," Bellows said. Danchuk jumped up on the ladder and with surprising speed and strength cut away a section of concertina wire wide enough for the team to scramble through in single file, then skipped aside. Bellows then launched himself up onto the top of the wall. Monaghan handed a shotgun up and the detective disappeared. Tom went next. Then Mike was on top of the wall, and as Monaghan passed him the remaining shotguns one at a time he handed them down to Tom on the other side. Mike jumped down and Monaghan and Singh quickly followed on his heels. Danchuk made a jump for the top of the wall but because of his height only got one arm over it. His feet scrabbled uselessly against the stone surface for a footing. I jumped onto the ladder, created a footstep with locked-together hands under the sole of one his boots, and heaved him up.

"No damn foolishness," he wheezed down at me. "Stay here." Then he dropped over the other side, hitting the ground with a hard thud. I heard him groan. "Bother," he hissed, before I heard him start running.

I got one arm over the wall and managed to wedge the toes of my boots into two small chinked gaps in the mortar lines holding the stones in place. From this precarious perch I was able to see into the grounds beyond the wall.

Danchuk was halfway to the spa building, but limping as if he had sprained an ankle. One of Dagleish's golf carts stood in the middle of the field. On the ground in front of it two security guards lay face down, hands linked behind their heads. Constable Tom, shotgun held level in one hand, quickly handcuffed the two men's hands behind their backs and then headed again toward the target building.

The others were already there, braced against the wall on either side of the main door with guns at the ready. When Mike reached out and pulled the door open, Bellows went in low and fast with the shotgun at the ready. A woman screamed in terror. I imagined Eleanor standing behind the reception desk and suddenly finding herself face-to-face with the open barrel of a cut-down shotgun.

The others followed on Bellows's heels, and I knew they would be fanning out by twos. Several of Walker's security guards were running about the property, but I quickly realized that they were mainly heading for the front gate. It appeared that, having seen two of their own taken into custody, the rest had decided to make themselves scarce. Suddenly from inside the building a shot rang out and was answered immediately by the hard boom of a shotgun.

I vaulted the wall and sprinted toward the spa as several more shots were fired and answered by a flurry of shotgun blasts. Lunging through the front door, I ducked to a position of cover behind the reception counter. Eleanor was huddled in a corner there with her arms wrapped around her knees, sobbing hysterically. I grabbed her by the shoulders. "Where's Vhanna Chan?" She shook her head and whimpered as several more shots rang out on the second floor. I shook her again, just hard enough to get her attention. "Where is she? Come on."

She let out a long sniffle. "I don't know. I … Mr. Ashton and Ms. Walker took her into the spa area about an hour ago. Mr. Ashton was carrying her, like she was asleep or something." In a little girl voice, she said, "I'm scared."

There was no sign of life in the pool area. Just the gentle splashing of the waterfalls and steam rising out of the hot pool. I walked slowly into the centre of the room, listening for movement. My heart was beating hard and I felt a deep sense of dread. Eleanor's words echoed in my brain. An hour ago. Like she was asleep or something. Drugged, knocked unconscious, *dead*.

I tried a door that led into a change room. Urinals on one wall, a common shower, and a bank of lockers opposite a long wooden bench. Empty. I went back to the pool area and crossed to the door leading to the women's change room. When I pushed the door open and stepped inside, I saw Vhanna lying naked on her stomach in the shower alcove. Jack Ashton crouched beside her. Vhanna's body was bent like a bow, ankles and throat circled by a length of gleaming barbed wire connected by a taut strand to which her wrists were also secured. She was breathing very slowly and deeply, eyes fixed on some point of middle distance, face etched with concentration. A single tear of blood pearled out from where a barb pressed into the centre of her throat.

Ashton had one hand on her ankles and the other pressed against the back of her head, as if he had been just about to push them in opposite directions. His expression as he looked up at me was more one of irritation at being interrupted than of surprise. Thrown in a careless heap by the changing bench was a stack of clothing that included a full-length Australian-style range coat, black leather motorcycle pants, a pair of scuffed black roper boots, and elbow-length heavy leather gloves; worn together the outfit would provide nearly impenetrable protection as Ashton worked with the barbed wire.

"Strong bitch," he said calmly. "Been like this for almost an hour." He had on nothing but the red bathing suit that he had worn the day before by the poolside, and the muscles of his arms, shoulders, and chest stood out like big rocks. Ashton could push Vhanna's legs and face flat against the floor in a second if he wanted to, and there was nothing I could do to stop him. "I was beginning to get bored. It's better when they squirm." He gave her ankles and head a teasing little push outward, causing the barbs to bite into the flesh. Vhanna bit her lip just hard enough to stifle any sound and her eyes met mine. There was fear in them, but a deep determination that gave me heart. Although I had no idea what to do to end the impasse.

"The police will be here any moment. It's all over, Ashton. They're upstairs right now. You must have heard the shots."

"I told Darren I'd take care of her. No fuss." He released Vhanna's ankles and waved an arm expansively around the shower stall. "Just wash it out, throw around a little bleach, stuff her in a rubber bag, and then toss her body somewhere. Maybe down at the homestead," he said with a chuckle. "Why not? That's where the killer struck before, right? She'd just be another victim. And nobody has a clue who the killer is."

He stared at me for a moment, like a thought was rising slowly to the surface. "You're the coroner. Supposed to be dead." He looked genuinely puzzled, even disappointed. "Wait here," he said to Vhanna with a grin and started to get up. "No time like the present, coroner."

I took a long step toward him and smashed the portable radio Bellows had given me against the side of his head. Pieces of plastic and electronics flew every which way, but Ashton never flinched. One fist slammed into my chest. I flew back across the room, crashed into a bank of lockers, and then slumped onto my butt on the floor with my legs up in front of me. The room spun and I sucked desperately for air as Ashton calmly padded toward me with his hands hanging loose at his sides. Blood was running down the side of his face where the radio had cut him, but he seemed oblivious to the injury. Let him get hold of me and I was dead. And so was Vhanna. I rolled and regained my feet, retreated toward the door leading out to the pool. "Don't run away, coroner."

Reaching behind me, I backed out into the area where the rattan chairs were grouped beside the pool. Ashton dropped his head and rushed at me. I waited with my legs apart and hands loose at my sides. When he was almost on me, I swivelled to the right and pushed hard against his left arm with the palms of both hands, using his momentum to send him stumbling past me. He smashed into one of the lounge chairs and went sprawling face forward over it to land with a hard thud on the tile floor. Ashton lifted his head, gave it a shake, and then started to get up as if nothing had happened.

Time was running out. Although Vhanna had patiently taught me a few Tai Chi Chen fighting techniques, I had not been a particularly attentive student. I had used Ashton's own power against him once in a simple deflection move, but doubted he would fall for that ruse again. Even if I could free Vhanna, she was in no shape to fight him. And I could never best him with just bare hands. I needed a weapon.

As he charged again I jumped back and spun a pot with a fake palm tree in front of him. He smacked the thing aside with such force that it soared out into the middle of the main pool, landed with a splash, and sank. Slowly he closed in, forcing me to retreat toward one of the fake limestone rock walls. I was being backed into a corner and could see no way to escape.

"Shoot him, Monaghan," I yelled.

When Ashton instinctively looked over his shoulder, I ducked past him and sent a wicker chair skittering his way. The big man just kicked it aside and started closing in again, herding me toward the pool. I kept tumbling furniture into his path, but I was gaining nothing more than a brief delay. And how much longer could Vhanna hold that position before her body weakened and started to unfold? Visions of Sparrow and the terrible wounds she had suffered flashed through my brain.

I tried dodging around him, but Ashton moved with a sudden speed and agility that caught me totally off guard. As I desperately ducked aside a fist grazed my temple and sent me sprawling across the hard tile floor.

My head felt like it was exploding, and I could feel blood leaking through the bandage. I scrabbled backward across the floor, trying to gain enough room to get back on my feet. Ashton was coming on slowly and calmly again, face impassive.

As I backed with a bang into one of the false limestone cliffs and used it to get upright, Monaghan came through the main entrance door. She took one look at the scene before her and raised her shotgun. "Police! Stop where you are and put your hands behind your neck!" Ashton halted and then looked over his shoulder at her.

Then he looked at me. "No bluff this time." His head moved back and forth between us. "Business to finish," he said, and started marching purposefully toward the change room.

"Monaghan, he's going to kill Vhanna. Shoot him," I yelled.

She swung the shotgun up and fired a slug into the ceiling. "Stop or I'll shoot."

Ashton kept going. Reached out and grabbed the door handle. I ran across the room — intent on tackling him, but knowing I was too far away. Monaghan's gun boomed as he pulled the door open and a huge hole opened in the wood in front of his face. "I mean it," Monaghan cried. Her voice was shaking.

The shot had caused Ashton to pause just long enough for me to reach him. I hit him in the back of the neck with a closed fist. He staggered forward and then spun back to strike me in the chest with an elbow that sent me sprawling. Through a haze of pain I saw him turn, and there in the change room doorway Sergeant Gary Danchuk aimed his pistol levelly at Ashton's chest. "Give me a reason," he said. Ashton didn't.

chapter twenty-four

Janet Ashton was buried in the family cemetery plot on a grey day heavy with mist. Her tombstone listed her name as Janet "Sparrow" Ashton. Devon Lysander was one of the few people who attended the funeral and burial ceremony conducted by Father Welch. Vhanna and I were also present.

Three days after we buried Janet Ashton, Moot opened her eyes and asked Devon Lysander for an ice cream cone. By the time he returned from the co-op with a two-scoop strawberry and chocolate waffle cone she was sitting upright and surrounded by a gaggle of nurses and orderlies.

Roberta Walker had been killed by gunfire when she tried to stop Bellows and the raiding party from capturing Darren Dagleish. There were no other casualties in the short, sharp exchange. Dagleish was caught in the middle of trying to erase data from his computers. His efforts failed, and Bellows recovered sufficient evidence to file an array of money laundering charges against him. He was also charged with conspiracy to commit murder — of Vhanna. Eventually he was convicted on all charges and confined to a federal penitentiary.

Jack Ashton was charged with the murders of his mother and sister, and the attempted murders of Meredith Ashley Bainsbridge-Stanton, Vhanna, and myself. He was convicted of all but the last charge. Although he was the owner of a dark blue Pathfinder that was matched with the one that ran me off the road, it was impossible to prove he was the driver. He is in solitary confinement in a federal penitentiary because killers of young women don't fare well in the general prison population. Surprisingly, Ashton never offered a defence against the charges of murdering his mother or sister or his assaults on Moot and Vhanna. He sat like a rock at the side of his attorney and ignored the frustrated man's attempts to discuss the evidence being piled up against him. After his conviction various reporters sent him written notes inquiring as to how and when he decided to use barbed wire on his victims. All went unanswered. Tully believes the old scarring on Janet Ashton's flesh might have resulted from her having been whipped by a strand of such wire, but there was no way to confirm such speculation. What we do know is that, according to Dagleish, it was Ashton who first proposed using barbed wire to establish perimeter fencing around Dagleish properties.

The question of the notebook arose during the trial, but what Sparrow had written in it was never learned because Ashton would never acknowledge that he burned its contents. Did she write of her family? Of the atrocities Jack Ashton had visited upon her and his murdering their mother? Or did she just scrawl down notes of what the Family needed to acquire, as Devon Lysander, who believed her a diligent quartermaster for the rest of them, thought had been the case. I suspected only Jack Ashton knew the answer. It was easy to imagine she wrote something that exposed him, but there was nothing left but fragments of ash. "So sorry, son," Nickerson told me on the phone, "but it's just a bunch of gas-soaked paper scorched to nothing. Hell of a thing, a shootout, for God's sake, not how we do things in Canada at all."

Monica Klassen was taken into custody, and Vhanna testified that it was the mayoralty candidate who had mixed her a drink, which must have been drugged. When Vhanna had awakened from a sudden stupor, she was bound in barbed wire. Bellows later reported that Klassen had played a fundamental role in Dagleish's money laundering operation. By running property acquisitions through her firm, Dagleish was able to pay one sum to the owner of land he purchased but report a higher price as paid. Klassen retained the unpaid balance and claimed it as extraordinary expenses and commissions for her services. Then she invested it back into Dagleish's company. The now "clean" money could be circulated back to Dagleish's drug lords as bonuses and profits paid to his board of directors. Monica Klassen quickly sang like a nightingale with details that enabled Bellows to wind up the whole laundering network. In return she got a greatly mitigated sentence.

One consequence of Klassen's arrest was that come election day, with the only viable opposition suddenly in custody, Doc Tully was handily re-elected to another term. Virtually everyone in town turned out to give him an uncontested vote. As he accepted a victory, the Chamber of Commerce sang loud and long about his virtues and said that the remaining candidates — one advocating the immediate establishment of pot plantations and the other the cessation of Scotch broom removal programs — had failed to capture the imagination of the electorate. Tully claims this will be his last term, but few believe him.

Moot's parents never did put in an attendance while she lay in the coma. She and Devon Lysander left Tofino the day of her release from hospital. They are rumoured to be living on the street in Victoria.

Constable Anne Monaghan still hopes for a transfer to Saskatchewan despite the fact that Sergeant Gary Danchuk now treats her like the rest of the detachment members. Which isn't saying much.

The Land Rover was pulled from the muddy pool and found to be little the worse for the experience. Its aluminum body suffered not even a dent because of the bogginess of the mud under the water's surface, and the various other damaged parts were all rather easily repaired or replaced.

Fergus proved to be only badly bruised. After a short bout of nervousness with regard to going for rides in the Land Rover he has returned to his old self.

Vhanna, too, suffered no visible physical injury from Ashton's assault. Her power of concentration and ability to attain a deep state of muscle discipline enabled her to maintain a static position throughout the time she was entangled in the barbed wire.

My own injuries were entirely superficial. I am, however, trying to be a better student when Vhanna teaches me Tai Chi fighting techniques.

Two days ago with dog alongside we walked down the beach and sat on a driftwood log in among the Family's former camp that fronted the Ashton property. A wind holding the cold promise of winter blew off the ocean. The barbed wire fence, "No Trespassing" signs, and Dagleish Development Corporation signs were all gone. We huddled together, arms around each other and Vhanna's head resting on my shoulder. I kissed her forehead and then her lips. The grey surf rolled in under a matching sky. There was no need to speak. We were together and safe. All that mattered.